3.50

Better Boxed and Forgotten

Andrew Charles Lark

Cover Art by
Pal Molnar & Andrew Charles Lark
Photograph by Kurt Fishwild

TO THE MEMORY OF
MY MOTHER THE POET

CONTENTS

PART I

There were three Nobel Laureates at my grandmother's funeral. As I drove down Jefferson Avenue, I kept replaying how my eulogy went over—the empty words, the anecdotes that didn't connect, the platitudes, and the forced sentiment. I looked up from my notes at the lectern. The many luminaries, politicians, and distinguished academics; a veritable who's who in the world of physics, sat in the cathedral, politely listening. Just as I was about to continue, I noticed one of the laureates raise his wrist to look at his watch, and my already-fragile confidence caved. *What am I doing?* I thought. *I mean, really! I barely knew my grandmother, and I'm going to connect with these geniuses who did know her and worked with her!*

I looked back down at my notes but the words blurred. I found my place and plodded on. I looked back up. Paige was in the second row, focused intently on her program. One of grandmother's former colleagues, an old woman sitting next to Paige, had her silver hair pulled back so tightly that her eyebrows were on top of her head. Paige averted her eyes when I looked at her—or was I just being paranoid? The old woman inhaled then ejected a cough that rattled around in the huge, domed space. The woman fished around in her purse, presumably for a tissue. Paige quickly offered her a handkerchief, then looked up at me, her eyes pleading for me to hurry it up.

I finally finished, gathered my notes and slinked off the dais, almost bumping into the retired dean of the department of physics, grandmother's former boss, who replaced me at the lectern and gave his side of things, knocking it out of the park.

He had sharp insights on her psyche, her outstanding work ethic, her tenacity, and her reputation as a tough professor who never suffered fools. He talked about how early in her career she fought hard to gain entry into what had been, until her arrival at Wayne State University's physics department, a men's only club, and that within a couple of years she was running the department more effectively than anyone prior. He pointedly added that her contributions greatly contributed to the work that eventually won a few people sitting in this cathedral some very prestigious awards, and more than a few people shouted, "Hear, hear!"

After the service, one of her colleagues—a short, thin, bald septuagenarian with a long, crooked nose—came up to me as my grandmother's coffin was being slid into the hearse and clapped my shoulder.

"Good job," he said. "Your grandmother would have been proud."

I looked at him and smiled. "Bullshit," I replied.

He cocked his head and squinted. The muscles in his jaw flexed. He looked down at the pavement before turning and recessing back into the fray of mourners that looked for all the world like a murder of crows—huddling in black overcoats, with upturned collars flapping in the whirls and gusts. Old, grey, and sallow-skinned, their pinched blue mouths exhaled steam in the unseasonable cold of this dank, miserable October day. Paige squeezed my arm tightly and yanked me closer to her.

"I'm sorry," I said, looking at her.

"He was just trying to be nice," she replied sharply.

"I know. I'm just... angry."

"Try not to be so obvious about it."

I turned north off Jefferson onto Seminole Street attempting to once again shake the memory of the funeral. Seminole, along with Burns and Iroquois, made up the historic Detroit neighborhood of Indian Village. Gorgeously designed and exquisitely built mansions of Detroit's turn-of-the-century elite nestled here in their meticulous and award-worthy landscaping. Many of these massive beauties were in a condition known in real estate lingo as diamonds in the rough, but more were still well-preserved, and each one, no matter its condition, was an architectural gem. Driving north and looking out the window of my pickup was like swallowing some mind-clearing elixir, and it was nice to reconnect with the neighborhood where I'd spent so much of my youth. I slowed down and took it all in.

There was 302 Seminole, a regal six-bedroom Tudor, recently featured on the front page of *The Detroit Free Press* real estate section. The original leaded panes, all 324 of them, had been re-glazed by a Scottish craftsman flown in at great expense. It also had a converted carriage house with doors that swung on hand-hammered hinges.

Next door, 308 Seminole was one of the smaller homes—an English arts-and-crafts-style cottage designed by Albert Kahn in 1912 that sadly had become a study in neglect. I recalled a conversation with my grandmother regarding the buzz stirred up by the president of the neighborhood association a couple of years back about a shoddy, yellow and white aluminum tool shed in the backyard at 308. Letters were sent and a compromise was worked out where the owner, a former city councilman, agreed to plant a row of arborvitae to conceal it from the street. However, it's been two years now and there are still no arbs.

Continuing north, I drove past 305, a stately three-story federalist-style colonial with white clapboard siding and functional black shutters. It sat majestically on the apex of its large elevated lot and was surrounded by a three-foot-high black wrought-iron fence.

I drove under century-old elms that towered over either side of the street, their branches meeting and mingling high above. These elms had miraculously escaped the slow death of Dutch Elm disease that wreaked havoc in the 1960s and 70s, and many of their massive trunks crept and folded over the heaved and cracked sidewalks, like molten lava slowly flowing over ancient cobbles.

I continued north toward grandmother's house, a massive three-story Dutch Colonial. She was born at 418 Seminole, lived here all her life, and inherited it from her father while in her 30s. He was among the great citizens of Detroit's past—a scientist, academic, and, as his daughter would be after him, chair of the physics department at what

4

was then the College of the City of Detroit.

Work on the mansion was completed in 1905. The stately home had flourished in the ensuing decades but sadly had become one of the more run-down places in the neighborhood. Pulling into the driveway, I now noticed it had fallen into a slightly more advanced state of decrepitude during the two years since I'd last seen it.

I felt a pang of guilt when I saw the overgrown lawn and noticed a mower that had been abandoned part way through the unfinished chore. A narrow row of short grass trailed the dead and rusting Briggs and Stratton, tall weeds and thistle blocking any further advancement, as though the mower decided to just give up and die right there on the spot. An array of tangled and overgrown juniper bushes grew with wild abandon against the house, obscuring the brick foundation, and an old, half-dead fruit tree, probably a crab-apple, groveled in a bed of white stone, like a crippled old hag.

Way up on the third floor gable was an octagon window that looked small from the street, but was actually quite large when one was on the other side of that window looking out. The line of the gambrel roof, the hallmark of all Dutch Colonials, was interrupted by three gabled dormers. This allowed for a maximum amount of light to pour into the large, third story ballroom. Grandmother's house actually had a ballroom—not that she ever used it, and not that she ever would. She had been dead ten days now, although the memory of her funeral still nagged at me.

I was here to meet with the executor of her will at the agreed upon time of 3 p.m. I was to formally tour the house, take an inventory of its contents, sign the deed, and become the third generation, sole member of my family to take ownership of this dilapidated piece of real estate.

I was about to exit my pickup but I stopped myself. I looked through the windshield and re-studied the exterior of this wreck of a house that I hadn't set foot in for over two years. I had always meant to visit again, but there was always something (or nothing) going on. Grandmother wasn't the most pleasant person to be around. Her thinly veiled questions were asked only to verify things she already knew—more judgment than query. I sat there trying to remember if I had ever seen her smile.

I put both hands on the steering wheel and crouched, looking up at the house's higher parts. There was gutter damage. Two of the panes in the octagon window were broken. The whole edifice was sorely in need of a fresh coat of paint, but to do that properly, the old paint would have to be stripped and rotted planks would have to be replaced. I considered vinyl-siding, but knew that I'd run into trouble with the neighborhood association on that front.

But actually this house was just the sort of challenge I needed to take my mind off the shaky times we were in. I had been laid off eight months ago and had quit looking for work. Paige had a good job that was paying the bills, and I was still collecting unemployment benefits, so between that, and some under-the-table freelancing, we were doing okay, but by no means thriving.

But who was thriving these days?

Like so many thousands in this great city that was once known as the Arsenal of Democracy, I was tired of looking, tired of worrying, and needed something to immerse my energies into.

Seminole Street typified what was going on in the city at large: one hulking ruin sadly stooped next to a proudly grand and glorious mansion. Two miles to the west, modern, shiny skyscrapers shadowed old and boarded-up blocks of city structures that vacancy and neglect had reduced to ruins. One of the buildings downtown had trees growing out of its upper story windows. An elevated train known as The People Mover continued to whirr by 25 feet above the street on a concrete track that snaked through downtown, despite being devoid of people to move.

Twenty miles to the north in Oakland County, entire subdivisions of McMansions were built in the boom-year 90s. The soil of suburban farmland was stripped away. Foundations were poured, then underground electricity and cables providing everything from telephone and high-speed whatever-your-heart-desired were laid, and through the clay, houses sprouted up.

For a time all was grand, and Green Day, Celine Dion, and classic rock blared out from backyard loud-speakers, mingling with the splash of in-ground pools. Then came the foreclosures and bankruptcy notices in the back pages of what were being passed off as newspapers.

For-sale signs littered almost every lawn, and five-bedroom, five-bath homes with open floor plans, granite countertops, three-car garages, and finished walk-out basements could be bought for pennies on the dollar. But no one was buying, and compared to the grand old ladies on Seminole Street, those houses were cardboard cutouts. How many of those Oakland County McMansions had genuine plaster ceiling medallions? Ballrooms? Old-growth stairway banisters? Servant's quarters? Stables? Service alleys? How many were designed by the likes of Albert Kahn? Exactly none. And how many people could afford such opulence? Hardly anyone, including me.

Mr. DuMichelle, the executor, had not yet arrived. It was ten minutes to three. I sat there looking at the hulk through the windshield while a Terry Gross interview droned on the radio. And that's what it was—a hulk—a huge hulking, broken down, ramshackle assembly of boards.

There was a slight drizzle and the wipers smeared tiny droplets to dirty arches.

Paige wanted no part of this and did not come along for the inventory. I sat alone in my truck and remembered the only time she had been here back when we were dating. She had an amateur, but enthusiastic interest in architecture, and would point out various details on the more interesting buildings we'd happen upon during our urban excursions; identifying this structure as Beaux-Arts inspired, adding that that particular style was rare here in the Midwest; or pointing out that a row of Doric columns high up on the Book Tower were fluted and that you'd never see an atrocious faux pas like that in real classic architecture.

I had brought her here that day on a lark. She too was mesmerized by Seminole Street, and I drove slowly so she could take it all in, inspect every passing house, and marvel. I pulled a sharp right up grandmother's driveway and stopped. She turned to me, puzzled.

"What're you doing? Do you know these people?" I

put the car into park and smiled.

"Yes," I said. "This is my grandmother's house."

Surprised, she raised her eyebrows and her jaw dropped slightly—just the reaction I had hoped for. Then suddenly her surprise appropriately gave way to etiquette. "Is she expecting us? I mean, is it okay that we're here?"

"No, she's not expecting us, but I don't think she'll mind."

Paige turned and looked at the house. Yes, it was a little run-down, but it was still a very impressive sight.

It was a crisp, sunny, Indian summer afternoon. We had just spent a couple of hours walking around Eastern Market, a bustling urban farmer's market where the scents of fruits, vegetables, flowers, and herbs mingled with barbeque smoke and the occasional wisp of propane exhaust left in the wake of hi-los—where vendors hawked their wares, shouting at passersby, some of whom pulled red rider wagons filled with Michigan-grown produce, bunches of fresh-cut flowers, toddlers, and other wares, much of it packed neatly in reusable, biodegradable bags.

Our jaunt through the market left us in a good mood, but pulling up to my grandmother's slightly complicated what had been, up until that moment, an idyllic day.

"If you don't think she'll mind," Paige replied. "Maybe we can give her some of the fruit we bought." I leaned over and kissed her and told her that was a perfect idea.

Fat drops of rain began to pelt the roof of my pickup and roused me from this long-ago memory. The drops ran down the windshield, multiplying, accumulating, quickly obliterating the depressing view outside. I looked in my rearview mirror and watched a massive, black Lincoln Continental Mark IV slow its trajectory and pull next to the curb in front of the house. It lurched to a stop. I recognized the car from the funeral as Mr. DuMichelle's.

I had heard his name mentioned a few times over the years. He was my grandmother's lawyer, so naturally he'd been appointed the executor of her will. I remembered him from the funeral. I saw him talking and laughing with some of her former colleagues both before and after the service. His car was this giant, older model monstrosity, a mint condition relic from the 70s, which followed our limousine in the funeral procession that meandered slowly through the city toward grandmother's final resting place. I wondered then as I wonder now why he hadn't introduced himself during the funeral. Certainly my status as sole heir warranted an introduction.

The rain petered down to a light drizzle.

He got out of his Lincoln carrying what looked like a very expensive briefcase and walked up the driveway. I quickly cleared my head and by the time he reached the sidewalk, I was out of my pickup. I turned toward him and extended my hand. He smiled and offered his.

He was an elegant man who looked to be in his 60s, but I knew he was actually much older than that—probably closer to 80. His hair was short with equal amounts of salt and pepper, and his suit was clearly tailored. He looked healthy and athletic and probably played tennis twice a week at whatever club he belonged to.

"Mr. Lintz?"

"Yes, Daniel. And you must be Mr. DuMichelle?"

"Please, call me David. I wish we were meeting under happier circumstances. I'm sorry for the loss of your grandmother. She was a very impressive woman and she'll be missed."

I thanked him and suggested we get out of the rain by gesturing toward the house. Out of nowhere he produced an umbrella and, with both of us canopied underneath, we made our way toward the front door. He mentioned he'd brought a copy of last Thursday's *The New York Times*.

"Her passing caused quite a stir in the world of physics and the *Times* wrote a very thoughtful obituary. I brought an extra copy in case you didn't already have one."

This was the kind of guy—gentleman actually—who apparently thought of everything, and his genuine friendliness and calm demeanor very quickly helped put me at ease. In spite of his top-drawer appearance, it would have been difficult not to like him. But there was something about him that bugged me. First impressions go a long way, and he hadn't even bothered making one at the funeral.

He took a key ring from his jacket pocket and unlocked the front door. We stepped into the foyer. It was ten degrees cooler in the house than it was outside. David collapsed his umbrella and dropped it into a hollowed-out elephant's foot sitting to the right of the heavily carved front door.

I took it all in, re-acclimatizing to the house's massive and ornate interior space. It had been at least two years since I last walked through the front door and I instantly felt sad and guilty, as though the house was somehow accusing me of criminal neglect.

I tried shaking off the oppressive feelings by doing a quick study of the foyer: there were large, leaded-mirror closet doors on either side of the entry, dark mahogany wainscoting and molding, and Tiffany sconces that matched a small Tiffany chandelier hanging above. Everything seemed to be in great condition, although a little dingy, and a once over with oil soap would do wonders. The black and white marble tiled floors were a little tired and worn with age and traffic, but were mostly in good shape and I considered the wear an acceptable patina that would not need restoration.

We entered the two-story main hall and I was immediately struck by how neat everything was and yet how empty it seemed. I remember my grandmother being something of a packrat, and I recalled previous visits where I had to negotiate through a lot of clutter when moving between rooms.

We turned right under an archway, walked through the formal dining room, through the butler's pantry, and into the kitchen. David put his briefcase on the tiled countertop and opened it. He pulled out the inventory paperwork and another large key ring festooned with at least a dozen keys. He then walked over to the east wall of the kitchen, which was oddly concealed by a curtain. He flung it open and revealed a metal door with a heavy deadbolt and the blood drained from my face. He noticed my reaction and subtly countered it with a calming gesture. "Shall we begin?" he asked.

"Ready when you are," I replied, attempting to mask my apprehension.

David unlocked and opened the door, and the basement

stairs beckoned. He gestured for me to lead the way and I thought it a little odd when he re-locked the door behind us, but I didn't say anything. We descended the stairs and he wasn't surprised when I told him this was the first time that I'd ever been down here.

"I actually forgot that door existed," I said. "I remember when I was a kid and there was just an old wood door that she kept locked and wouldn't let anyone near. I feel like I'm breaking one of her cardinal rules by walking down these steps."

"You'll see in a minute what it was she was protecting," David said behind me.

As I reached the bottom of the stairs, David flipped a switch and a row of industrial pot lights turned on, brightly illuminating a long, central hallway with doors on either side. The concrete floor was painted gray, the plaster walls were painted white, and I noticed upon closer inspection that it was apparent that my great-grandfather had gone to great lengths to make sure the basement was waterproof and well-ventilated. It was cool down here but not musty and again, I was struck by the organization and cleanliness; I didn't even see any cobwebs.

David led me down the hallway, opening the doors as we passed each one. It looked like the heavy metal doors were meant to both fireproof and dustproof the contents stored within each room. Several doors opened into rooms filled with orderly rows of filing cabinets that had been placed on pallets, ostensibly to keep them elevated off the floor in the event of a flood. There were other rooms filled with rows of shelves loaded down with wooden crates, some of them stamped, "Property of U.S. Government -

Contents Secret." David said that at the very least I was now the owner of a very important archive—my great-grandfather's life's work—and that it would be a good idea to contact the Detroit Public Library, or one of the local universities, as they would certainly be interested in procuring his papers.

"I tried talking your grandmother into having the papers moved to a more suitable location, but she wouldn't hear of it. You may remember she was not the most trusting of people," David said. His demeanor was like that of a friendly museum docent. He clearly knew a lot about the archive and seemed eager to divulge its secrets.

"Do you have any idea what's inside those crates marked secret?" I asked, my sense of apprehension completely wiped away by awe.

"I do not. The inventory only states the existence of the crates, but not their contents." He then showed me a page for the basement, each line reading something like, "1 wood crate, 24"x 36"x 36", contents unknown."

"I knew my great-grandfather was an important person but, to be honest, I never really understood what it was that made him so influential. I had no idea any of this stuff was even down here!"

"No one alive knows these boxes are here except you and me, and you have the sole privilege of discovering what it was that made him such an influential person."

I asked David if he would allow me a few moments to myself.

"Of course," he said, looking at his watch before he exited the room.

I walked over to one of the filing cabinets and pulled

open a drawer labeled, "February 1923." I reached in and took out the front-most file and opened it. The document on top was written on French Embassy letterhead dated February 1, 1923, addressed to my great-grandfather, and written entirely in French. I closed the file and stuck it back into the drawer where it came from. I was in the presence of some very important stuff, but incapable of understanding what it was that made it so important. I couldn't help comparing myself to him and began to feel like a medieval peasant gaping at a Roman ruin.

I walked to another cabinet and opened the second drawer down, this one labeled "April 1926." I pulled out another file and opened it. It contained a large, folded-up, schematic drawing. It was very complicated and the only thing I could ascertain from all the lines, squiggles, and incomprehensible engineering and electrical jargon, was that I was most likely holding it right-side up.

I put the file back and closed the drawer, deciding to not open any more cabinets lest I devolve from peasant to Neanderthal. I walked out of the room and joined David in the hallway.

"I want to show you something else," he said. "Follow me. You're going to be amazed by this."

We walked down to the end of the hallway and turned right. Here was a narrower hallway, about ten feet long, which ended at the base of a small, two-step stairway. He ascended the steps and stopped at a solid, six-panel door, which was larger and more ornate than all the other more utilitarian basement doors. He pulled out the large key ring, instantly picked the correct key, and unlocked the door.

It opened on a very pleasant library lined from floor to ceiling with bookshelves filled with leather-bound books. The parquet floor was mostly covered by a massive oriental rug. In the center of the room was a large, square, arts-and-crafts style table with a bronze pharmacy lamp mounted to its surface. Ahead and to our right was an arrangement of oversized, tufted leather couches and chairs surrounding a large coffee table, all grouped comfortably near a massive limestone fireplace. In the opposite corner was a spiral staircase that ascended through an oculus in the ceiling.

This library, the furniture, the carpeting, the books—all were in pristine condition. We hadn't even left the basement and already my head was reeling.

"This is your great-grandfather's private library. He, a few of his colleagues, and your grandmother, obviously, were the only ones who knew of the existence of this room."

"Where does the spiral staircase lead to?" I asked, dumbfounded. "Or is it just decoration?"

"No, it's functional. It leads to the library on the main floor."

"I've been in the main floor library a hundred times! I think I would have noticed a spiral staircase!"

"Yes, but you obviously never noticed the secret panel which, when opened, leads to the spiral staircase."

"No," I admitted. "I never noticed the secret panel which, when opened, leads to the spiral staircase!"

We both laughed, but mine was tinged with bedazzlement. We stood there for a few seconds, and I saw that certain wheels began spinning in David's head. He was enjoying the show he was putting on for me but, for a split second, I detected a hint of reluctance in his demeanor.

"But wait!" he said, swiping the reluctance away with a quick gesture. "There's more!"

He walked toward the fireplace, turned left and continued a few paces. I followed. He felt around on the wall then grabbed a section of the dark mahogany trim and pulled downward on it. There was a mechanical *click*, two of the mahogany panels slowly swung open, and a large, ornate, art deco style bar rolled outward on a track. Hidden lights blinked on behind the bar, bathing the mirrored shelves in warm light. Dozens of bottles and decanters filled with the liquors and spirits that my great-grandfather and his collogues enjoyed almost a hundred years ago glowed in the amber colored light.

"Are you kidding me!?" I said, dumbfounded, as the bar came to a stop. "Look at this!"

"It was the ratification of the Eighteenth Amendment that inspired the construction of this wonder," said David, walking behind the bar. He reached up and snatched a crystal decanter that was three-quarters full off the top shelf.

"The Eighteenth was Prohibition?" I asked.

"Yes, and the Twenty-first rendered this whole mess obsolete. Still, I think your great-grandfather kept it around because *it is* a rather interesting feat of engineering," David said.

"How many other hidden panels and passages are in this house?" I asked.

"Perhaps you'll find that out on your own," he replied rather cryptically, handing me the decanter.

"That cognac is over a hundred years old, and I'm sure

your great-grandfather was the last person to pull out that stopper."

I held up the decanter and looked at the cognac through the warm light. It was a rich, reddish, caramel color. Not exactly a connoisseur of fine cognac, I wondered if it still tasted the way cognac should taste. I was really starting to feel intimidated by the amazing secrets in this house, and we hadn't even left the basement.

Behind one of the grated cabinet doors below the bar top, I noticed lit shelves of neatly stacked decks of playing cards, a poker chip carousel, and a small but beautifully crafted roulette wheel. I smiled as I imagined all the Prohibition era parties great-granddaddy hosted here in his private library—all, of course, in the name of science.

He was dead long before I was born and I always pictured a serious, dour academic, pondering the great questions of his day. Assessing the cards, the poker chips, and other gambling implements tucked away, *and* the hidden bar, my mental picture of him began to change, and I saw a smile starting to form on the black and white photograph of his mustachioed face I've had in my mind since I was a kid.

"When we finish the tour, I think we need to come back down here," I said, putting the decanter on the bar.

"Why's that?"

I reached up and took down two snifters and set them in front of the decanter.

"Well, I think we need to see how this cognac has held up over the years, and I'd be honored if you'd join me in a toast to the memory of my grandmother and great-grandfather."

"In that case, I'd be delighted," David said, a warm smile lighting up his face.

He gestured toward the spiral staircase and, as we trounced upward, he very politely suggested I wear archival gloves whenever I decided to explore the contents of the archive.

We were halfway up when a tremendous crash reverberated from the archive. I swung around and looked at David, who was a couple steps behind me. He stopped and looked at me blankly.

"What the fuck was that?" I whispered loudly. My heartbeat throbbed down my arms, numbing my hands. "Someone's in this house!"

He swallowed and almost took too long to answer.

"I guarantee you we're the only ones here."

"Didn't you hear that? It sounded like one of the filing cabinets was knocked over!"

"More like someone picked one up and threw it against a wall!" he replied. I snatched out my cell phone and flipped it open.

"I'm calling the police!"

"Hold on! This is Detroit. It'll take them an hour to get here. That is if they even bother to show. Put your phone away and calm down. Let's go back and have a look."

"That's crazy! What if..." He raised a hand to silence me.

"...When we go back, I guarantee we won't find anything out of the ordinary."

Walking back through the archive, a genuine case of the creeps mingled with my alarm and, still, I thought

David was wrong in that we would surprise some crackhead hiding behind one of the doors. But after a thorough inspection of the archive, we found no one. The steel door at the top of the kitchen stairs was still locked, all the crates were intact, and all of the filing cabinets were undisturbed.

We slowly walked back down the hallway toward the library and that's when I realized that it felt *a lot colder* than during our first walk through. I reluctantly turned around for another look, but all I saw was a long, well-lit hallway with many closed doors on either side. I turned to David.

"I mean, I know what I heard. You heard it too, right?"

"Sure I did."

"What do you think's going on down here?"

"Are you asking me if I think this place is haunted?"

"We both heard that noise!"

We turned the corner and walked back into the library.

"I thought there was a chance something like that would happen during the tour," he said, turning around and locking the archive door.

"Why would you think that?" I asked.

"I've spent a lot of time in this house since your grandmother died. This is not the first time that's happened, but it was definitely the loudest." We walked over to the table in the center of the library. He looked tired and took a deep breath.

"Do you mind if we sit down for a few minutes?" He took out a monogrammed handkerchief and wiped his brow. He started looking his age, and his tailored suit now seemed too big.

"Not at all, please."

He sat on one of the chairs surrounding the table and I took the one opposite him.

"I've known your grandmother since before you were born. She was never what I would consider—excuse me for saying this—an overly friendly client. We met in October of 1962 and that meeting completely changed my life. I very quickly came to learn that she was a formidable person and not someone to be trifled with. Now back in those days you didn't run into many female college professors. And her subject wasn't art appreciation, or advanced domestic engineering. It was physics for God's sake!"

"You're not telling me anything I don't already know. I mean, she was never what I would consider a milk-and-cookies kind of grandmother."

He laughed. "No. I can't imagine your grandmother rolling out the cookie dough, although she was a great cook."

His arms rested on the table with the thick inventory folder near his right elbow. He was more relaxed and his breath resumed a normal pace. By now I also noticed that he had a disconcerting habit of looking me directly in the eye when he spoke, and I wasn't sure if he was sizing me up, or if he was just an intense person who had to make sure his points were being taken.

"As I told you earlier, I'd spoken to your grandmother, *many times* about moving the archive to a more suitable location: Wayne State University, the University of Michigan, Michigan State—they'd all be capable of taking the archive, correctly cataloging its contents, *and* making it available to scholars for study, but more importantly..." he pointed toward the archive door, still looking me in the eye. "... a university would put to practical use the *science* that's boxed up and forgotten down here."

He rested his chin on folded hands and waited for me to reply. I met his look. He wasn't wasting any time trying to talk me into what he had tried to talk my grandmother into.

"What's in that archive, David?"

He leaned toward me and placed his hand on top of the folder. "You have no idea."

"What's your interest in the archive?" I asked.

He smiled and I immediately realized that this question was offensive, but so what. I was starting to feel a little pressured and, as far as I was concerned, this conversation had taken an inappropriate turn. We really had only just begun the inventory, and already he was talking to me about giving up a very important (and no doubt valuable) piece of my property.

"I have no personal interest in the archive. Your great-grandfather was a very accomplished man, and he deserves his place in the pantheon alongside other great men. Men like Thomas Edison and Henry Ford. Eastman, Fermi, Tesla, Hubble—*Einstein* even! I could go on, but I think you know what I mean. That's not going to happen as long as the archive remains down here, again, boxed up and forgotten."

This was condescension, pure and simple, and I don't know who he thought he was dealing with. If he had dismissed me as an easy mark, then he was going to be disappointed.

"David, you mentioned a moment ago that my grandmother was a formidable person and not someone to be trifled with. I think you'll come to the same conclusion about me." I stood up and opened the inventory folder to the first page. "Now if you don't mind, I'd prefer we proceed with the inventory line by line."

David took a deep breath and shrunk as he exhaled and his shoulders slumped in resignation.

"Daniel, I apologize. It's not my intention to try to get you to do anything against your will. This house and its contents are yours to do with as you please," he said.

I suddenly felt bad, but held my ground. "I understand what you're saying about the archive, but you know— you're jumping the gun on me, alright? I mean, let's finish the inventory first. Let me settle in, explore a little, you know? I don't know or even understand what that stuff is in there, and you're already asking me to give it away."

"You're right, and I apologize. And, I lied. I do have a personal interest in the archive." The air had cleared and the level of stress from the mysterious crash had subsided a little.

"Aha! I knew there was something! So what's in it for you?" I asked, pointing at him in a mock prosecutorial tone. Again he smiled then expressed himself with what I interpreted as merely a veneer of compassion and integrity.

"Only that your great-grandfather *and* grandmother receive the recognition they deserve. That's it, pure and simple. As a lawyer, I'll consider it my duty to see that that comes to pass."

I looked down at him sitting there and, just as

inappropriate as it was for him to introduce the idea of selling the archive, I thought it equally inappropriate to tell him I had no intention whatsoever of selling or donating it. I had made up my mind, right there on the spot, and decided to grant him the courtesy of having to wait to hear my decision. I changed the subject.

"You still haven't told me what you think that noise was all about."

He slowly stood up, stretched his arms, then tugged at his lapels. "Good question. What do I *think* caused that noise? Truthfully, I have no idea. The house is old. The foundations are settling. Spirits, ghosts, poltergeists—who knows! This place is over a hundred years old and it's filled with memories. There's stuff like this on TV all the time. Perhaps these memories for some reason play themselves out from time to time."

"That all sounds like a bunch of b.s. to me," I replied turning toward the spiral staircase.

"Well, you asked. If you want a better answer, call a paranormal outfit, or a priest. Things that go bump in the night are just a little outside of my professional experience," David said a few steps behind me.

What *was* within David's professional experience, however, was the remainder of the inventory, which was exceptionally well-organized, making the task of reviewing it relatively easy.

Once again we ascended the spiral stairs, this time making it all the way up without incident. We walked into the main floor library through the cleverly hidden panel, similar to, but smaller than, the one hiding the bar, then spent the rest of the day going through the house floor by floor. Grandmother must have either hired someone to help organize and document the house's contents, or perhaps David had arranged it. I had no idea and didn't ask.

We finished the first and second floors within the span of five hours and every room, with the exception of grandmother's bedroom, was neat and organized. I opened the door to her bedroom and the smell of vapor rub was enough to stop me from going in. Gray light leaked into the dim room through a gap between the side jamb and a large piece of cardboard she had fastened over the windows. There was a clothesline strung from one wall to the other with underclothes hanging from it. I quickly closed the door and told David I'd deal with her room another time.

The basement and the first and second floors were in phenomenal shape, and I was very relieved I wouldn't have to spend money I didn't have making extensive repairs. I would, however, have to spend a lot of time cleaning and painting.

We made our way to the end of the second story hallway, walked under an archway, ascended a double winder stairway, and stopped at a set of very large pocket doors. As I slid one of them open, a hidden pulley neatly slid the other door open and into its pocket.

"I'm glad the pulley still works," I said. "I love these doors! I remember coming up here and playing with them when I was a kid. I could never figure out how they worked, and thought it was magic." My enthusiasm for the doors vanished, however, when I saw the disaster that waited on the other side.

"I'm glad about your pulley doors, but here's the room

that's going to break the bank," David said.

He wasn't kidding. I just stared into the vast room and made a mental list of all of the problems. There was water damage to the parquet floor, mold infestation on the walls, and pieces of the ceiling had begun to break off in chunks, exposing the lath.

The ceiling was very high, perhaps 15 feet, and I'd need scaffolding to safely make repairs. The only thing left of the chandelier that had once hung under the large plaster ceiling medallion were two short wires poking down through the center—one black, the other white. I also saw the telltale signs of aviary infestation and heard the flapping of unseen wings.

I walked over to the large octagon window that faced north and stepped up onto the sill. My outstretched arms and legs fit easily into the jamb, and I imagined (or rather wished) I looked like da Vinci's *Vitruvian Man* boxed inside the geometric shape. I looked up at the two broken pieces of glass and didn't think it would be too difficult or expensive to replace them. I put this project at the top of my long to-do list. I looked down at the driveway and was seized with the reality of just how high up I was. I stepped off the sill and backed away.

The floor creaked and popped as I slowly walked the perimeter of the room, and my voice echoed in the vast, empty space as I casually replied to David's earlier remark.

"It looks like it could break the bank, but I'm going to do the work myself. That'll save me a lot of money." Up until now, David and I had mostly maintained a respectful silence and spoke only while going over the inventory.

He quickly caught the thread of my comment and

asked if I was good with my hands.

"As good as the next guy, I guess. I did all the work on the house I live in now, except the electrical. I don't mess with electricity."

"Are you and your wife going to move in eventually?"

Instead of answering, I just laughed, but hearing the word *wife* brought on a mild panic attack. I still had no idea how I was going to broach inheriting this mansion to Paige. I had asked her to come with me today but she flat-out refused. I didn't want to sell this place—I wanted to restore and resurrect it. I wanted to cash in my 401k, deplete my savings, and sell the house in St. Clair Shores to finance this endeavor. I wanted to move in and start renovating immediately, and I had no idea how I was going to tell Paige about what I had decided. I did, however, have a very good idea about how she would react.

I stepped up onto a stage, which stretched across the width of the south wall. Red velvet curtains, heavy with dust, hung limply on both sides of the stage. Looking up behind them, I noticed a few stage lights attached to a metal bar. There were pigeon nests woven into some of the lights, and generations of bird shit littered the floor. Off to the side were a bunch of folded chairs stacked against the wall, and a few music stands.

I walked out to the edge of the stage and looked at the room from my slightly higher vantage. It was a mess, but it wasn't insurmountable. I looked back up at the ceiling medallion with the two wires poking through its center. I tried to recall ever having seen a chandelier, but I couldn't remember. The last time I was in this room I was probably all of 10 or 11 years old. David's voice echoed from across the room.

"Five bar tables. Do you see them?" He was sitting on a chair a few feet from the pocket doors. The half-moon glasses he had put on earlier were perched at the end of his nose and he was looking down at the inventory.

"Yep. They're in the corner."

"Twenty wooden folding chairs."

"They're here on the stage."

"Count them."

"There's only nineteen. No worr…"

"I'm sitting on the twentieth."

"Oh…"

"Five music stands."

"Got 'em."

After a few more lines David slapped the folder shut then lifted it above his head.

"That's it! We're finished." He pushed a button on his watch and announced that the inventory took just over 6 hours.

"Are those 6 billable hours?" I asked, a little worried that there would be a fee attached to his services.

He shot me a quick look above his glasses, not hiding his irritation.

"It's been taken care of," he replied curtly.

⚱   ⚱   ⚱

I poured a dram of the cognac into each of the snifters I had taken down earlier and handed one to David. We had both tired of each other's company and any remaining vestige of friendly banter had long since run its course, but the

28

promise of sampling 100-year-old cognac was worth trudging back down three stories to the private library. As soon as David saw me reach for the decanter the friendly banter magically resumed. We walked over to the table and sat. David took two cigars out of his briefcase and gave one to me.

"Do you know anything about cigars? This is a Baron de Rothschild—a macanudo."

"I've got to hand it to you, David. I think you knew I'd share some of this cognac when you showed it to me."

He smiled and hoisted his snifter.

"Well, I'd hoped anyway. What about that toast?"

David really was the kind of gentleman who seemed to think of everything. But could I trust him? He was fairly candid in his assessment of the archive without really saying anything. What did he mean when he said that the science that's down here could be put to practical use? The only thing I could figure is that maybe there were discoveries my great-grandfather made that, to this day, no one else had yet discovered. Maybe what I had down here was something like what some high-ranking political official—I don't remember who—alluded to during some long ago press conference: "an unknown-unknown." It would take me years to figure it out given that there were more than a dozen rooms to pick through, and even though it was all very organized, how could I even begin when I didn't have the slightest clue about my great-grandfather's work?

There were other things to consider. Did he file for patents? Would these patents have expired? Would the intellectual property boxed up down here belong to me?

Could this stuff make me rich? These questions could have easily been cleared up by a lawyer, and here I had one sitting across from me, but I decided that, no, I didn't trust David—not after remembering the funeral and how he had laughed and cajoled with grandmother's colleagues, his whispers and backslaps echoing throughout the great cathedral. I wondered if he had been so brazen as to discuss the archive with those arrogant university types before grandmother was even in the ground.

And what about the science down in the archive? The only way to find out about that was to dive in and start picking around and learn about my great-grandfather's work by going through it. Treat the archive as though it were an instruction manual. But for now there were more pressing and important things to worry about.

I hoisted my snifter.

"To Beatrice and Alois Lintz! Geniuses through and through!"

"Hear, hear!" David said, raising his own snifter and clinking mine.

The smoke from our macanudos folded and slowly curled upward, and the pleasure of understanding the complexities of this good and very old cognac eluded me for the moment. It only burned in my mouth. David advised me to "sip gingerly" and "take only very small amounts at a time." He was enjoying it immensely and I was half-way tempted to just give him the decanter but didn't, rationalizing that the cognac would probably come in handy in the event of any future visits.

There would be other opportunities to learn to enjoy and savor, but the weight of the day and the promise of everything it would bring was only now just beginning to sink in. I had many rooms to clean and paint. I had a ballroom to restore. I had a wife who wanted nothing to do with this mansion.

⇧   ⇧   ⇧

David handed me the two key rings and a folder bulging with my copy of the inventory and other documents we didn't bother with. We shook hands and he climbed into his mint condition relic.

"This is quite a car you've got here" I said, holding its long, heavy door open. "You sure don't see these old Mark IVs on the roads much these days."

David turned the key and the giant V8 snarled to life under the long, black hood. He smiled up at me.

"Danny, I have three essential people in my life who operate on the peripheries: my barber, who knows more about sports than anyone I know; my bartender, whose skills with a martini shaker are deadly; and my mechanic, who's kept this baby humming along since 1976."

"Well, they must be a pretty dedicated bunch," I replied.

"Especially the bartender, Danny boy. He's one dedicated son-of-a-bitch!" Then, in one swift move, David grabbed both the door and the shifter, slammed one shut, the other into drive, and sped off, not bothering with the seatbelt.

"Took the words right out of my mouth," I said, as he sped off. "Jesus! There goes one old school bastard." I watched his taillights bob and diminish off into the distance and climbed into my lowly pickup.

It was dark. Instead of hopping onto I-94, which would have gotten me home within 15 minutes, I took Jefferson Avenue east. It would take me a half hour to get home this way, but the route was more interesting and it would give me more time to formulate some convincing plan that Paige might buy into.

Yeah, right, I thought. The reality of what I saw through the windshield contradicted anything resembling logic, and I'd need the persuasive powers of Svengali to get her on board. I drove by empty lots littered with filth and cars that had been torched and abandoned. A beefy prostitute dressed in bicycle shorts and a dirty tank top grooved to the beat of whatever played on her giant headphones near a glass-shattered bus stop. Her eyes locked on mine and within the span of time it took a few thousand key synapses to fire off, I was dismissed. She turned indifferently to search out another passerby.

I continued east. Much of the blight hid just out of sight in the shadows on this very dark and moonless night. I passed the mouth of the river, where Belle Isle clots the flow of water running down from places like Port Austin, St. Ignace, Marquette, and Duluth; where the mile-wide river balloons open like an aneurysm, forming Lake St. Clair, then crossing north over Alter Road, I left Detroit behind and entered the Grosse Pointes, where Jefferson Avenue, like a constrictor sloughing off its ragged skin, turns into the patrician Lake Shore Drive, and the difference between two places on earth couldn't be more pronounced.

I remember when people used to compare Detroit to Beirut, but the comparison is no longer applicable. Beirut has moved on and recovered its cachet as a Paris of the Middle East. Detroit remains stuck in its one step forward, two steps backward infamy, the mother of all rust-belt urban wastelands.

I flipped open my cell phone and called Paige.

"Hi," she answered.

"Hi."

"What's happening? Are you on your way home?"

"Yeah."

"Where are you now?"

"On Lake Shore about ten minutes away."

"I knew you'd take that way. I got take-out," Paige said.

"Lebanese?" I asked, suddenly realizing how hungry I was.

"Yeah. I got you a chicken shawarma and some rice."

"Thanks, I'm starving."

There was a long pause.

"So how'd it go?" she asked finally, a little detached.

"It went alright. David was pretty cool, I guess."

"Were you there this whole time?"

"I left about fifteen minutes ago."

"Took quite a while."

"Well honey, it's a frickin' mansion! Lots of rooms and stuff."

"This is so bizarre. You own a mansion now."

"*We* own a mansion now. It's really not in that bad of shape."

"Don't get too attached," she said, repeating herself from an argument that started before I'd left the house to meet with David.

"I'd rather talk to you in person about it."

There was another pause. The rawness from this morning's argument was there, lingering, and she wasn't going to disguise it anymore, and not that she could; we'd known each other too long for her to even try.

"We can't afford this," she snapped.

"I know."

"I mean it! We can't afford this in our lives right now."

"I know! I'll see you in a few, okay?" I replied, no longer masking my irritation.

"I've said all I'm going to say!"

"Okay!"

I didn't want to argue and number one on the list of things I didn't want was to hurt Paige. I loved her more than anything. And she was right. We didn't need this goddamn mansion in our lives right now, but it didn't matter—I wanted it and there was nothing she could say or do to change my mind. I drove with my ear plastered to the cell phone.

"Are you crying?" I asked.

"Just come home. And I don't want to talk about this tonight, okay?"

"All right. We don't have to talk about it," I replied suddenly feeling like a jerk.

"I've got something to tell you," she said.

I was irritated and didn't feel like talking anymore, so I pulled out one of my old standards. "I gotta go. There's a cop behind me. I'll be home in a bit," I said a little too abruptly.

"Okay! I wasn't going to tell you until you got home anyway," her voice starting to crack.

"Fine. This day's been one surprise after another. One more's not gonna kill me, but there's just one more thing, then I'll drop it."

"What?" she asked. I could hear the tears running down her cheeks.

"We're rich." I snapped the phone shut and tossed it onto the passenger seat. I didn't say goodbye.

Ten minutes later I pulled into the driveway of our nondescript three-bedroom, one-and-a-half bath, now woefully inadequate, ranch-style home.

Paige was in the living room watching TV. The coffee table was set for dinner but her plate, littered with balled up wax paper and streaked with hummus trails, bore evidence that she had already eaten. My food sat on its plate still in wrappers, the shawarma looking like a greasy party favor. She looked up at me. Her short, wavy blonde hair was tousled, and she was already in her pajamas.

"Hi, again," she said. Her eyes were red and swollen.

"Hi." I offered a weak smile and she returned one in spite of everything while a fresh tear welled then streamed down her cheek.

"Did you shake that cop?" she asked, still smiling, clearly onto my bullshit.

"Yeah. I kicked it into high gear and left him choking on my smoke."

"That's nice, rich guy," she said, looking down at my

plate, then added, "You should probably toss your shawarma in the microwave."

I took her advice then sat down with her and quickly became absorbed in the drama of watching celebrities I'd never heard of dance their way toward career redemption, or maybe it was a trophy they were after. I wasn't sure. Regardless, it was mindless, mildly entertaining, and it took my mind off the dozen or so physical and emotional tasks that loomed.

There we were, like so many other millions of post-boom Americans, safely ensconced within our living room, engaged in an act of communal disconnection. College educated, married 13 years, childless, surviving but not thriving, one employed full-time at a well-paying job in fashion merchandising, the other sporadically employed, about to enter into the expensive, time consuming, and profitless world of mansion restoration.

Paige waited until a commercial interrupted the dance show to inform me that she was pregnant.

⬆   ⬆   ⬆

Over the next few months I became a familiar face at the local, big-box hardware retailers—huge, soulless entities that existed merely for the pleasure of their major stockholders.

I sometimes worked myself into a real indignant, self-righteous lather when I thought about the workers and their poor wages and lack of benefits; though in actuality, my anger really just amounted to mental cover. Deep down, I truly liked these places. They had everything I needed and were conveniently located near the on-ramps.

I befriended the people who worked in these places, many of whom used to work high-paying union jobs making things, now reduced to selling things mostly made in China.

They walked the buffed-to-a-high-sheen concrete floors in their primary colored aprons that, like depression era sandwich boards, had cheerful slogans written all over them. They worked their aisles in eight-hour shifts, ten on holidays. They knew how to mix paint, how to install hot water heaters, and how to glaze a pane of glass. They knew when I'd need an anchor over a simple Phillips-head screw.

I engaged them and showed them pictures of my progress. They became my partners in the successful completion of difficult tasks, and expressed pride whenever I thanked them for a bit of advice I did (or did not) use. I knew their names, their spouses' names, and feigned interest in the grades their children were getting in school, the part a daughter got in a local production of *Annie*, or the prowess of someone's boy on the high school gridiron.

One cold and rainy day I was loading 200 two-by-fours into my pickup underneath the loading port when suddenly one of my big box buddies approached me from behind and clapped his hand on my shoulder.

"Busted!" he said, with a nod and wink.

Fuck, I thought, almost pissing myself. *Did I forget to pay?* I turned to see a smile on his craggy face, his gloved hand reeking of cigarette smoke.

"Lemme help you out there, chief," he said, practically shoving me out of the way. When he finished he slammed the tailgate shut and sent me off with two loud knocks and a wave.

No matter how much I tried to avoid it, I ended up spending a great deal of money on the house over the next few months by borrowing significantly from my 401k. Paige was mostly on board with the renovation—to a point— but her thoughts incorporated phrases like "return on investment" and "profitability." She didn't want me spending too much money on the house, and didn't mind me devoting a certain amount of time on it, thinking that it would ultimately pay off when we put it on the market. She just had no idea that I had no intention of selling it. I would let her see it in its completed state then wait and see the kind of effect it had on her.

She was still a romantic at heart and knew a good thing when she saw it, but she still had not come to see the place.

The most expensive project naturally was the roof. The original slate tiles were pitted and mossed over with decay, cracked to shambles, or completely broken, and this was the reason for most of the damage in the ballroom. I hired roofers to do a complete tear-off. They also replaced the plywood under-sheathing, much of which had rotted completely through, and when they finished, the gambrel roof, re-clad in its architectural, slate-style asphalt shingles, was watertight and mimicked the look of slate so convincingly that no one would be able to tell the difference.

It made sense to start at the top of the house and work my way down. It would have been pointless beginning a major renovation in the ballroom had the roof not been repaired first, and the roofers finished their five-figure task inside a month.

Whenever Paige asked about the progress, I downplayed my accomplishments, not wanting to provoke too many questions about money. I left out huge chunks and I said nothing about the roof. Had she seen the bill for that one, I would have been served papers the next day. My impression was that she was allowing me to have my fun with the place; that we had come to a *détente* of sorts. The problem would be convincing her that what we had was, in fact, a good thing, so I would allow the house to do the talking.

I prepared for my part of the renovation by rolling up my sleeves. I knew I could handle most of the work, but other things like electrical and plumbing I'd leave to some friends in the building trades. There would be a lot of trial and error, but I didn't have enough money for error, so I started slowly and with caution. I checked out how-to books from the library and consulted with experts. I bought scaffolding for cheap on Craigslist, and a machine that stripped wood floors too. I set up a huge work bench and repaired and re-glazed the octagon window piece by piece. I demolished the plaster ceiling in the ballroom and replaced it with drywall. It was heartbreaking to ruin the original plasterwork, but nothing was salvageable.

I got into a rhythm and within a couple of months I was almost finished. But something was taking hold. I arrived early every morning and worked until very late at night. I had never focused so much concentrated energy on anything in my life. It was like being on auto-pilot. The renovation became easy—almost too easy. I worked as if in a trance. I was exhausted, but there was an elation to my exhaustion. I'd look up from my work and notice suddenly what an incredible amount of progress had taken place. It was as if I were receiving help of some kind.

And, like the day David and I had first walked through the house, I heard things—things that were not easy to dismiss.

I was up on the scaffolding completely absorbed in the task of hanging drywall when suddenly a coin rolled across the floor. It began its trek near the pocket doors, and continued to roll toward the scaffolding. It was enough for me to drop what I was doing.

"Who's there?" I shouted.

No one answered. I climbed off the scaffolding. A layer of drywall dust coated the papered-over floor, which made the trail left by the coin easy to see. It began at the doors and ended at the base of the scaffolding, where the coin wobbled to a stop. I picked it up. It was an old quarter dated 1955.

I picked up a piece of two-by-four, walked out of the ballroom and into the stairway vestibule. Nothing was there but my footprints. Looking at the floor, it would have been impossible for a coin to roll all that way without being obstructed by one of a dozen things, but the quarter simply rolled around the obstructions. My alarm subsided a little when I remembered what David had said about the house being over a hundred years old, and that old houses make noises. I reasoned it away thinking that perhaps there's a stash of old coins in the ceiling, and my work, the roofers' work, and all the accompanying vibrations and bumping caused the coin to fall from its yet to be discovered hiding place.

However, I never found a stash of old coins. And there were other incidents.

There was an old wheelchair stowed away in grandmother's bedroom. One morning I found it perched at the top of the stairs. The easy thing to do was to simply wheel the chair back into grandmother's room and treat it as though it were the most natural thing in the world. Coming back down from the ballroom for lunch, the wheelchair was out in the hallway again facing the stairs I'd just descended. I thought about putting the wheelchair out on the curb but didn't.

Things like this did not happen every day but when they did I wondered if there was a connection between these incidents and my meddling with the bones of this house. Something objected to my intrusion and I often felt a palpable dread while walking through the hallways. It followed me and lurked behind doors. I saw shadows and movement at the terminations of my peripheral vision—or imagined that I had. The house wanted to die but I was there to resuscitate it. Even though it belonged to me, I felt like I had to chase my interloper status away every time I unlocked the front door. So I began to explore.

I became intimate with the house. I established dominance and took ownership by force. I opened bedroom doors and rummaged through dressers that probably hadn't been rummaged through since the 1920s. I pulled books off the shelves in the library and riffled through their pages. I opened a curio cabinet to inspect the condition of some Lalique vases that were decorated in relief with goldfish, nymphs, and geometric shapes.

⚱   ⚱   ⚱

Paige left town for a manager's meeting for a few days, so I took advantage of her absence by sleeping overnight in my great-grandfather's bedroom. I often imagined the day I would finally show Paige the finished house—watching her face as I open the front door—she catches sight of the grand foyer, the black and white marble tiles, and further up, the grand stairway and its banister polished to a high sheen. I see her eyebrows rise and her jaw drops. She turns to me and smiles.

This was the reaction I was fantasizing about as I stripped down, leaving a trail of clothes that led toward the bathroom in great-grandfather's master suite.

You couldn't turn a corner in this house without running into shelves filled with books and the suite was no exception. There was an entire wall of books next to the entryway with a desk set at an angle in front of the shelves; more bookshelves lined the south wall, flanked by a large bay window with a tufted leather chaise lounge and a small Pewabic tiled fireplace in the corner. The bed, wardrobe, dresser, chests, even the moldings, were large, dark and very masculine. Tiffany lamps bathed everything in a warm glow and an oriental rug covered the wood floor. Other than the gloom and dust of ages, the room was in impeccable condition.

The bathroom was spartan, but not completely without decoration. There was a subtle Roman bath motif with a classical key pattern bordering the perimeter of the tiled floor. The walls were tiled in off-white subway tile with a key border set at roughly head level, handsomely matching the floor. By today's standards, the bathroom wasn't luxurious, but everything down to the smallest detail was high quality and, like so much else in the house, I would leave it just as it was.

I turned the nickel-plated faucets, which probably hadn't been touched since the great depression, and listened as the pipes buried deep within the bowels of the house groaned in protest. Thirty seconds later rusty water puked out of the spigots. I waited another two minutes for it to turn a more acceptable shade before stepping into the massive, old-fashioned porcelain tub, which stood on stubby ball and claw feet. I snapped the shower curtain closed and allowed the hot, umber-colored water to relax my knotted-up shoulders.

Days of hanging drywall had taken its toll, not to mention the mounting stress over the impending day of reckoning with Paige regarding the house. It felt good under the steamy water, no matter the color. I stood there, closed my eyes, and turned my back to the showerhead.

Something bashed into the closed door. I reeled around and watched a dark figure emerge through the door and lurch into the bathroom. It rose from a crouch and stood stock still, facing me, the opaque curtain separating us. It was tall, thin, and jagged, and I could just make out its face through the opacity of the curtain. The light in the room dimmed and other shadows formed, closing in, blotting out the light. Water streaming through the showerhead hissed and mingled with the whispers, moans, and whistles of the shadows, and the noise became deafening through the ringing in my ears. The shadow figure drew closer, its mouth yawing wide open. I backed away until I pressed against the cold tiles. The thing's skeletal arm rose and jabbed at the thin film separating us. My fight-or-flight instinct kicked in and I lunged toward the figure, tackling it in a bear hug and landed hard on the bathroom floor in a tangle of curtain and broken metal rod. I slowly got up but there was no one or nothing beneath me. Adrenaline surged into my bloodstream and wiped out my capacity for reason. None of this made sense and a blind anger and rage swelled up in me as I stood. I tore through the door and blindly ran into the bedroom, naked and dripping wet, and tripped over the wheelchair that now obstructed the doorway. My shin must have wracked the edge of the tub and a goose egg, already starting to bruise, formed mid-shin.

I grabbed the handles of the wheelchair and rolled it out into the hallway before turning toward the stairs limping, gaining momentum, and shouting.

"I don't know who you are, but know this: I own this house and you are not welcome here, so get out! GET THE FUCK OUT NOW!"

I lurched toward the stairs and shoved with all my might, sending the wheelchair tumbling down in a cacophony of metal, rubber, and wood. It landed upright and wobbled toward the foyer, its wheels crippled and bent. It bounced off one of the wood columns and stopped. I stood at the top of the stairs waiting for a reaction. Except for the whooshing in my ears and my heart slamming against my bruised ribs, I heard nothing.

Gradually I calmed down enough to hear the shower still running in great-grandfather's suite. I limped back into the bathroom and my nostrils were accosted with a rotting stench. My hand shot up to cover my nose. I looked in the bathtub and my body went numb.

Now it was blood that streamed from the showerhead, filling the tub with a foamy, crimson soup, giving off a metallic stench. I tried to reason it away, *It's nothing!* I thought. *The water running through the pipes has dislodged more rust.* But the substance filling the tub was not rust.

I slowly walked toward the tub. I turned off the spigots, bent down, and immersed my hand into the soup to unclog the drain and grabbed what felt like long strands of hair. I pulled it away from the drain and felt something attached to the hair bounce against the bottom of the tub. I yanked my hand out and fell backward, slipping on the wet shower curtain, and landed hard on my ass.

A head bobbed to the surface. It rolled slowly over and bloody ropes of hair separated, revealing a small crimson ear. It rolled further and out of the blood a face emerged sucking and gasping desperately, like it had been holding its breath for a century. It gurgled and choked, coughing and spraying offal and clotted jets of blood all over the tiles. It submerged back into the red foam, coughing and spurting, desperately trying to form words that couldn't be understood. I jumped back and bashed my head on the underside of the sink and blacked out.

🏛 🏛 🏛

I was awakened the next morning by light streaming in through the bay window in my great-grandfather's bedroom. I lay in the bed with my eyes open, staring at the spidery cracks in the ceiling. A dream slowly unreeled from the roll of my memory—or what I thought was a dream. In it, I was lying in great-grandfather's bed when I heard the strangest chant, half-sung, half-spoken:

I had a little birdy
His name was Enza
I opened up the winda
In-flu-enza

I was lying on my side and my lower arm hung off the edge of the bed. I was in a deep sleep, but the song roused me. I heard it again:

I had a little birdy
His name was Enza
I opened up the winda
In-flu-enza

I slowly woke to the sounds of this incantation and a peaceful, warm feeling enveloped me. It was too dark to see clearly, but I felt safe in spite of the disturbing lyric and the horrifying spectacle in the bathroom earlier.

I felt a small, cold hand touch my wrist and cold fingers intertwine with mine, and I heard a far-off voice, so happy, so peaceful.

"Oh, Papa I've missed you. I've missed you so, and I knew you'd come back to me."

I opened my eyes and there was a girl standing next to the bed, holding my hand. She looked to be in her early teens. Her hair was long, shiny, and black, and she had thick bangs that covered her eyes completely. She wore a very fine, maroon velvet dress like she was going to a party or perhaps a more somber event.

"Help me Papa, would you please? Please help me, Papa."

I was flooded with compassion and got up. She led me out of the room and into the hallway.

"I've been looking for so long and I cannot remember where I put them." she said sadly.

"I'll help you find what you're looking for," I told her.

She looked up at me and smiled. We walked down the hall together, hand in hand, descended the stairs, and walked up to the crippled wheelchair where she stopped. She looked at it.

"She doesn't like you, Papa," said the girl, smiling, her hand tightening its grip.

"Who? Who doesn't like me?"

"The lady in the wheelchair."

"Why doesn't she like me?

"She won't say. She just hates you. But I can protect you, Papa," she said, her head snapping up. She stared at me through her bangs. "I know what she's scared of," she added proudly. "I know how to call them back—those who did her in."

"Who did her in?" I asked, alarmed at the idea that anyone or anything in this house could hate me.

She looked up at me and her visage filled with malice. Her pale, porcelain skin became ashen, and her rosy cheeks and lips withered to blue. Her icy hand gripped mine vice-like.

"The shadow people," she said.

"Who are the shadow people? Are they bad?"

"The others think so, but I know different. Would you like to hear my song, Papa?"

"Yes, sing me a song."

She let go of my hand and skipped off into the library, disappearing around the corner. I heard her laugh.

"Come find me, Papa!"

"What about your song?" I asked heading in the direction of her voice.

Again she laughed, but the sound was faint and further off.

I had a little birdy
His name was Enza
I opened up the winda
In-flu-enza

The chant came from everywhere and nowhere. I turned in a circle looking for the source of the voice before walking into the library and noticing that the secret panel leading to the spiral staircase was open. A chill ran over me and I was reluctant to follow her.

"Come find me Papa!" she beckoned with a shade of threat in her voice.

I walked through the panel and descended the spiral stairway. I stopped at the foot of the stairs and looked around. She wasn't down here in the secret library, but the archive door was wide open.

"Where are you?" I asked unable to mask my fear. Laughter came again from the archive. I wondered if this game would stop if I got firm with her.

"You come out of there right now, young lady! You know better than to go into the archive!"

"But you told me you'd help me find them! You told me you'd help me, Papa!" She began to cry a low, muffled whine that chilled my blood.

"I'm frightened, Papa! Come get me. Come to me, Papa!"

I walked into the archive. Her whining cry stopped when I walked down the hallway and that's when I heard scratching. A wispy haze floated inches off the floor and ahead to the left one of the doors was open. I turned into the room and there she was, kneeling on the floor in front of a large crate. She desperately scratched the crate's wooden side with bloody fingertips. Her hair was no longer shiny and straight, but blown-out and wild. Her beautiful, maroon velvet dress was threadbare and faded. One of her fingernails was lodged into the wood.

"What are you doing? You're bleeding!" I asked, frightened and alarmed at the transformation in her appearance. She continued scratching obsessively.

"I think they're in the box, Papa!"

I couldn't reply. I was too frightened, but I wondered— what was in the crate? It was like she read my mind. She turned and faced me, smiling maniacally. Instead of eyes, two black, gaping holes stared up at me.

"My eyes, Papa! My eyes are in the box."

⇑ ⇑ ⇑

Generally speaking I'm something of a neatnik, but over the course of the last couple of months I have really let the interior of my truck go to hell. Fast food and plastic grocery bags have accumulated on the floorboards and offered a window into my buying and eating habits. Empty CD covers, newspapers, and junk mail littered the passenger seat. Every cup holder was pulled out, each holding an empty paper cup that bore testimony to my expensive taste in coffee. More fast food bags were strewn on the backseat floorboards along with tools galore, a five-gallon bucket filled with half-empty spackle cartons and, shoved into the back door compartment, the paperwork David had given me months before.

I knew this was stupid. I had to get that paperwork out of my truck and into my office but for whatever reason I kept putting it off. I was pulling out of the St. Clair Shores driveway, vowing that tonight was the night I would take the paperwork out of the truck and bring it into the house, when I suddenly slammed on the brakes.

Fuck that! Do it now, dumbass! I yelled at myself. *What if someone breaks into the truck and steals everything?*

This had been gnawing at me for months, but having the paperwork in-hand as I walked down the hall toward the small office, was transformational. I wasn't allowing some important paperwork, covered in road dust and permanently curled in the shape of the compartment it had been crammed into, to serve as a barometer into how screwed-up everything was. I was a detail-oriented person who sometimes allowed himself to get distracted, and this was just a minor, temporary lapse in judgment. Now that the paperwork was in the office, what was I stressed about.

I placed the curled folder on top of a pile of papers on my desk and turned to go when it dawned on me that I had never actually looked through it. I opened the file and riffled through the contents, thinking that at the very least I could get a minor grasp of what lay inside. It wasn't considered procrastination if I was educating myself on the complexities of my inheritance. This was akin to research. Driving down to Seminole to sandpaper the now almost complete ballroom for its first coat of primer would have to wait an hour or so.

I looked through the folder's contents. On top was the inventory, which I was familiar with. Underneath was the deed David and I had both signed, he as a witness. Next was a surveyor's plot indicating the length, depth, and directional orientation of the lot. Then a large envelope with a wax seal and my name scrawled across it in my grandmother's handwriting. I gasped.

David hadn't said anything about a letter from my grandmother. I turned the large envelope over, cracked the seal, and carefully opened the partially glued flap. I unfolded the four-page, handwritten letter and another, legal-size envelope fell out onto the floor. I picked it up and debated whether or not I should open it before reading the letter. I decided to read the letter first.

Dear Daniel,

I'm going to my grave knowing that I have not been, in the traditional sense of the word, a very good grandmother. This letter is not a confession and I make no apologies. I'm writing this rather to help you understand what you're coming into, and also to provide you with a short history into your ancestral past. None of it is really very important, but people like to know where they come from, what stock they're made of, and about the accomplishments of their ancestors. That said, you should know that you come from some very fine stock, indeed.

Your great-grandfather was a great and very accomplished man but, due to a succession of personal tragedies and misfortunes that occurred in rather short order, he became quite miserable in his later years. You would think, and rightly so, that I inherited some of his more miserable traits. But you should also know that for every action, there is an equal and opposite reaction.

I was very ambitious as a young girl and my sister, your Great-aunt Nora, and I were very competitive for our father's affections. Nora was very dear to me, and I to her, and her sudden death during a short convalescence at the 11th Street Academy in Traverse City was a huge blow to your great-grandfather and me. My mother (your great-grandmother, to whom I was not very close) died three months prior to Nora's death, and after Nora died, your great-grandfather never fully recovered his passion for continuing on with his life's work. Nora's death, so close on the heels of mother's, was just too much for father to bear. I did what I could to help him regain his enthusiasm, but his heart was no longer in it. He resigned from his positions at the college, the hospital, and the various boards on which he served, then he locked himself up into this house and set about putting his life's work in a semblance of order that bordered on what could be considered obsessive. But more on this later.

By this time I had been away for a few years working on my Ph.D. at Cornell and had no idea of the depth of his obsession with what I refer to as the archive.

I met your grandfather at Cornell, but that was a short and rather disastrous union of which the only good thing to emerge was your dear mother, whom I loved with all my heart. Her death in that house fire in 1977 is still too painful for me to address, even here in this letter. I only want you to know that I loved her very much in spite of some of the choices she made that I didn't agree with. I will not go into details. Just know that you are now older than she was when she died and it is not my intention to taint (as if I were capable of any such thing) the many fond memories you surely have of her. You are fully a man now and you know and can surely empathize when I say that a mother/daughter relationship can be a very complicated thing, indeed. I do want you to know this: She loved you very much. You were the one, bright, shining light in her life, and from everything I observed, she was a very good and loving mother to you. You may never understand why I put you into foster care after her death, perhaps until your dying day, but you just have to trust me when I say that this was for your own good. I did not want a young boy living in and being poisoned by the memories this house harbors.

You will no doubt be spending a great deal of time in the house; perhaps you will even choose to move in. Here's some valuable advice:

The best way to deal with them is to ignore them.

I give you free and unfettered reign as the house and its contents now belong to you. I'm demanding only one thing, and this is very important: You have by now been shown the archive. It is my wish, just as it was your great-grandfather's wish, that the archive remain undisturbed. David DuMichelle has been instructed to inform you of my wishes. The formulas, the papers, the research and development, the mathematical work, and the scientific instruments, all filed away in the basement are to remain undisturbed. I cannot stress to you enough how important it is that you adhere to these instructions. I can only tell you that even to the day of this writing (November 16, 20_), science does not have the ability to explain, nor the capacity to contain, the negative phenomena that manifests whenever your great-grandfather's machines are turned on.

There were other accomplishments that made your great-grandfather, me, and now you, very wealthy. Money is something I never had a firm grasp of, but that doesn't mean I was careless. I had my work and that was always enough for me.

Enclosed in the envelope is your monetary inheritance. I want you to remember that this enormous sum is the result of almost 100 years of hard work, discipline, and brilliance. Don't fritter it away. Invest it wisely. Be good to your wife. I liked her from the moment I met her. She's strong and worthy of your love. Be worthy of hers.

Goodbye-
Beatrice Lintz (Grandma)

⇧   ⇧   ⇧

I sat for a while looking down at the letter. I read it again. I remembered a day trip my mother and I took to Cedar Point with the man whose house she died in. There's a snapshot somewhere of a young woman beaming a million-dollar smile with long, brown hair, dressed in cut-off shorts and a red tank-top posing next to Snoopy and her 12-year-old son who's not at all amused. I remember how jealous I was of the man who'd taken us to Cedar Point that day. No matter how hard she tried she could not make me laugh. And I feel so bad about not laughing and being so absorbed in my self-pity, and it's still so goddamn painful.

I remember the ride home in the dark, sitting in the backseat of his Camaro and looking between the bucket seats at how they held hands and how badly that burned me. I could see right through this curly-headed, chest hair, motherfucker who called me "Little Dude" all day long because he couldn't remember my name. She would be dead two days later, and that son-of-a-bitch is still alive because he's such a fucking coward he couldn't rescue her, or better yet, die in her stead.

My hands were shaking when I picked up the envelope, my eyes blurred and burned, and, even though I hadn't smoked in over two years, I was so craving a cigarette. I was still so angry with my grandmother. I didn't realize how much so until I read that letter. She was correct in assuming that I still, to this day, have problems understanding some of the decisions she made regarding the disposition of a 12-year-old orphan over 20 years ago. On many points her letter was vague or maybe purposefully evasive; or maybe she just forgot, which is somehow just as painful.

I opened the envelope and read a notarized form from an investment house stating that funds in the amount of $___,___,___.__ had been transferred into my care and that certain documents await my signature.

I did not drive to Seminole that day.

I called the investment house and made an appointment to meet with the vice-president. I finished cleaning out my truck and looked for more paperwork that might have fallen out of the folder, but there wasn't any. I drove to the investment house, signed a bunch of documents, and became a multi-millionaire.

I thought about the paperwork stashed in the compartment for all those months and the multitude of times I left the truck running while I dashed into a party store to buy something. I thought about all the times I left the truck unlocked on Seminole, where cars are broken into and stolen with aggravating regularity. I marveled at both my luck and stupidity.

I drove to a florist and arranged for them to deliver a very expensive bouquet to Paige's work. She called a couple of hours later.

"Honey! Oh my god, they're beautiful!"

"What? What're you talking about?" I asked like I'd just been crowned with a halo.

"My beautiful surprise!"

"What beautiful surprise?"

"My flowers!"

"Flowers!?! Who's sending you flowers?" I asked feigning jealousy.

"The card says they're from a secret admirer," she airily replied.

"We're gonna have to see about this secret admirer."

"These must've been expensive! I love them, but... honey!"

When she got home I gave her the letter to read. I showed her the documents from the investment house and pointed to the line indicating how much we were worth.

We sat in the living room and looked out the window in the direction of our neighbor's house across the street. Cars drove by too fast. People walked by with their dogs. A rail-thin, emo teenager with bad acne glowered at us as he walked by, all hunched over, his hands crammed into his pockets, and later, other teenagers with a basketball. We didn't say anything to each other for an hour.

The light outside suddenly broke to gloaming when everything ordinary becomes extraordinary and that's when Paige said that now might be a good time to quit her job and focus on raising our soon-to-be-born son. I crawled into the chair next to her and we held each other for a long time.

As we sat there enveloped in each other's arms, I thought about the incident in great-grandfather's suite. I thought about grandmother's advice: "The best way to deal with them is to ignore them." I guess she was telling me that the house was haunted, but nothing else had happened since that night. I had even spent a few other nights there after that, and nothing—no dreams, no bloody bathtubs, and no mysterious, meandering wheelchairs.

I fixated on that bad dream about the strange girl in the maroon velvet dress. I remembered that when I woke up the next morning in great-grandfather's bed, I was sore as hell. My shin was swollen and my arms were bruised. I got up and when I walked into the bathroom, nothing was amiss. The shower curtain was still on its rod and no blood stains smeared the tiles. I had walked out of the suite and, true to form, the wheelchair was in the hallway with no evidence of any damage. It wasn't until I walked downstairs into the library that things got weird. The secret panel to the spiral stairway was open. The archive door was open and so was the door to the room where the crate was stored. I walked over to the crate and it had scratches and blood stains streaked up and down its side. I bent down and noticed something glinting in the dim light. Imbedded in the wood was a small fingernail.

� ☖ 🝑

The next few years brought many changes. The sudden windfall of money erased all of Paige's objections regarding the mansion, so we happily moved in. But the most important change was the birth of our son, Elliot. His birth was physically and emotionally difficult for Paige. She was bedridden the last two months of his third trimester, and once he was born, she suffered through a severe bout of post-partum depression.

At first she gave Elliot the requisite care that any infant would require. She held him, breast-fed him, changed him, bought him clothes, played with him, and outwardly showered him with love and attention; but inwardly, she later confessed, her heart was not into being a mother. She came to feel like a fraud and emotionally withdrew. She was horrified when she'd look down at him as he slept in his crib and felt nothing at all. He might as well have been a porcelain doll or a stone lying there all tucked in; this utter lack of feeling began to consume her. She bravely fought her indifference thinking she would be able to work through it on her own, but came to realize that when given the choice between lying in bed all day in a fetal position or providing Elliot the care and attention he needed, she craved the first—the depression was bigger than her ability to do anything about it so she sought professional help.

Anti-depressants were prescribed and therapy sessions, in time, diminished her symptoms, but Elliot was three by the time she got a handle on it. Elliot and I would wait for her at the front door when we saw her car pull into the driveway. I'd say how excited I was that she was home and he would invariably complain that he wanted to go back upstairs to play. She'd walk in, scoop him up and shower him with kisses, but he'd react by squirming away and reaching toward me. She'd hand him over and beeline into our bedroom, where she stayed for the rest of the evening.

I'd told her that the guilt she felt was, in itself, validation that she loved Elliot. She looked at me puzzled then inhaled. She almost replied but the words caught in her throat. She waved off my comment and laid back down on her side. What a stupid thing to say. She looked tiny on great-grandfather's giant, ancient bed, and her eyes stared past the fireplace completely devoid of hope. I'd told her to give it time and that I knew, and Elliot knew, that she loved him. Plus she had to factor in that he was three and operated on a different level.

According to Paige's therapist, I was partially to blame for the state of their relationship. I had a tendency to overcompensate whenever her depression manifested to the point where her withdrawal became obvious to him. On top of her depression, and because of the dramatic changes in our lives over the last few years, I, too, was weighed down with a guilt that tainted the air, making everything bitter.

I came to realize that Paige was right when she said that we did not need this mansion in our lives. But we were fully immersed now and there would be no turning back. Money was no longer an issue, but the money was not a salve that solved our problems; on the contrary—often it only compounded them.

A thousand tasks were accomplished in Elliot's first three years, every one of which could have waited for a more ideal time. By re-roofing the mansion, I had stabilized the decay before he was born, and we could have mothballed the project, re-starting once he began kindergarten, but hindsight, as they say, is always 20/20.

After we gave our old house in the Shores to Paige's sister and brother-in-law, we moved in and set about turning the partially restored hulk into a fully restored work of art.

Too many things were being attended to at once and it was a great strain on all of us, but that's not to say we lacked enthusiasm. On the contrary, once we moved in Paige, too, became obsessed, and whatever feelings she initially lacked for Elliot, the opposite was true of the mansion. She thrust herself fully into its restoration. Her therapist suggested lots of "mom and Elliot time." Playing in his room, taking him shopping, or reading to him was all well and good, but it turned out that the key to Elliot's heart was making him her construction partner.

Slowly over the course of the next year their relationship improved. Elliot loved construction. She bought him a play workbench with all the requisite play tools, but the brightly colored plastic play things didn't cut it—he preferred the real deal. So under her supervision he learned how to use the "big boy" tools. She gave him a piece of wood with three small nails driven in most of the way and his task was to pound them in without denting the wood. Elliot got very good at this and other small tasks, which not only developed his coordination, but it also drew him and Paige closer together. Paige's guilt, like the gloom that used to float through the halls of this place, slowly dissipated to trace amounts. So when I came home one day I was surprised to find her crying in the library.

"What's the matter?" I asked.

"Look at this."

She handed me a crayon drawing Elliot had drawn in pre-school earlier that day. It was a picture of the three of us standing in front of the mansion all holding hands: jellybean bodies with stick arms and legs and big smiles on our happy face heads. Hearts floated above and Elliot gave the mansion a face that smiled too. There was another face looking out of an upstairs window that was small and difficult to notice at first glance. It was colored black and blue and it did not smile. I put the drawing on the coffee table.

"See? He's coming around. He loves his mommy very much."

"Do you think so?"

"I know so!"

I was relieved that I no longer had to assure her daily that the post-partum depression was not her fault. I was also relieved that Elliot was, in fact, coming around; he had begun to reciprocate some of the love and attention Paige gave him. But a wisp of distance still lingered, as did certain wisps of dread I'd feel while turning down a darkened hall or reaching toward the spigots in the bathroom. Looking back, an enormous amount of work had been accomplished in a relatively short period of time and I hadn't, up until that point, begun to draw a connection between the mansion and Elliot and Paige's troubles.

Elliot enjoyed his solitude and sometimes got angry if we intruded on his alone time. If anything good had come from Paige's battle with post-partum depression, it was that Elliot grew to become an independent little boy. He spoke his mind when something bothered him and he, too, seemed charmed by the mansion and its restoration.

Things calmed down to the point where I felt comfortable enough to enroll in a Bachelor's program at Wayne State. Paige took the lead role in the renovation and became a very adept project manager. We hired plumbers and electricians and paid them hundreds of thousands of dollars to work their magic. Carpenters re-clad the house with pressure-treated wood siding. The shutters were repaired and reinstalled with their original bronze hardware. Painters came and coated the house in period colors that the neighborhood association put their stamp of approval on. Landscapers installed subtle landscape accoutrements, period paving stones, and a beautiful lawn.

Neighbors slowly began to introduce themselves. Many had lived on Seminole, Burns, and Iroquois streets for years and a couple of our more immediate neighbors brought us faded old photographs of the house so that we could see what it looked like back in the day.

Tall, gaunt Mr. Evans, our neighbor at 411 Seminole, retired judge and self-proclaimed techno-geek, offered to scan, enlarge, and clean up the photos. "That way you can study them in order to more faithfully restore the house to its original condition," he had told us. We dutifully accepted the manila folder filled with the new and improved photographs he had brought over and listened as he repeated his mantra on the importance of a faithful restoration. We promised to not disappoint.

Everyone seemed delighted at the progress we were making. Mr. Hintermann, the neighborhood historian, made an appointment with us and arrived promptly at the allotted time. We greeted him at the door, where he gave me a very firm handshake and kissed Paige on both cheeks. He brought a basket filled with goodies along with some forms and a questionnaire for us to fill out, "at our discretion, of course." We escorted him into the library and he whistled as he took it all in.

"What a gorgeous home you have here, Mrs. Lintz. You should be very proud of the progress you've made."

"Thank you, Mr. Hintermann. And please, call me Paige. And my husband's name is Daniel."

"Of course. And please, call me Charlie."

"Is this your first visit, Charlie, or have you been here before?" I asked, genuinely interested, wondering if he had any insights or opinions on my grandmother.

"This is one of the few houses I've never been invited into. The lady who lived here before was very private and something of a recluse. I believe she was a professor or something? I never actually had the pleasure of meeting her."

"Actually she *was* a professor," I said. "A physics professor, and also my grandmother."

"Well bless her soul. So you inherited the house, then?"

"Yes."

"How wonderful of her to have kept it in the family," replied Charlie, genuinely touched.

He was a pleasant, portly, General Motors retiree, and let us know that he was considered by many around here to be the neighborhood eccentric, a role he gladly admitted to reveling in. He was a lifetime bachelor, flamboyant in his dress and mannerisms, but too old to comfortably out himself, so instead he used innuendo, allowing us to fill in the occasional blanks.

"I stopped caring what people thought years ago!" he brayed.

We drank coffee in the library and he helped himself to some of the delicacies in the basket he brought us.

"I moved to The Village before it was fashionable to do so—back when everyone still lived in Palmer Park."

Paige suggested a tour of the house and his reaction was one of pure, unadulterated joy—as if she had just ceremoniously popped open a bottle of champagne. I excused myself and told them I would meet them on the third floor. I had a couple of chores I wanted to attend to.

"Don't worry about us—we'll find our way around, won't we Paige?"

"Oh, yes. I think we'll manage," she said smiling at him, then turning toward me with a look that said, "Thanks a lot!"

Still, I could tell she was enjoying his company. He knew everyone in the neighborhood and within an hour she'd have the skinny on every last one of them.

I hurried up to the ballroom and beelined to the worktable that was now covered with cans of paint, turpentine, and assorted brushes. I walked over to the octagon window with a cup of paint and a brush and looked out through the panes. I noticed lately how our renovations had spurred more activity up and down the street. Three other homes were now clad in their own cages of scaffolding and a landscaping crew was tearing out an old lawn across the street.

I gave the paint a few stirs as I walked toward the last dormer window that needed attention. Brush met wood as I carefully began on the last casing. I would be finished within the hour.

If the house was a queen then the ballroom was her crown, and the very large room was nothing short of spectacular. Carpenters picked up where I'd left off a couple of years ago and I had them restore the room to its original style. The plaster work, the wood moldings, the parquet floor, and the stage were pristine and gleamed in the mid-afternoon sunlight that beamed in through the three dormer windows. The only glaring exception to the otherwise finished room was that the chandelier still had not been installed. Those two bare wires—one black, the other white—still poked out through the center of a newly hand-crafted plaster ceiling medallion.

I really fretted about this. I did not want to buy a new chandelier, or even an antique one; not until I had the chance to really explore the entire house. I thought maybe I'd find the original somewhere in the basement all crated up, but I still hadn't conducted a thorough examination of the archive and honestly I preferred to not go down there. In a way I was honoring grandmother's last wishes, but that was not my primary motivation. In all actuality, the archive gave me the creeps. The few times I had ventured down there I felt like I was being watched. Paige didn't like it down there either, and Elliot didn't even know we had a basement, which was just fine for now. Thus like my grandmother, I preferred to keep it locked up—out of sight, out of mind; but the task of finding the missing chandelier loomed, and I'd be making the trek down into the archive to find it soon enough. It had to be in one of a couple hundred crates down there. I just had to look.

When I finished with the window I took the cup of paint back to the table and looked around for more work to do: Nothing. Except for the missing chandelier, the ballroom was completely finished. I hopped up onto the stage and admired my handiwork. Everything was perfect. I marveled at the incredible changes we'd made in this room from the day I walked into it with David over four years ago. That memory with David triggered a reminder: Paige took a call from him a couple days before and I still hadn't returned it. I had thought a lot about our inventory tour over the past few years and my ire at his pushiness had completely subsided. I was anxious to return his call. I was going to invite him over to see the transformation, but I also wanted to interrogate him on why he didn't tell me about my grandmother's letter and why he deliberately went against her instructions by encouraging me to donate the archive.   Maybe   it   was   all   some   huge miscommunication, but I doubted it. In spite of everything, I still liked him. I mean, I barely knew him and already our relationship was complicated. He was one charming son-of-a-bitch. Goddamn lawyers.

Just then I heard Paige and Charlie coming up the steps. I'd rather have had the chance to clear the paints and stow the table away before our first visitor walked into the newly completed ballroom, but, oh well. I allowed that his status as neighborhood historian warranted a preview. The pocket doors opened and Paige's *"Voilà!"* echoed through the huge, empty space.

"Oh, now this is spectacular," said Charlie. "Just spectacular!"

He walked around the room and took it all in. I looked at Paige and cocked my thumb in his direction, still wondering if he was okay or just a whacko. She nodded quickly, letting me know he was cool.

"Thank you, Charlie," I said. "This room was a challenge. There's so much going on architecturally."

"I see what you mean. It's almost like they let their hair down in here a little, so to speak. And all these different styles were here before you started the restoration?"

"Yes, and believe me, the restoration was painful." I hopped back off the stage and walked toward the paints, still self-conscious about the messy table.

"Mm-hm." He walked around and studied everything with the eye of a connoisseur. "It's delightful! This shouldn't work but it does—splendidly so! I see Arts and Crafts, Federalist! Jesus, there's even a hint of Rococo here and there!" He turned to me. "Mr. Lintz, this room is a masterpiece!"

Paige beamed proudly and walked over and put her arm around me.

"That's so kind of you, Charlie," she said, clearly moved. "Thank you very much. Daniel's worked very hard up here."

"No, but I mean it! This room is one-of-a-kind! And it's wonderful to see that you kept so much of the house original. You wouldn't believe how many yuppies have moved down here over the years. They buy some gorgeous piece of history—they have no idea what—then gut the place, turning it into some Pottery Barn monstrosity!"

"There's no way that would happen," I said. "There's just too much family history here."

Charlie was now looking up at the medallion with the two wires poking through.

"That's right, you said you inherited this place. How long has it been in your family, if you don't mind my asking?"

"Daniel's great-grandfather built it, when was it—1905?"

"Yes, 1905," I replied.

"So you're the third, or fourth generation owner?" asked Charlie, rather excitedly.

"I'm the fourth."

"And the house has stayed in the family since it was built?" he asked.

"That's correct."

"Would you be interested in mounting a red letter marker under your address plate?"

"I've noticed those on some of the houses," said Paige. "What do they signify?"

"It means that the house has stayed in the same family since it was built. There are only 17 red letter markers out of a couple hundred homes. It's considered prestigious to have one."

"I don't know…" I said, hesitantly.

"We should get one," said Paige. "That would be cool!"

I shrugged. Charlie looked at me, expecting me to say something.

"Think about it," Charlie said, after a pause. "You're eligible." Then he shifted his attention back to the medallion. "What's going on with the chandelier? Are you having it restored?"

"No, I've got to find it first. I think I remember it hanging up here when I was a kid, but I don't know what happened to it."

"That's a shame. It's going to be hard finding one that works with all this going on," Charlie said scanning the room. "I mean you could go all sorts of different ways."

"I'm sure the original will turn up. There are a lot of nooks and crannies in this house. I just haven't had the time to really look," I replied.

"I'm sure you're right. Regardless, I'd love to come back and have a look after you have it re-hung."

Picking up on his cue, Paige walked over to him and offered her arm. He hooked his in hers as they walked toward the pocket doors.

"You have an open invitation, Charlie. Anytime. And we'll take a look at your questionnaire," said Paige.

She turned back to me and I got from the arch in her brow that this time she wanted me to follow. I obeyed and the three of us descended the double-winder stairway.

"Will you two be participating in the home and garden tour this year?" asked Charlie. "I'm on the organizing committee and would love for you to participate. I can tell you right now that you'll steal the show."

We were now headed toward the grand stairway. I walked by Elliot's bedroom door, which was open slightly.

"The dust is only just now settling," said Paige to Charlie, still arm-in-arm walking a little ahead of me. "We're a little exhausted from all of the restoration, but we'll do it next year. That's a promise."

I peeked into Elliot's room. He was on the floor vrooming his cars and trucks on a big rug that had a picture of a town with streets that twisted and turned between the buildings. A menagerie of stuffed animals sat next to him.

"Hi, daddy!" he said, looking up at me.

"Hey, buddy. Playing trucks?" I walked into the messy room that was filled with a mishmash of old antique furniture and newer, little-boy-cool-stuff.

"Yeah. Is that guy with Mommy a worker?"

"That's Mr. Hintermann, our neighbor."

"I know, Mommy told me. Is he gonna do some work on the house?" Elliot asked, hopefully.

"Nope. He just wants to be friends. But that's okay too, right?"

"Yeah," he replied, with a trace of dejection.

"He brought a basket of goodies for us. I bet there's something in there you'd like."

"Did he bring gummy worms?" he asked, brightening.

"I don't know. We can look through it and find out."

"Okay."

"We're going to eat soon, so why don't you clean up a little then come down, okay?"

"Okay."

I tousled his thick mop of dark hair and walked out of the room. His reality from the time he was born was renovation. He had developed a fascination with construction and knew the name and age of every worker that walked into our house. He won all of them over and was known as the little foreman and actually developed an eye for quality work.

Lately he'd been missing the hum and activity of all the construction and we were in a period of transition with him. He was in the midst of construction withdrawal and was having a tough time. As I turned to walk down the stairs, I heard him get up and toss things into bins. I heard the pad of his small feet running around his room. He was my joy, my love, my little guy, my smart little worker. He began to sing something that at first I thought was a song he learned at pre-school—the, "Let's put our toys away" song—but the lyrics froze me and made my blood run cold.

I had a little birdy
His name was Enza

I opened up the winda
In-flew-enza

⇑   ⇑   ⇑

"I've been dying to come to this place for ages," I said to Paige wiping barbecue sauce off my face. "I think it was worth the wait. What do you think?"

Paige picked at her food. "I like it. The food's good," she lied.

"You don't like it?" I asked.

She shrugged. I wanted to have a good time tonight. I wanted *her* to have a good time tonight, and God knows we both needed a few hours away from Seminole Street. Elliot was safe at Paige's mother's where we had dropped him off earlier. He would be spending the night there so we had the whole evening to ourselves.

Normally, Paige would have really been into an evening like this: a foray into our urban wasteland, exploring, marveling, and commenting on the ruins. This time, however, she could take in the scenery from the vantage of a comfortable restaurant booth with a spectacular view of the massive, fourteen-story Michigan Central Railway ruin—the tallest train station in the world when it was built a century ago.

I wanted to help her realize that her suspicions about the house were unfounded, and if I couldn't do that at least I could distract her for an evening. I charged on talking and masticating, washing it all down with some heavenly local microbrew, heroically plodding on, trying to cleverly diss our immediate surroundings, but there wasn't much to diss.

"I mean, it's cool they opened this place, and it got great reviews and all, but they need to chill a little on the enthusiasm," I said, feeling a little buzzed.

She didn't really care for barbecue so she opted for the fish, which wasn't this restaurant's specialty. She was usually a trooper when it was my turn to pick where to eat, but her lack of enthusiasm was obvious by the way she stirred her fork around her plate. Still, the cuisine at Slows Bar-B-Q ranked low on her stress list; something else was bothering her, but she was doing her best and seemed to at least enjoy the restaurant's hip, rustic ambiance—and it *was* a great place to people watch. I rambled on halfway through my third beer.

"They talk about this place like it's the greatest thing that's happened to this town since the goddamn assembly line," I said, raising my glass.

She smiled then looked out the window and winced.

We watched as the sun's red orb descended behind the railway station, winking through the thousand broken windows of the massive Beaux-Arts silhouette, looking like it had been there for a millennium. It was the western hemisphere's most famous urban ruin thanks in part to armies of Euro-trash photographers posting their ruin porn all over the internet.

Slows was packed with a collection of thirty-something hipsters, students, artists, suburbanites, and a smattering of high-rise professionals in suits who'd recently been relocated downtown from the suburbs. Conversation petered down to a whisper as everyone turned to watch the sunset. What we were witnessing was almost spiritual and, if only for a moment, it connected us and our faces were lit in the warm red glow. As if on cue, everyone donned sunglasses like soldiers lined up to watch a test detonation.

The red orb dipped below the cracked horizon and the light dialed down to purple. The din of conversation returned to its previous volume.

"You're awfully quiet tonight. What're you thinking about?" I asked.

"I don't know. We're finished with the house. Now what?"

"I know. I've been thinking about that, too."

"In a way it's so cool and I'm really happy with the results. The place is incredible, beyond anything I could have imagined; but there's something that, I don't know, bothers me about the place," she said, placing her fork onto her plate.

"Maybe we're going through post-construction blues, like Elliot," I offered.

She smiled but only briefly, then got to the point. "Did you know that Elliot has an imaginary friend? When I say friend, I don't mean, like, a friendly friend."

"No, I didn't. How'd you find out? I mean kids are secretive about that stuff sometimes, aren't they?"

"I got up to go to the bathroom last night and decided to check on him before hopping back into bed. I got to his door and heard him talking. At first I wondered if maybe he was talking in his sleep. It was so late. I stood there crouched by the door for a few seconds and listened. Then I swear it sounded like someone shushed him. I panicked thinking someone was in there with him. I opened the door and he was out of his bed and standing there staring into his closet, and the door was wide open."

"Wait. What time was this?" I asked, realizing that dispelling her fears would be more difficult than I'd anticipated.

"Like three in the morning! I asked him, 'Sweetheart, what are you doing out of bed?' And he just looked at me like he was in a daze. Then he ran to me and hugged me. I picked him up and took him to the rocking chair, and sat him on my lap, and we rocked for a little while. I soothed him and told him it was okay and that he was only having a bad dream. And I thought, yes, that must be it; my four-year-old son, for some reason, is walking and talking in his sleep and having a bad dream. Then I noticed his big toe."

"What? What about his big toe? What happened?" I asked.

"The nail on the big toe of his right foot was all black and blue."

I listened and immediately came up with a litany of logical explanations.

"Well, he likes playing with tools. Maybe he dropped a hammer on his toe, or something."

"He's four years old," she said, leaning in toward me. "He would have come screaming to one of us if that'd happened."

"Well, what happened? Did you ask him about it?"

She was still sensitive about the post-partum depression and this question triggered a defensive reaction.

"Of course I asked him about it! You think I'm going to notice an injury on my son and *not* ask him about it?"

"I'm sorry! Of course you asked him! What did he say?"

"He said he couldn't tell me; that *she'd* get mad if he told anyone."

"Who told him this? Did he tell you?" I asked, a little alarmed at this revelation.

She looked at me and bit her lip. She took a sip of wine and pushed her plate out of the way.

"Did your grandmother have a sister named Nora?"

A chill ran down my spine. "I don't know—I don't remember. I know she had a…"

Paige interrupted. "Back when we lived on Grove I remember you had me read that letter your grandmother wrote you. She mentioned that she has a sister named Nora. That was her name, right?"

"Yes. I remember now. Nora was her name. What about it?"

"Elliot told me that Nora did it. That Nora comes to him and wants him to help her and when he says no she pinches his toe. He told me that she pinches his toe really hard."

I didn't want to believe what I was hearing. I remembered my own experience a few years ago that first night I spent in the house. I'd never told Paige about it. I hadn't made any connections between the little girl who led me to that box in the archive and Nora, my grandmother's long-dead sister, until that moment sitting across from Paige in that booth. Paige leaned in a little closer.

"Now I'm going to ask you a question and I want you to be perfectly honest with me. Can you do that?"

"Yes… I think I can be perfectly honest."

"Because I know how important that mansion is to you, but I'm going to be perfectly honest with *you*. If there's anything in that place that can hurt my son, we will hightail it out of there so fast it'll make your head spin!"

"What's your question?" I asked dryly, not appreciating the hysterical turn the conversation had taken.

"What do you know about the mansion? What's going on in that house?"

"I don't know what you mean," I lied.

"Has anything weird ever happened to you there?"

"I mean, sometimes I get the creeps when I'm upstairs by myself. Sometimes I hear things, but I always attribute that to the fact that the house is old. The foundation is settling. There's been a lot of activity with all the construction and I'm sure it's been a great strain on the bones of the house. But if you're asking me if I think the place is haunted, then no, I don't think it is," I said pointedly.

"That's not what I'm asking you," she said looking me directly in the eye. "Your grandmother's letter said, 'the best way to deal with them is to ignore them,' or something like that. Do you remember? What do you think she meant?"

"I don't know what she meant."

"Okay, then I'll just come out and ask: Has anything, I don't know… paranormal, ever happened to you in that house?"

I thought long and hard about how to answer that question. The only thing I had experienced was a very lucid dream that somehow crossed into reality in the form of a small fingernail imbedded in a wood crate buried deep in the archive. I had long ago rationalized that the whole thing was just a dream and that I had probably glimpsed the crate and fingernail while taking the tour with David without even realizing it, and later my subconscious flushed it into consciousness in the form of a seriously creepy dream. I remembered it being a very stressful time in our lives and the mind can play tricks.

"No," I said. "Nothing paranormal has ever happened to me while living in the house. And what about you—has anything paranormal happened to you since we've lived there?"

"No," she replied, holding the stem of her wine glass.

"Okay. Do you think that maybe we're dealing with the overactive imagination of a four-year-old boy?"

"You need to look at his toe. He's going to lose his toenail."

"It's that bad!?" I asked, surprised.

"Yes! It's all purple and black underneath! The nail is dead."

"Why am I only hearing about this now?"

"I didn't want to make a big deal out of it last night. It was three in the morning and I wanted to keep the drama to a minimum," she replied, looking down at her wine glass, her fingertips twirling the stem.

"What's that supposed to mean?" I asked a little hurt.

"If I would have told you, you would have rushed into his room and scooped him up and babied him."

"And that's a bad thing?"

"I don't want to reward his fears. I don't want him to start sleeping with us every time he hears something go bump in the night. And we don't need to be over-reacting around him."

"Well, should we at least have taken him to the doctor?"

"I told my mom about it. She's going to look at it."

"Well, she's the nurse," I replied. "You don't think it's broken, do you?

"No, it's not broken. It's just bruised. It doesn't hurt when he wiggles his toes, I asked him," she said, matter-of-factly.

I didn't want to believe Paige's story, but I knew it was true. Nora, if that's who she was, was visiting Elliot. How else could he have known that song?

"Do you recall ever mentioning Nora to him?" she asked.

"Hmm, let me think… have I ever mentioned my long-dead, great-aunt Nora to Elliot? Gee, I don't think so!"

"You don't need to get sarcastic. I'm only asking."

"I'm sorry. Maybe there's a logical explanation," I said, knowing in-fact, that there was no logical explanation.

"Well, when you think of one let me know, because I'm telling you right now, I don't like this. I don't like this one bit."

"Well, neither do I!"

I paid the bill. We drove through downtown and passed a sea of orange traffic cones and blinking yellow arrows where construction had begun on a light-rail system that would eventually run all the way up Woodward Avenue out to Pontiac. The original light-rail system (street cars, as they had once been known) had been dismantled in the 1950s, making Detroit the largest city in the United States without street cars or subways. I wanted to say to Paige that all of this expensive construction was like nails being pulled out of a coffin, but she was talking to her mother Marian on her cell phone.

From what I could gather by listening in, Elliot's toe was fine in that it wasn't broken. He would probably lose his toenail, but that was the extent of his injury. I don't think Paige had said anything to Marian about Elliot's "imaginary friend."

Elliot adored his grandmother and loved visiting her. I was sure that he'd tell Marian about Nora and that she'd find a way of dispelling his fears. She was a retired emergency room nurse who now taught classes at Macomb Community College. Paige continued talking with her mother, staring out of her window, looking blankly in the direction of Windsor. I listened as she spoke.

"Yes," she was happy with the house, and "Yes, the lack of a neighborhood grocery store was a pain in the ass, but Whole Foods and Meijer would be opening soon," and "Yes, there's been a lot of construction around here; we're driving through some now," and "Actually it's not so bad down here, I've gotten used to it," and "Our neighbors are super nice, wait till you meet Charlie!" and "You've seen the house—it makes up for a whole lot, trust me."

We drove by the massive General Motors world headquarters, also known as the Renaissance Center, a collection of ugly, cylindrical glass towers that has dominated the Detroit skyline since the 1970s. A Cadillac sat displayed in front of the Jefferson Avenue entrance, illuminated brightly under an array of strategically oriented digital lighting designed to maximize impact.

We continued east over the I-375 interchange. Paige said good-bye to her mother.

"My mom told us not to worry. The toe's not broken. Just bruised," Paige said slipping her phone back into her purse.

"Well, that's a relief," I replied.

"I'm going to sleep in Elliot's room tonight," she said as we turned left onto Seminole.

I couldn't help but sigh. "Whatever."

"This isn't about you!" she said, suddenly angry. "I just want to make sure!"

"Make sure of what? That if Nora comes you can tell her to leave our son alone?" I asked, pulling up onto our driveway. She turned to me. Moonlight glinted in the tear that ran down her cheek.

"Yes! That's exactly what I'm going to do," she replied, grabbing the door handle and yanking it open.

⇧   ⇧   ⇧

Paige was in our room getting ready for bed. I went into Elliot's room and opened his closet door. I didn't see anything out of the ordinary. Nora was not hiding in there, I noted, thinking how ridiculous it was to even look. I retrieved the baby monitor we had stowed away a couple of years ago and plugged it back in. I placed the microphone prominently on Elliot's dresser and brought the receiver into our room.

Paige was wearing one of my t-shirts and walking toward the bedroom door with her pillow, cell phone, and a couple magazines.

"I thought it would be a good idea to hook the baby monitor back up," I said, placing the receiver on her nightstand.

"That is a good idea," she replied, turning to me. She was so beautiful standing there, and so strong. I could practically see the love she had for Elliot surging through her veins.

"I wish you'd stay," I said to her. "I'm worried about the situation too, but seriously, how will sleeping in his room prove anything?"

"I'll be able to tell him about it when we pick him up tomorrow, and that nothing happened."

"Well, we have the baby monitor now," I offered weakly. "We'll be able to hear if anything happens."

"It won't be the same. I have to sleep in his room."

I couldn't help but stare at Paige with longing. She looked so hot wearing nothing but my t-shirt, and she knew the effect it was having on me.

"You know it gets awfully drafty in here at night. I'm probably going to freeze to death all by myself," I pouted.

Nothing turned me on more than when Paige wore one of my t-shirts and nothing else. I was never one for sexy lingerie. Lace, straps, garters—they had very little impact on me, and I've always regarded them as more akin to a costume that needed an instruction manual to be properly removed. She lingered by the door, and the mixed signals were driving me crazy.

"Then why don't you light a fire?" she replied, indicating the fireplace, still lingering.

"You already did that."

"Well then maybe I just need to come over there and give you a goodnight kiss."

She dropped her burden of pillow, magazines, and cell phone onto the floor and walked toward me. Her t-shirt was on the floor, too, by the time she reached me. She whispered into my ear after giving me a long, deep, kiss.

"I know there's probably nothing going on in this house, but I'm still sleeping in Elliot's room."

I cupped her head into my hands and looked her in the eyes. "I know. I understand. I really do."

"You know what still turns me on about you even after all these years?" She asked, her fingers undoing my belt. "The thing that makes me crazy, but still turns me on?"

"No. Tell me," I whispered, kissing her neck.

"Your total immersion; your total dedication. There's no stopping you once you've made up your mind."

"Then I think we need to dedicate ourselves to some total immersion right now."

⇑   ⇑   ⇑

I dozed off for what seemed like a few minutes but when I came to, Paige was no longer in bed with me. I walked into the bathroom suite not bothering to turn the light on and beelined to the toilet where I stood peeing more than half asleep. I had a slight headache and my nostrils registered a metallic stench, but I dismissed it, too tired for its familiarity to register.

A drop released its grip from the spigot behind me and plopped into the bathtub, then a faint swirling of liquid, like an arm swishing soap bubbles away. I silenced my stream, re-aiming it onto the porcelain, then I froze and listened. Another drop fell into the tub, its sonar-like ping reverberating off the tiles.

"Paige?"

How peculiar. Why is Paige taking a bath in the dark?

"Paige? Is that you?"

Another swirl of liquid. Then another and my hair stood on end.

The air in the room suddenly became stifling, the metallic stench dialing up to a nauseating level. A shadow crawled across the wall by the door and the door suddenly closed. Other shadows tumbled out from behind the radiator, the toilet, cupboards, and corners, and they converged, turning the dark to total blackness. I didn't want a repeat of that first night I slept in the house, but that's what I was getting and I knew I had to get to Paige. Where was she? She was in Elliot's room—I had to get there to see, to make sure she was okay. I had to reach Paige and comfort her and tell her that it's nothing—just memories. The house is sick but we can make it better. We can chase the memories away and purge the house. I had to reach Paige. I needed her so bad. We can get a priest to come and bless the house. We can get rid of them. We can make them go away.

I felt my way toward the door and as I did, whatever was in the tub suddenly stood, causing the liquid to slosh onto the floor. I felt for the light switch, found it, and snapped it on. The shadows blinked back into their hiding places and the tub was empty and dry. Not a drop of liquid. It was as if the light had suddenly broken a spell and I stood there puzzled and pissed-off.

I didn't want, nor did I accept this intrusion on our otherwise peaceful home; it had been too easy for me to dismiss these bizarre events but I couldn't ignore them anymore. *But I was told to ignore them!* I had to take stock. I inspected the spigots, showerhead, and drain. A swirl of thick black hair, coated in a crust of clotted blood, lay matted over the drain. I leaned over to inspect it when a single crimson drop fell from the showerhead, punctuating the white porcelain with a shocking red blot. The drop trailed toward the drain in a straight line before disappearing, taking the hair and clotted blood with it, leaving not a trace of either.

My eyes shot up to the showerhead, but there was nothing out of the ordinary to see. I sat on the edge of the tub with my face in my hands. I couldn't deny this any longer.

"The best way to deal with them is to ignore them." My grandmother's words kept reverberating in my consciousness. But how was that possible when they would not be ignored? Nora was visiting Elliot. She has been teaching him songs and pinching his toes—how do you get a four-year-old to ignore that! *Maybe we should leave this place,* I thought, but another part of me screamed back, *NO! We're not leaving!* I had to figure this out. What did Nora want? Eyes! She wanted her eyes. But where were they? The crate! I'll go into the archive and open the crate!

The hinges creaked as I opened the bathroom door. I stopped. They never creak. I walked back into the bedroom and heard something running down the hallway, but it stopped abruptly. Did it hear the creak?

"Paige? Is that you?" I called out, unable to contain the fear in my voice.

Sure, Paige decided to run laps down the hall at 3 a.m., my brain retorted sarcastically.

The glow from a night-light in the hallway leaked into the bedroom from under the door. All I focused on was getting to Paige. The entity, or whatever it was, ran down the hall again from the direction of the ballroom stairs and stopped at my door. My heart was beating loud enough to be heard throughout the house. The light under the bedroom door dimmed as the shadow of two small feet shuffled to the foot of the door. It stood there on the other side, waiting, before a whisper hissed through the keyhole.

"Help me, Papa!" It was Nora.

I crouched forward and banged my head on the bedroom door. I closed my eyes and pounded on the door with my clenched fists and whispered back through the door, matching its malevolence, "Go away! Go away!"

Then I felt it. It was slight at first, then excruciating. I opened my eyes and a small, spidery, shriveled hand had reached under the door and gripped my big toe, crushing it between its boney thumb and index finger.

"Find them!" the voice hissed.

Nora had crushed Elliot's toe too, and a wave of rage washed over me. I yanked my foot away from the spidery, withered hand then stomped on it. The hand, wrist, and forearm—all of it—exploded into a puff of dust.

I opened the door and walked out into the hallway. The night-light had been kicked out of its socket and it lay there next to the runner, the plug twisted and bent. Moonlight leached in through the grand stair window and shadows spindled down the hall, slicing through the dim. The hallway was freezing and I wished I was wearing more than just my pajama bottoms.

I opened Elliot's bedroom door and peeked in. It felt twenty degrees warmer in here, and I was surprised, but happy, to see that Paige was sound asleep. Part of me wanted to crawl in with her, but Elliot's twin bed was too small for both of us and I didn't want to wake Paige. I just wanted to make sure she was safe, and she was. I couldn't have been more relieved, because she didn't need to know anything about what I had just gone through.

I walked down the grand stair and beelined to the butler's pantry where I kept a small tool box, then fished the keys from their hiding place. I unlocked the metal door and descended the basement stairs. I turned on the lights. A hazy, dry ice-like fog undulated inches off the floor and eddies and whirls formed and dissipated as though the floor were a boiling liquid.

I walked down the hall to the room where the crate was stored and opened the door. The crate was in its place, tucked in halfway between the corner and the entrance to the room. Elliot's tiny tool belt sat on the floor next to it. The little hammer Paige had bought him was on top of the crate and there were hammer dents pockmarked into it and splinters of wood littering the floor. Nora must have led him down here and forced him to try and open the crate, but he couldn't do it. It was too strong for a little guy like him to open. Since living here we've never let him in the basement; we never even mentioned having a basement. For Elliot the basement was an unknown-unknown. He never asked about it, and we never brought it up. We always thought that one day he'd ask about the steel door in the kitchen and where it led to, and we'd deal with it then. Nora obviously had other plans.

I stormed out into the hall, the haze parting in my wake. I whispered, calling out to Nora, my voice reverberating off the hard surfaces.

"Nora! I'm going to open the box now. Let's find your eyes! Come and get them," I said, daring her to materialize.

A dry, hissing, cackle came from everywhere and nowhere, and further down near the library hall, a swirl in the fog grew taller, pulling the rest in toward it. I backed into the room, opened my toolbox, and pulled out a hammer.

The doorway darkened as a figure floated into the room, still forming, the hazy apparition coalescing into the form of Nora, back-lit in silhouette with hazy tendrils and wisps of plasma slowly whipping and lashing to and fro. The scent of rot and earth mingled, putrefying the dank air. I backed away as Nora drew closer, but I held my anger in check remembering why I was down here.

"Let's see what's in the box, Nora! Let's find your eyes!" I said, resisting the urge to back away from her.

The entity floated toward the crate as her figure became more formed and solid. The wisps and tendrils disappeared into her frame, and standing before me was the familiar pretty girl wearing the maroon dress with the lacy collar and sleeves, the white stockings and patent leather shoes. She stared down at the crate through her bangs, like an addict fixated on her drug.

I dug the claws of the hammer into the top of the crate and levered the top loose. I pulled off the top and detached the sides, which collapsed onto the floor. The object inside the crate was wrapped in canvas and bound with ropes. I shuddered and paused, wondering if it was Nora's body I'd find cloaked under the canvas. I untied the rope and tossed it aside and slowly pulled at the canvas revealing a multi-colored globe-shaped object comprised of thousands of pieces of tiffany art glass. Was it the ballroom chandelier? I wasn't sure, but pulling the canvas off was like lifting the lid off a treasure chest. But there were no eyes, and why would Nora's eyes have been stored in the crate along with this boxed-up and forgotten treasure? It made absolutely no sense.

"Your eyes aren't in the box, Nora," I said, looking up at her. "You need to leave now."

She gazed down at the object through her bangs and her smile gave way to shock. Her visage crinkled, and her maroon dress became threadbare and tea-stained with age. Her smooth, young skin yellowed and stretched like crepe-paper over her skull. She shuffled toward the object, her dagger-like fingertips quivering as her arms reached outward. Her empty eye sockets registered horror and desperation.

"They're not here, Nora!" I shouted, anger shutting out any vestige of fear. "Your eyes are not in the box! They're gone and you have to leave this house." I stood and pointed toward the door. "Leave and never come back! NOW!"

She turned to me and her mouth opened wide in a frozen scream. Her fingers clawed the air in front of her face. Then she collapsed, crumbling onto the floor in a cloud of dust. I watched it dissipate in a whirl until it disappeared completely.

She was gone and wouldn't come back.

No more dreams and visions. No more pinching, no more black-and-blue toenails and no more cold spots. No more sleep-walking and midnight trips down into the archive. I had cleansed the house. All it took was showing Nora that what she was looking for could not be found. She wouldn't be back and now we could live in peace. We could raise our son in this house without fear. I could now sincerely attribute those things that go bump in the night to foundations that settle, to the recently completed work that, after all, had been a great strain on the bones of the house, because, really, wasn't that all it was? All this commotion, fear, and talk of ghosts? Ridiculous!

⇑   ⇑   ⇑

I turned my attention to the object. Was it the chandelier I remembered seeing up in the ballroom when I was a boy? I wasn't sure, but it was an incredible find. I examined it and there was what I thought might be a Tiffany hallmark in the spidery, titanium framework that held the pieces of art glass in place. A little online research would answer that question. But there was something strange about the chandelier. It had what could only be described as an industrial, utilitarian look to it. It reminded me of some of the gorgeously designed, 19th-century machinery on display at the Henry Ford Museum. The more I looked at it, the more I realized that it was probably an optical instrument of some sort and not a chandelier.

It was large, perhaps four feet in circumference. It was globular, but unlike anything I had ever seen before. Steam punk came to mind. *This couldn't be the same chandelier,* I thought to myself. I didn't remember it looking this way, but it didn't matter because I knew it would be perfect. The ballroom was slightly odd and what it needed was an odd centerpiece. Nothing could be more appropriate as the ballroom's centerpiece.

Within a month it would be hanging under the hand-crafted plaster ceiling medallion in the ballroom on the third floor of our newly restored home on Seminole Street.

PART II

The next day my electrician friend Al came by to help me schlep the chandelier to the ballroom and wire it up. It weighed well over 100 pounds so we had to be very careful trudging up the three stories, carrying it by hand and taking frequent breaks.

There were a lot of strange things about it that I didn't notice upon first inspection. The light bulbs inside were unlike any I'd ever seen: Each was very large and had three filaments, and each filament was fixed to its own base, each of which spun in circles around a center axis. I found another box filled with 12 of the strange bulbs, each one carefully packaged in its own compartment. The equator of the chandelier was ringed with a lens that probably magnified and focused light—similar to a Fresnel lens in the lantern room of a lighthouse. The lens consisted of three thick bands of multi-colored glass, one on top of the other, and each band rotated independent of the others. Attached by a thick, three-foot-long cable to the top of it was a small, rectangular, gunmetal box. It was probably some sort of transformer, but why a chandelier would need its own transformer was beyond me. I knew very little about electricity and didn't like messing with it. The upper and lower hemispheres of the globe-shaped chandelier were composed of hundreds of pieces of multi-colored art glass. Each piece was faceted like a gemstone on the side facing outward and as smooth as a telescope mirror on the inward side. I couldn't wait to see how each piece would refract the light emanating from the strange bulbs inside.

Much to my dismay, I discovered that two of the crystals were missing from the lower hemisphere of the globe. It would be very difficult to find replacements for the two missing pieces as every single piece was of a different shape and color from the other. It would be glaringly obvious once the chandelier was connected and lit that the two pieces were missing. Al picked up the box connected to the light and shook it and we heard what sounded like broken glass inside. I shot him a what-the-hell look.

"Well, whatever's broken in there *was* broken!" he said.

"I know, but still," I replied, sharply.

Al had been a good friend of mine for years. I met him back when we had worked for the same construction company. He spoke in a rich baritone voice and had a booming laugh that could be heard above everyone else's in a crowd. His thick shock of hair was a lot more gray than the last time I saw him and he was 20 pounds heavier, too. He was also sporting a waxed handlebar mustache, which caught me completely off guard.

"I've got to ask," I said, as I slid the pocket doors open. "What's up with the 'stache?"

"Promise you won't laugh?" he said a little apprehensively.

"I'm not promising anything," I chuckled.

"I joined a barbershop quartet," he said almost embarrassed.

I looked at him incredulously. We picked the object back up and carried it into the ballroom, grunting and groaning.

"Barbershop? What, like, 'My Sweet Adeline.' That kind of barbershop quartet?"

"Yeah, except that's old school. We don't sing 'My Sweet Adeline.'"

"Oh, you're on to more modern stuff, like 'Daisy?'"

"Shut up, dick!" he laughed, only half-kidding. I laughed too.

"We actually sing a lot of Beatles tunes. And we totally rock some Journey," he said.

We made our way to the scaffolding I'd erected earlier that day and set the object onto a large piece of Styrofoam. Al picked up the gunmetal box, took a small screwdriver from his tool belt, and unscrewed the side. He opened it and looked inside. There was a broken vacuum tube.

"So what's the box for?" I asked.

"I don't know. I thought it might be a transformer, but I've never seen tubes in a transformer."

He put the box down and we carefully slid the object into place, directly below the plaster medallion. Al picked the box back up and raised a safety issue.

"I'd feel a lot better if I knew what this box was for. I'd like to take it home and look it over," he said staring into its guts.

"You said it's probably just some kind of transformer, right? It should be okay," I said dismissing his concern, anxious to get the object hooked up.

"No! It's not okay! You've got a broken vacuum tube in here that'll have to be replaced, and... holy shit!" he said aiming a small flashlight into the box. "This thing's been wired with gold!"

"What gold? Why would they use gold?"

"It's a great conductor—like a hundred times better than copper."

"Cool! Gold wiring!"

"Still, I don't know what this box is for... and wish me luck finding a vacuum tube to replace the broken one. And this thing is old, you know? I just want to make sure it's safe."

"Well, what could go wrong?"

"Hmm, let's see... it could short out and burn your house to the ground for starters. That would kinda suck, wouldn't it?" Al said matter-of-factly.

"Uh, yeah, that would definitely suck."

"And I'm not connecting this thing until I know what it's for and that it's 100 percent safe."

I felt like a kid who wanted a BB gun for Christmas but got a slingshot instead. I couldn't wait to get the object connected and I was dying to see what it looked like all lit up.

"Well do me a favor at least. I can't wait to see what this thing does. Just bypass the box for now. See if it'll work if you wire it up directly."

"Dude, you gotta cool your jets! This box serves some important purpose."

"What could happen? Just do it!" I pleaded.

"No! See all those delicate moving parts inside that thing? All those wires and fancy bulbs?" he said pointing at the object. "If I bypass it, this thing could go up in a puff of blue smoke! My guess is that this box is some kind of regulator. Let me take it apart, look it over, and replace the broken parts—like this tube here. Seriously, I'll start working on it tonight and we'll have this thing up and connected in a couple days. That's a promise."

Despite my excitement and impatience, I knew Al was right. We'd been living in the house for five years, so a few more days without the crowning touch wouldn't kill me. Still, for whatever reason, my exuberance was over the top and I had to check myself. I calmed down, acknowledging Al's concerns.

"Sorry. I've been looking for that chandelier since we've lived here and I guess I got caught up in the moment. You're right; safety first."

"That's okay, Danny boy. Don't worry about it. We'll get it done and do it right," Al said then added, "Can I tell you something? This thing is not a chandelier."

I looked at him skeptically. "What is it then?" I asked.

"I don't know but we'll find out, won't we!?"

Al disconnected the cable and box assembly from the chandelier—or whatever it was, and coiled it. We left it sitting on the Styrofoam and I took one last look as I slid the pocket doors closed. It was odd. The further I walked away from it the darker it got, its features melding until it looked black; like a giant, round star sapphire resting on a bed of cotton.

We walked back downstairs to the kitchen and I made

BETTER BOXED AND FORGOTTEN

a couple of sandwiches that we ate at the small table in the breakfast nook. I told Al that Paige and I were going to throw a house warming party soon and that I'd love for his barbershop quartet to come and perform as a surprise for Paige.

"We're not cheap!" he said, smiling, giving his mustache a twist.

"Name your price," I replied.

We made an agreement then clinked our glasses of Vernor's together.

⚜   ⚜   ⚜

"You've done some pretty miraculous things up here. I can't believe the transformation!" David said. It had been just over 5 years since the inventory, and he was clearly impressed with the restoration.

He was standing in the middle of the ballroom slightly stooped over, his balled-up fists resting on his hips. I had invited him over for the inaugural activation of the device. He was a lot thinner now and doing his best to hide a slight shuffle in his step. Paige heard that he had a minor stroke and said it would be a good idea to invite him over soon (which, in my mind, was her saying that we should basically get him over here before he croaks) and this was as good an occasion as any. She knew I had some questions for him but I didn't want this to turn an interrogation session. There was a lot he could tell me and there would be a price attached—a quid pro quo—but my inquiries could wait for now. We were here to watch what would happen when we flipped the switch.

Even though he was a little more frail than the last time we'd seen each other, David was still a formidable presence. I felt out of my league around him because he had a lot of guile, kept his cards close, and was an expert in things like non-verbal communication. Despite his intimidating demeanor, he seemed a bit tense at the prospect of us fiddling with the device and I wondered if he knew more about it than he was letting on. He still practiced law, but only sporadically and, despite the stroke, he was as sharp as ever. Other than the weight loss, he really hadn't changed that much from the time we shared that cognac in the secret library, but he seemed vulnerable and brittle, like a delicate glass figurine teetering too close to the edge of a shelf, and he was doing his best to hide his debilitated state with a thick layer of make-up.

Al was on the stage wiring-up a temporary control panel that was equipped with a series of rheostats to regulate the amount of power going into the different parts of the device. The wall switches were already installed by the pocket doors, but Al bypassed them for now, wanting to conduct some tests with the panel. It had taken him a little longer than a couple days to get it up and running (more like a month actually), but he completed everything by the book and even had to rewrite a few pages due to the many unanticipated complexities.

The inner workings of the device were as complicated as a Swiss watch. Many moving parts had to be inspected, tweaked, repaired, and lubricated. He sent away for new vacuum tubes and, while he cleaned, repaired, and rewired it, he figured out that the box and cable assembly was in fact a regulator. Neither of us realized what we were getting into and Al said that the project turned out to be more complicated than repairing a gutted-out pinball machine. Al had devoted over a hundred hours to the device's restoration and was well paid for his efforts.

David walked toward Al and the control panel, which was set up at the edge of the stage.

"So, Mr. Laborde," David asked looking up at Al, "What do you think this device was designed to do?"

He held out his hand; Al grabbed it and pulled, hoisting the old man on to the stage. David walked around to the front of the control panel and looked down at all the dials and knobs.

"I still don't know what the hell it's for," Al replied, plugging a cable into the back of the panel. "But I can tell you this: it sure as hell isn't a chandelier!"

"Do you think it's safe?" David asked.

"Safety is why he's got it hooked up to a control panel," I interjected. "He can power it up slowly and if anything goes wrong he can shut it down."

"Is that true?" David asked with a hint of skepticism.

"That's it in a nutshell," Al replied.

"This seems like an awful lot of precaution," David said. "What are your concerns?"

Al looked at me a little exasperated. David caught the look. He felt the need to take control of the situation so he qualified his question, throwing in a little volume.

"I only ask because none of us has any idea what this device actually does!"

"And that's why we're here," I said, bundling the thick black cables and zip-tying them together. "To find out!"

I walked to each window and closed the curtains. My

eyes adjusted to the dark as the only light in the room now emanated from a work lamp that lit Al's control panel.

David took his glasses off and wiped the lenses with the fat end of his tie. He stuck them back on the end of his nose and inspected the control panel, probably rationalizing that cleaning his glasses would help him understand what he was looking at.

"You know, your great-grandfather had his own research lab—his own Menlo Park, as it were."

"I didn't know that," I said, appreciating the information. "Tell me about it."

"This device you're playing with was probably invented there. You haven't come across any information about it in the archive?"

"Nothing that says what it's for. The only things I found relating to it were some letters from the Tiffany Glassworks. He contracted them to fabricate the glass and frame."

"Well it's a very impressive piece of machinery and, for whatever it's worth, I'm going to throw my two cents in," said David, the anger in his frail voice sounding almost comical. "This isn't some goddamn toy! It's a scientific instrument and God only knows what purpose it serves! You haven't turned it on yet?"

"No, and I can't wait to see what it does." I looked at Al who was still behind the control panel labeling the dials. "How much longer, Al?"

"Just a few more minutes," he replied.

"I see that a couple of the crystals are missing. Is that going to affect anything?" David asked.

"That's actually one of the reasons I wired it up to the

control panel," Al said. "While I was working on it, I couldn't believe the craftsmanship that went into it. All the moving parts on it are perfectly balanced. I want to bring it up slowly in case those two missing pieces throw it out of whack."

"We think what we've got here is some kind of gyroscope that'll throw off light," I said walking up to the panel and turning to Al. "Can you think of anything we might have missed?"

"I think we're okay, but I'm going to take one last look-see."

He jumped off the stage and walked around under the device, aiming his flashlight up at the various connections, joints, and cables, like a pilot giving his plane one last inspection before climbing into the cockpit.

The device hung, centered underneath the plaster ceiling medallion, from a pole that was just over four feet long and attached to a complicated universal joint bracket that would allow for spinning and tilting.

"I think we're good," he said jumping back onto the stage.

The control panel was wired directly into a fuse box located just off stage. The knobs were set to zero. Al tripped a breaker to the "on" position, walked to the control panel, and tapped a switch. It lit up and began to hum as the dials danced and blinked to life.

He slowly turned the knob that controlled the strange light bulbs inside the device to three and the hum increased in pitch and volume. Slowly the globe warmed with a very slight glow, fluttering to life in dim but colorful tones. Al turned the dial up a little higher and the three filaments inside each of the bulbs began spinning on their individual bases and light suddenly pulsed out of the globe. Al turned it up higher still and millions of multi-colored pin-pricks suddenly appeared, quivering on the ceiling, walls, and floor, but two blotches of bright white light beamed out of the holes where the missing crystals otherwise would have been, almost ruining the whole effect.

"Damn, it's too bad about those missing pieces," David said, commenting on the obvious.

By now I regretted inviting him because he was being such a worry-wart, but I had to admit that even though his concerns were categorically ignored, they were justified. He was right in saying that none of us knew what we were dealing with.

"I'm going to power up the upper and lower hemispheres now," Al said.

He turned another knob and the upper and lower halves of the globe slowly began spinning in opposite directions. The effect was immediately bewildering. Half of the pinpricks spun in one direction and the other half spun in the other. I felt the urge to grab something to steady myself. Al slowly dialed-up the knob and the globes spun faster. The multi-colored pinpricks of light bounced off the ceiling, walls, and floor as they hit a velocity fast enough to meld into straight bands of light in every color imaginable.

"I'm going to power up the mid-section now," Al said as he turned another knob.

The three Fresnel bands that separated the upper and lower parts began to spin, making the entire device slowly tilt upward on the universal joint, then the entire globe slowly began to orbit around the support pole, acting just like a gyroscope. The bands threw off another type of light entirely and the effect was like existing in the negative of a photograph: when I looked at Al and David I was astounded at what I saw. Their skin became translucent and I could see their veins, arteries, nerves, and skeletons. Al looked at me and I could tell that he was astounded, too. I saw every tooth in his skull and his fillings glowed bright in the negative light. I saw through David's skin, his rib cage, and his rapidly beating heart suspended in his chest cavity—his frail C-shaped spine and how osteoporosis was taking its toll.

"Can you believe this?" I yelled to them over the electrical din of the rapidly spinning device.

"This is incredible!" David shouted.

"Should I take it up a little higher? I've only got the knobs half-way up!" Al shouted, his skeleton hands poised over the knobs.

"No! Hold it here for a while!" David shouted. "We still don't know what we're dealing with."

"C'mon, Danny boy! Let me crank it up!" Al yelled, his skeletal fingers now grasping the knobs.

"Okay, but just a little—one number at a time," I replied, both fascinated and worried about what may happen next.

I held my hand before my face and saw my bones. I watched blood coursing through my veins and capillaries. I heard the device dial up a little higher.

"Oh lord, oh lord! What have we got here?" David shouted fearfully.

I looked out at the ballroom and it was a cacophony of whirling swirls, chaotic shapes, and images twisting over themselves, as though some black-hole tornado was ripping every molecule to shreds and annihilating the room down to its very atoms. Then the vibration started, slight at first, then pounding.

"Take it down! Take it down!" I yelled to Al.

I looked at him and he was staring down at the control panel bewildered, wondering which knobs to turn first. Then I heard a loud crack and the blood drained from my head.

"Turn it off!" I shouted.

Al reached and switched the master control off. The swirls of chaos, wisps of plasma, and eerie light vanished instantly.

The electrical hum silenced and the room was suddenly pitch-black, but when I blinked I still saw ghostly swirls and dervishes that had burned into my retinas. I slowly got my bearings and noticed the control panel's work lamp lighting us in its dim glow. I looked at my hand again and skin covered my bones. Al and David were back to their normal, flesh-covered selves, and they were inspecting their hands, too. I could hear the device still spinning on the pole, but now there was a disturbing wobble as though it had somehow become unbalanced during the test.

"Fuck! I hope we didn't break it!" I jumped off the stage but fell to the ground, completely disoriented.

"Watch it there, Danny! You alright?" Al inquired, hearing my fall.

"Yeah, just dizzy," I replied.

I got up and made my way with some difficulty to the nearest dormer window where I yanked the curtains open.

Sun streamed in, partially lighting the ballroom. I looked around. Nothing had changed. There was no evidence of molecular or atomic carnage. I stumbled toward the object and looked up. It was still spinning very fast. The pole wobbled slightly, but I was impressed at how quiet the globe was as it spun. It was, as Al had said, a solid piece of engineering; however, there was a long, thin crack in the plaster ceiling medallion that started at the center and jutted outward like a jagged bolt of lightning.

"How's it look?" Al asked, still behind the control panel.

David was sitting on a folding chair, wiping his brow with a monogrammed handkerchief.

"I don't know," I said. "It's a little wobbly but it seems okay. It's still spinning so we'll know in a few minutes for sure."

"Daniel," David said. He folded his handkerchief and stuffed it back into his jacket pocket as he stood up. "Do you realize what you've got here? That was the most incredible thing…"

He was suddenly at a loss for words, which was unusual. He walked over to the edge of the stage, looking a little unsteady. I pointed at him and Al walked over to help him step off the stage. He walked toward me slowly, pointing up at the device.

"Do you realize what you've got here? Do you realize what you've found?" David asked.

Al disappeared behind the stage left wall. I heard him flip some switches and the ceiling lights blinked on.

"No, David. I have no idea what the hell that was," I replied, standing directly under the device.

There was a palpable energy in the air and the unmistakable scent of ozone.

"Think of the possibilities!" David exclaimed. "This one device; this, this... thing we just witnessed! The applications boggle the mind! Medical, military, industrial! Daniel! This device will make you a very rich man!"

"But David, I'm already rich."

"Chicken scratch! This device could potentially make you a billionaire!"

"But David," I said, taking a couple steps toward him. "There's the matter of my grandmother's wishes—the ones in the letter in the inventory packet? Do you remember?"

David looked at me blankly.

"Letter? I recall putting a letter from your grandmother into the packet, but it was sealed. I wasn't privy to its contents. What about it?"

Al had returned to the control panel and started coiling cables. We made eye contact and he seemed a little embarrassed to be in the vicinity of what was clearly a private conversation.

"We'll talk about it another time," I said. "We've got some work to do."

David turned around to see Al and turned his gaze down to his shoes.

"Yes, you're right. We'll discuss it later."

The device came to a stop and from my vantage there appeared to be no visible damage other than the crack in the ceiling, but a more thorough inspection would have to be conducted.

⇪   ⇪   ⇪

We celebrated Elliot's first day of kindergarten with a special breakfast of blueberry pancakes. Paige's and my emotions fluctuated between wistful and happy. How quickly this milestone day came upon us and it was difficult to believe that our son was already starting school.

We took some pictures of him standing in front of the fireplace wearing his new school clothes and backpack. He fidgeted with his buckles and laces and paced nervously. Paige gave Elliot's hair a subtle lift with some gel and he was fascinated with the results—suddenly he was cool and kept checking himself in the foyer mirror. He kept asking what time it was and reminded us repeatedly that we had to be there at 8:45 a.m. sharp.

It was about a 20-minute drive to Elliot's school and we still had a half hour before we had to leave.

Paige and I were carrying the syrup-and-blueberry-smeared plates to the sink when my cell phone rang; the caller ID showed an out-of-state number. It could wait, especially after I caught the wrinkle in Paige's brow when she heard the ring. This was an important morning and it didn't need to be interrupted by any phone calls. The area code was familiar but not enough to pique my immediate interest; whoever it was could leave a message. A minute later a *ding* indicated a new message just as I remembered the area code: Cornell, New York!

I snatched up the phone and ducked into the butler's pantry to listen to the voicemail, bringing a stack of plates with me to disguise my momentary act of truancy in familial fidelity. It was the person I had been waiting to hear from for weeks. I listened.

"Hello Mr. Lintz, this is Dr. Harlan Lappe. I'm the curator of the Tiffany Glassworks Museum in Cornell, New York. I received the packet you sent to me and I'd certainly appreciate it if you'd return my call. We have a lot to discuss. Thanks and I look forward to hearing from you. Bye for now."

In the weeks since Al and I had powered up the device, we were no further along in figuring it out for ourselves. If anything, we were more perplexed. A few weeks prior I had taken a bunch of pictures and measurements and, along with copies of what little documentation I had relating to the device, assembled a package for Dr. Lappe asking if he could help me determine exactly what the device was designed to do.

The letter in the packet received a finely crafted revision by David, ensuring that the contents of the packet, and any information Dr. Lappe might provide about the device, would be kept in strictest confidence. David's revision turned out to be a very artful composition of legalese that bore little resemblance to my original. He knew what he was doing.

In the letter to Dr. Lappe, I also asked if it would be possible to manufacture replacements for the two missing crystals. David let me know that Tiffany had gone out of business years ago and that the request was futile. Still, I didn't think it would hurt to ask.

The entry to the pantry darkened with Paige's shadow and I quickly stowed the phone into my pocket.

"You'd better not be on that phone!" she said, brushing beside me to put some silverware away.

"I was just listening to a voicemail." She gave me a disgusted look. "I had to! It was the curator of the Tiffany Glassworks Museum in Cornell. He finally called."

"It can wait, right? I mean, it's great that he called you back and everything, and I hope he's got some good news for you, but seriously, it can wait."

"Yes, it can, you're right. I'm sorry, I know this is Elliot's big day. It's just I've been dying to hear back from this guy."

She took a deep breath and relaxed a little, enveloping me in a hug.

"I know you're excited, but I need you today. Elliot needs you today. He's two minutes from a major melt-down and hanging by a thread. Now get out there and be a dad!"

I made my way to the foyer, but Elliot was nowhere to be found. I ducked my head into the library, but he wasn't there either.

"Elliot!" I called upstairs. Nothing.

"ELLIOT!" Still nothing. I trounced up the stairs.

"ELLIOT! C'mon buddy, it's time to go, there's no time for hide and seek."

Still no reply. I looked around and noticed his backpack down the hall at the foot of the double-winder stairway. I mounted the stairs and halfway up I found his right tennis shoe strewn on its side on one of the risers. I got to the top and saw that the pocket doors were open slightly—just enough for a five-year-old boy to slip through. I walked into the ballroom.

Elliot was staring at the device, left shoe on, right shoe off, and his thumb was in his mouth. This was new. Elliot was not a thumb-sucker. Only one of the drapes was open and the room was cast in bluish light. The device hung on its complicated pole, centered in the room, looking like a black hole sucking the dim light into its dark orb.

"Elliot? C'mon buddy, we've got to go. Let's put your shoe back on."

He didn't respond; he just continued staring upward at the device. I walked to him and touched his shoulder. No response. My worry now turned to alarm, but I tried to hide it so I wouldn't upset him.

"What's wrong buddy? What're you staring at?"

I looked up in the direction he was staring and he seemed fixated on the holes where the two crystals were missing. I looked back at Elliot and pulled his thumb out of his mouth. For the first time he looked at me.

"She wants her eyes back, Papa, but we can't let her have them," he said before he popped his thumb back into his mouth.

I walked around to face him and crouched. A pee stain darkened his new khakis and he was standing in a small puddle of urine. His right sock was soaking wet. I choked back tears wondering what the hell had happened to my son.

"Elliot? What's wrong, buddy? Talk to me."

He continued staring up at the device.

"She's wants to open the shadow hole but she can't do it without her eyes," he said, staring upward.

Now my alarm turned to panic and I didn't know how to respond. I thought all of this ghost nonsense was behind us. Now it's back and Elliot's talking about shadow holes? I wanted to think that this was a severe case of first-day-of-school jitters gone amuck. That's how I'd explain it to Paige.

"Elliot, look at me! There is no shadow hole, okay? Shadows cannot hurt us."

He pulled his thumb out of his mouth and looked at me, but his eyes kept darting back to the device like he was expecting to see something happen. But nothing would nor could happen. Al had disconnected the control panel and taken it with him, and all of the circuit breakers were off.

"The shadows in the hole were dead, but now they're waking up and they want out," Elliot whispered, his eyes darting back and forth unnaturally.

It dawned on me that he might have been having a seizure of some kind, so I scooped him up into my arms and walked out of the ballroom. He was stock-stiff as I held him and his thumb never left his mouth. Just as we reached the second floor Paige called up from the foyer.

"What's going on you two? Chop, chop! We've got to go!"

"Uh, Houston, we've got a problem!" I called back down.

I took Elliot into his room and sat him on his bed. I heard Paige running up the stairs and down the hall toward Elliot's room; she was behind me within seconds.

"Aw, Elliot what happened?" she asked, seeing his pants. She looked at his face and panicked. Elliot continued staring, his eyes still darting in their sockets. I had pulled his thumb out of his mouth before she ran into the room. I didn't want her seeing that.

"Elliot!" she said, practically shoving me out of the way. "What's wrong, buddy?" She looked at me, her body starting to shake.

"What's wrong with him? What did you do?" she yelled at me.

I was dumbfounded—what in the world did Paige think *I* did to him!?

"I didn't do anything! I think he's having a seizure! I found him in the ballroom like this! I have no idea what happened!"

"I'm calling a doctor!"

She ran out of the room and a minute later I heard her faint but panicked voice shouting into her cell phone.

Within a half hour, Dr. Singh was beside Elliot's bed. His eyes had stopped their darting and he was a lot more present. I asked him what happened and why he went upstairs to the ballroom but he had absolutely no memory of having gone there.

Dr. Singh was a middle-aged and slightly overweight man with thick glasses and an accent just as thick. We relayed everything that had happened prior to me finding him in the ballroom. The doctor didn't find anything physically wrong with Elliot's foot other than his big toe being freshly crushed. Then he asked us to take Elliot's shirt off. A hundred small bruises dotted Elliot's chest, stomach, shoulders, and back. Paige and I looked at each other dumbfounded. It was as though some mood switch had been flipped and the doctor didn't bother hiding a sudden disgust with us. He began to examine Elliot. When he touched a couple of the bruises Elliot flinched but remained silent.

"How did yer son get all these bruises?" asked Dr. Singh, looking alternately at me and Paige. Paige and I looked at each other, then back at him.

"I found him up in a room we have on the third floor," I offered. "Halfway up the stairs I found one of his shoes. Maybe he stumbled when it came off. I don't know." I was completely mystified how Elliot could have gotten so bruised up. "Elliot," I asked, "How did you get all those bruises?" Elliot averted my question by looking away and he remained silent.

Dr. Singh scratched the back of his head with the tip of his pen. He grabbed his bag off the floor and opened it. He cleaned Elliot's toe, wrapped it in some gauze, and taped the whole thing up. He told us the nail would die and fall off in a few weeks. It wasn't serious and it would grow back. We just needed to keep it clean and dressed.

"Just like the last time," I said and Paige shot me a look. Dr. Singh noticed the exchange and looked me in the eye.

"This has happened before?" he asked, turning from me to Paige.

"Well, with the toe, yes," I replied. "About a year ago. But he's never been bruised up like this before; I can assure you of that." Dr. Singh lifted his glasses and rubbed his eyes. Then he exhaled a big sigh and put his scissors, swabs, and bandages back into his bag.

It was obvious that certain wheels had begun turning in Dr. Singh's head upon seeing the bruises. We sat in the library with Dr. Singh. Paige's arms were tightly crossed over her chest and the muscles in her jaw flexed as she ground her teeth, listening to the doctor's questions that, for all intents and purposes, were accusations he didn't bother trying to sugarcoat.

"Do you hit yer child?" he snapped.

It felt like an interrogation and Dr. Singh's mounting anger was obvious, his words growing more and more difficult to understand as the tone in his voice grew more and more agitated.

"How much do you lose yer temper when he is doing bad tings?" he asked, his questions laden with accusation.

It was difficult to be rational with all the false conclusions about us being abusive parents. Rage, frustration, and hopelessness made me feel as if there was nothing that could be said to alter the opinion of this doctor, who probably had the power to bring social workers into the mix.

It quickly became clear that he would rather speak than listen, and that he was someone who drew conclusions based only on what he saw.

"Doctor, I know what you're thinking but I can assure you we do not abuse our son. We don't even spank him!" I said, almost pleading. "Neither of us has ever laid a finger on him in any way that could cause him harm."

Dr. Singh looked at me quickly then back down at the clipboard on his lap. He jotted down notes as he talked.

"I want to believe you, Mr. Lintz, but you do not offer a satisfactory answer to yer son's injuries. What am I supposed to tink?"

Now it was Paige's turn. "Let me ask you something, Dr. Singh. Are you a social worker?"

"No, I am not. I am a medical doctor."

"Are you a psychiatrist?"

"As I have told you, I am a medical doctor. I practice family medicine."

"Are you a neurologist?"

"I am not."

Paige uncrossed her arms and leaned into the conversation. "You just asked my husband what you're supposed to think. We're not paying you to think. We're not paying you to make judgments you're not qualified to make."

"I only know what I see, Mrs. Lintz," said Dr. Singh, unperturbed.

I've never seen Paige so furious. She stood up, no longer able to contain herself.

"We told you when you first got here that he seemed to be having a seizure of some kind! His eyes were darting uncontrollably, he wasn't making any sense, and he seemed, I don't know, mentally locked-in somehow! Is it possible, remotely possible, doctor, that he could have injured himself while in the throes of a seizure?"

Dr. Singh exhaled, put his pen into his pocket, and rested his hands on his lap. There was a long silence.

"You wouldn't believe some of the tings I see on my rounds. Perhaps it has become too easy for me to draw conclusions. Clearly I jumped to a harsh conclusion about you both and for this I apologize."

Paige sat back down on the sofa next to me and began to sob. I wrapped my arm around her shoulder and squeezed.

"Does he have a history of epilepsy?" Dr. Singh asked.

"Now you're on the right track, Doctor," I replied.

Elliot missed his first, second, and third day of school.

⇧   ⇧   ⇧

Every test for Elliot's episode came back inconclusive. His doctors would not rule out epilepsy, but for now they were cautiously optimistic that what had happened to him was an isolated incident brought on by any number of factors, which included everything from diet to stress to poor choices on our part as parents. We were mystified. We were good parents. We always fed him healthy foods like fresh fruits and vegetables. We considered ourselves model parents. Yes, Paige had suffered through a long bout of post-partum depression, but that was completely under control, so much so that she was now off her meds.

Elliot was outwardly a very happy child. He loved us very much and acted like any typical five-year-old boy but, like many parents, we thought of our son as gifted. He was always comfortable in the company of adults. He also had a lot of confidence and a very impressive vocabulary for a kid his age. At the very least, Elliot was bright, and his unresponsiveness to Dr. Singh on the day of his episode was an anomaly, and an understandable one given the circumstances. Of course he had a tendency to work himself up into a high state of excitability, but I always chalked that up to the times we lived in.

One of Elliot's specialists thought it could have been an absence seizure, another type of epilepsy, which made more sense to us because he had been displaying signs of excitability prior to the episode, but nothing we considered alarming. He told us that absence seizures can be brought on by hyperventilation and it's possible that Elliot could have been hyperventilating and we just didn't notice it at the time.

Then there was the injury to his big toe. Neither of us had forgotten about the first time that happened. Nothing weird had happened in ages, at least not since my supposed encounter with Nora in the basement, and I'd long since discounted that entire incident as a hallucinatory delusion on my part. There were a thousand other explanations for Elliot's toe getting injured, the least of them being visits from the dead. But we still could not reasonably explain the bruises. Perhaps he had some sort of grand mal seizure prior to my walking into the ballroom which somehow caused all the bruising.

Paige wasn't ruling out anything. She became very protective and didn't let Elliot out of her sight. She insisted we mount cameras with ultraviolet capability all over the house, including his bedroom, so we could watch what was going on while he was alone, day and night, via closed circuit monitors.

As for Elliot, he had absolutely no memory of his episode, which is also typical of an absence seizure. We were instructed to be watchful of specific behaviors and to keep a detailed log of the foods we fed him, his bed times, how long he slept, anomalies during sleep such as nightmares or sleepwalking, and to be careful to note all seizure-like occurrences. We were also told to instruct him to calm down when appropriate, and that we should anticipate challenging behaviors in kindergarten.

Over the next few months, the memories of that stressful week subsided and we slowly fell back into our

ıtrary to what we were told, Elliot did not turn
ıllenging student and instead became a model
ıor the other kids to emulate. He learned quickly and was
popular with his classmates.

During our first parent-teacher conference we were
elated to learn that his teacher, Mrs. Bonham, often had to
assign him additional work because he typically finished
long before his fellow students and got bored waiting for
them to catch up. Mrs. Bonham told us that occasionally
she had him pass out assignments just so he could start his
own a bit later. She'd been teaching for years and this was
one of the strategies she employed for her more gifted
students. She actually used the word "gifted" and Paige
and I beamed.

When we picked him up from Marian's we lavished
him with praise and on the way home stopped at Whistle
Stop Toy and Hobby to pick out something as a reward for
being such a good student. He immediately beelined to his
favorite aisle and picked out a Matchbox car to add to his
already large collection.

I'd anticipated more blow-back from Paige and was
prepared for the worst, thinking we'd be packing our bags
right after Dr. Singh walked out of the house, but that
didn't happen. Perhaps it occurred to her how daunting it
would be to pull up stakes and just move after we'd spent
so much time, money, and energy on restoring the house to
a state better than its original glory.

⚑   ⚑   ⚑

Paige and Charlie had become fast friends. She even

partnered with him to have our house and gardens featured in a multi-page spread in *Hour Magazine*, with an accompanying article on the revitalization of Detroit and the many properties that have recently undergone extensive renovation, both commercial and residential.

David heard about the impending article and called us, insisting that no photographs be taken of the device. Since the day we had powered up the device with Al, David had become a man obsessed, and often asked if I had any plans to explore its potential as a scientific instrument; but where I saw only a unique chandelier, David saw dollar signs, and the device had to be protected from prying eyes. Paige was disappointed but understood.

We were in the midst of planning a spectacular open house party, which Charlie was heavily involved with. In fact, I was alarmed when I found out that over 200 people had been invited and almost as many RSVP'd in the affirmative. A very expensive catering company was hired and I recalled grandmother's advice about not frittering away our family fortune as I looked over the estimates.

Strange people began showing up, oohing and ahhing, taking photographs, measuring rooms, and discussing which ones would be the most suitable for the event. I suggested the gardens, but Charlie nixed that idea, naturally suggesting the ballroom instead.

David had a fit when I told him about where the party would be taking place, and he was over within a half-hour to try and talk Paige out of it. We assembled in the dining room to hash it out, David sitting on one side of the table with Paige and me across from him. Paige came armed with a file full of papers, estimates, and invoices all related to the party.

"I know you want to show off the house and deservedly so, it's fantastic! But we've got to keep the device under wraps for now," David said.

Paige looked at me, mystified, and cocked her thumb in David's direction, wondering if I knew what planet he'd come from.

"What are you telling me? I can't have a party in my ballroom?" she asked, baffled by David's suggestion.

"No, I'm not telling you any such thing! I just think it would be a good idea to either temporarily remove the device, or cover it with a tarp. I don't want anyone seeing it until we sort out some legal issues," David replied.

"Legal issues? What are you talking about?" she asked.

David was a little taken aback at Paige's vehemence and apparently didn't answer quickly enough.

"What's he talking about, legal issues?" she asked me. I held my hands up unsure of what to say.

"David, I think you're overreacting a little," I said. "As far as anyone's concerned, all we've got is a strange looking chandelier up there. No one has to know what it does."

Paige sighed and calmed down a little. She got up and walked toward the kitchen. I heard the refrigerator door open and things being pulled out and placed on the island counter.

"It's a chandelier that we found in our basement!" she said from the kitchen. "It's suddenly illegal to hang a chandelier in a ballroom?"

She walked back into the dining room carrying a tray filled with cheese and crackers. I got up and went to the kitchen and fetched the pitcher of iced tea from the counter.

"First of all, it's not a *chandelier*. It's a device of some sort—one of Daniel's great-grandfather's scientific instruments. We don't know exactly what it is," David said, correcting Paige. I walked back in with a tray topped with a pitcher and glasses and poured us some iced tea.

"Well, whatever it is, it stays up and we're not covering it with a tarp!" Paige said with finality.

David exhaled and gave me a pleading look. I shrugged my shoulders and grinned, letting him know the matter was settled.

"Have you heard back from Dr. Lappe yet?" he asked looking at me, a little wounded that his professional advice was being ignored because of a party.

"Yes. He's flying in next week."

David was surprised at the revelation.

"Oh! I'd like to meet him! Do you mind?" he asked, sarcastically.

"Of course not. I'd prefer it if you did. There will be a lot to discuss!"

David slid his chair back and stood up. He was dressed a little more casually than usual in a short-sleeve polo, and I noticed a cotton ball taped in the crook of his elbow and a couple of bruises on his forearm. It looked as though he had gained a few needed pounds over the last couple of months, and whatever they were doing at the hospital seemed to be working. He was looking healthier and I was genuinely glad about that. He reached for the windbreaker that hung on the back of his chair and put it on.

"I've got to say something to both of you, and please don't take this the wrong way," he said, with a hint of irritation in his voice. "You've got to start looking out for your interests with a little more caution. You're in the big leagues now, and you'd better get used to the fact that you need a lawyer involved in some of the decisions you make."

Paige and I looked at each other.

"Go on," said Paige.

David sat back down.

"Now, I'll admit that you made a valid assumption. Perhaps everyone will assume that it's just a chandelier. But I don't make decisions based on assumptions and neither should you. What happens if someone asks you to turn it on? What are you going to do?"

"Well naturally we're going to turn it on," Paige said.

"It would be a little weird if we didn't, don't you think? People will be expecting it."

David's eyebrows shot up in alarm.

"You cannot possibly... "

I didn't let him finish. "I've already talked to Al about it. He said we can just turn the bulbs on. We don't have to power it up any further than that."

"And Al is willing to stake his professional livelihood on it being 100 percent safe? He's willing to put it in writing?"

"Well, it never occurred to me to ask him," I replied. "I mean, you were there when we turned it on. Other than getting a little dizzy, did you suffer any serious side effects?"

"No, I didn't, but you and Al cannot guarantee that someone else won't. And guess what—Al won't be the one held liable! Listen, some people will do anything to take advantage of you, and lawsuits, justified or not, are the perfect inroad. Here's something else to chew on: You have no idea how often your grandmother was the victim of frivolous lawsuits. I have no objection to your having a party—as a matter of fact I'm looking forward to it—but if you insist that it take place in the ballroom, I'm advising you that, A, the device not be turned on, and B, no photographs."

Paige stood up and pushed her chair in. She lingered there for a second wanting to say something. It was obvious that she wasn't happy with the advice David was giving us but, after all, that's all it was—advice. We could take it or leave it. He said things neither of us had even thought about, and Paige and I would definitely have to talk about it.

"I've got to pick Elliot up from school," she said. "Thanks for the input, David."

"I'm sorry if I upset you," he responded, getting up.

"Not at all. It's a buzzkill, but I'll get over it."

She kissed me goodbye then swept out of the room. I heard the familiar sounds of her departure ritual, then the swoosh of the front door opening and closing just a little louder than normal. She was pissed but, under the circumstances, doing her best to conceal it.

"So what did Dr. Lappe say?" David asked, as we walked toward the front door.

🏛   🏛   🏛

The three of us—Dr. Lappe, David, and I—trounced up the stairs, David a little further behind. I slid open the pocket doors and Dr. Lappe rushed in ahead and gasped when he caught sight of the object.

Earlier, when we picked him up at the airport, he expressed his excitement in finally getting to see "the Cyclops," as he called it.

"Cyclops?" I replied.

"The military always gave code names to the secret devices that were under development at their research labs. This device," he said, pointing up at it, "was code named Cyclops."

"Hm. Okay, then Cyclops it is," I said, looking up at it.

He had been hearing rumors about the Cyclops for years in the world of Tiffany scholarship, but dismissed them as antique urban legends. As we drove, Dr. Lappe told me that there were a hundred or so people around the world who actually made a living studying the works of Louis Comfort Tiffany and Dr. Lappe, as it turned out, was the world's foremost expert.

He spoke with what I guessed was a Boston accent and looked like someone capable of giving professional antique appraisals on PBS. He had a thick mop of sandy colored hair that was greying over and wore large tortoise shell-colored glasses. He was short in stature with the beginnings of a middle-aged paunch, was dressed in khakis, a white button-down shirt, blue blazer, and penny loafers, and he had an old brown leather satchel draped over his shoulder.

"The old black-and-white photographs I found do not do this justice! It's magnificent! And a lot bigger than I pictured!" Dr. Lappe said, looking up at it.

"If you thought the Cyclops was some urban legend then how do you account for the photographs you found?" David asked. "You obviously didn't find them in your museum's archive."

"No. I know our archive from A to Z and I knew we didn't have anything. That's mostly why I thought it was just a legend," Dr. Lappe replied. "We have the most extensive collection of Tiffany *objets d'art* in the world, and our archive is unparalleled. About 80 percent of our collection consists of papers, photographs, art glass, and formulas, and it's all tucked away in our vaults, never seen by the general public. You'd better be a scholar, expert, or have a damn good reason before we let you down there."

"Well, where'd you find the documentation, then?" I asked.

"I had to file a Freedom of Information Act request then I flew to Washington to search through miles of shelves at the National Archives," Dr. Lappe answered.

"You flew to Washington for this?" I asked, shocked that he went to all the trouble.

"Daniel, when your packet arrived on my desk I dropped everything! In my world this is comparable to finding a lost da Vinci! This is huge!"

"Did you hear that, Daniel? I knew this was something!" David said.

"It took me days, but I finally found that I was looking for: photographs, documents, and a partial schematic. And I also received some documentation from my Freedom of Information request, but I've got to warn you that some of the text on almost every document has been redacted."

"What does that mean, redacted?" I asked.

"It means that someone with a security clearance actually took the time to black out chunks of the text," David answered.

"So this Cyclops thing is actually some secret military device?" I asked.

"Yes. The documents pertaining to it were secret too, at least until my Freedom of Information request went through," Dr. Lappe replied.

"It's too bad about the redaction," David said. "It would've been great to know everything about it."

"Actually, in spite of the redaction, what I have is still very interesting. But personally, I like a good mystery—it gives us something to solve. We'll go over the documentation in a bit, but for now, do you mind if I take a closer look?" Dr. Lappe asked.

"Not at all, please," I replied.

David saddled onto a barstool and placed his briefcase on a bar table. I looked at him and smiled. He returned it with his own kind of smile then snapped his briefcase open.

"I certainly appreciate the scaffolding. It makes my job a lot easier," Dr. Lappe said as he climbed upward.

He opened his satchel when he got to the top and pulled out a large magnifying glass.

"I'm 99.9 percent certain that this is Cyclops, but there are three things I need to find before I'm 100 percent positive."

He slowly walked around the Cyclops studying the lower hemisphere of the globe then stopped. He took a closer look with his magnifying glass.

"I think I found what I'm looking for. Yes, here it is."

I stood at the foot of the scaffolding looking up at Dr. Lappe. It was very interesting watching a professional antique scholar at work.

He started fiddling with a section of the lower globe. He took a small tool out of his satchel and started working a part of the titanium frame. I heard a click and suddenly a hatch opened downward. Al and I hadn't noticed this hatch and I was surprised when Dr. Lappe found it. He studied the inside of the hatch with his magnifying glass and began talking to himself.

"Yes… each piece of art glass is numbered in a very small font. Check!"

"And that's a good thing?" David called out, a little preoccupied with the contents of his briefcase, though very calm under the circumstances.

"Yes sir, a good thing indeed!" Dr. Lappe said, more to himself.

He stuck his head inside and I almost laughed at how ridiculous he suddenly looked. I heard his muffled voice commenting from inside. He pulled his head back out and put his magnifying glass back into his satchel. He closed the small hatch and re-locked the clasps with his tool.

"Check, check, and checkmate! This is code name Cyclops! I am 100 percent certain." He hooked his satchel over his shoulder then climbed down off the scaffolding.

"And that's a good thing!" David replied.

It suddenly dawned on me why David was so calm: there was no doubt about the Cyclops' authenticity and Dr. Lappe's inspection was really just a formality. "That's a good thing indeed, sir!" Dr. Lappe replied, pacing to and fro, unable to contain his excitement. "Now I'm going to tell you something and I hope you don't find it too shocking." Dr. Lappe stopped pacing and walked to me. He put his hands on my shoulders and looked me dead in the eye. "Daniel, this is the single most important Tiffany object in the company's history. Its reemergence will make international waves in the world of antique scholarship. This will make the six-o'clock news all over the world! Congratulations! You are the owner of a priceless national treasure!"

"Well, let's hold off on any press releases for now, Dr. Lappe," David said. He had laid a few documents out on the table while Dr. Lappe was busy inspecting the Cyclops.

"We're not ready for any major announcements right now, and we've got a few very important matters to consider, like insurance and security."

"Of course," Dr. Lappe said. "I would never even contemplate the idea of a press release until it's feasible for all parties."

"Well, just so we understand each other, I've got a confidentiality agreement I'd like your signature on."

David went over the documents and Dr. Lappe signed them after they hashed out a few changes. In addition to being the curator of a prestigious museum, Dr. Lappe was also a lawyer, and David began to warm up to him when he complimented us on all of the precautions we were taking. This was another instance of David holding his cards close, and it was on this day I finally began to trust him—almost completely.

⇑   ⇑   ⇑

It had been a long time since I'd been in great-grandfather's private library, but since this was most likely where the Cyclops was designed, I thought it was appropriate to conduct our meeting there. Before we began, I gave Dr. Lappe a tour of the archive similar to the one David had given me all those years ago, but what I thought would be a quick jaunt through turned into a two-hour marathon.

Being a professional archivist and curator, Dr. Lappe very quickly figured out great-grandfather's methods of organization.

"It was common practice to arrange documents in this manner back in your great-grandfather's day," he said as he perused some of the files. "If you'd permit it, I might be able to find more documentation on the Cyclops down here, but it'll probably take me a few hours."

Clearly bored but too polite to say anything, David finally cracked and became a study in skepticism.

"Good luck with that! I've had access to these rooms for years and I've never been able to find anything."

This was a revelation. David had never said anything to me about being privy to the archive for years, and my level of trust in him ratcheted back down a notch. I wondered: what did he mean by not being able to find anything? What had he been looking for?

"Did you know what you were looking for?" Dr. Lappe asked, almost reading my mind.

David's torso was practically splayed across the top of a cabinet near the door and he looked exhausted.

"Not really," he admitted reluctantly. I looked at him but he averted my gaze. David's admission was difficult for someone who was used to being the smartest guy in the room, but the scope of Dr. Lappe's knowledge was daunting, and David had no choice but to begrudgingly acquiesce his superior link on the smart chain. It was amusing to watch, but it was getting late and we still had a lot to go over.

"Dr. Lappe," I said.

He interrupted me. "Daniel. My friends call me Harlan, so please, it's Harlan. Both of you, please call me Harlan."

"Of course, Harlan. I don't want to be rude," I said, "and I'm more than happy to allow you to search the archive—you have an open invitation—but for now we need to get down to brass tacks."

I saw relief shoot across David's face as he disembodied himself from the cabinet and disappeared into the hallway. I caught up with him and commented on what an impressive man Harlan was.

"Don't be too taken by all that east coast grandiosity. He puts his pants on one leg at a time just like you and me."

I detected a little jealousy so I egged him on a little.

"But David, I looked him up online. He's Harvard Law! He taught at Cambridge *and* he's the curator of a world famous museum!"

"Pshh! I've got a couple of diplomas lying around, too," he said, getting a little pissed. "And I taught a few classes at U of D. Big deal."

Harlan was a few feet behind us and seemed to be in his glory. Some people are born historians and Harlan was clearly one of them. He opened every door we walked by, snapped the lights on, then peered inside. He couldn't wait to dive in.

"What did you say your great-grandfather did?" he asked, peeking into yet another room.

"I didn't," I replied, spinning around mid-stride to face him.

"So the plot thickens!" he said, smiling.

We turned the corner and made our way to the ornate, six-panel door. David was trembling as I unlocked it. I looked at him and noticed he was sweating.

"I'm sorry, David," I said, feeling bad that this was taking so long.

"Don't worry about me, I'm fine," he lied.

It was stupid for us to have gone on as long as we had without eating—David was getting hypoglycemic. I led them to the large arts and crafts table, where Harlan hooked the strap of his satchel over a chair back and David placed his briefcase on the table.

"Feel free to roam around, you two. I'll be back in a few minutes with some lunch," I said.

As I wound my way up the spiral staircase I watched from above as David led Harlan toward the hidden mahogany latch. I heard a click and the panels swung open, the bar rolled outward, the recessed lights flickered on, and the library was suddenly bathed in the warm glow emanating from behind the dozens of bottles of spirits and crystal decanters, all backlit against the antiqued mirror.

"I bet you've never seen anything like this in all your travels," I heard David's faint voice say. I smiled, assuming he was reaching for one decanter in particular.

⚑ ⚑ ⚑

We finished our lunch. I cleared the table and brought out the crystal decanter, the object of David's interest, and three snifters to the table.

"I assume that David's already told you about this," I said as I poured us each a dram.

David looked up at me and smiled guiltily as he eagerly reached for his snifter. The lunch of cold chicken and coleslaw did him some good and he was back to his charmingly devious self.

"I'm really not supposed to imbibe anymore, but to hell with it!" he said. "This is a special occasion."

"Amen to that!" Harlan replied, accepting his.

David proposed a toast to the genius of my dearly departed ancestors as we allowed the cognac to work its magic, and this time it didn't just burn in my mouth.

Harlan opened his satchel and pulled out a folder filled with papers and some old black-and-white photographs.

"Before I go over my findings," he said. "I noticed a few things during my inspection."

"What's that?" I asked. "Is anything wrong?"

"No! Not at all," he assured me. "I just noticed some repairs that looked recent. Did you have some work done on the Cyclops?"

"Yes, I did. It wasn't in great condition when I found

it down here, so I hired my friend Al to take a look. Does that hurt the value?"

"It could. There are purists out there who prefer a 100 percent original piece, but I don't see where you did anything that affected the aesthetics of the piece and, really, that's the most important thing. A Tiffany lamp can be completely re-wired and it doesn't affect the value one iota. It's the glass and patina that everyone's most concerned with; cracks, chips, and missing pieces *will* affect the value though."

"Shit, I've got two missing pieces! That affects the value?"

"Well this is such a special, one-of-a-kind object that it doesn't really affect it. You can have a craftsman color match and replace the missing pieces, but all the repairs need to be documented if you ever decide to sell it."

"Well, I have absolutely no intention of selling it," I said. "It's not going anywhere."

"Harlan," David said. "you mentioned that each piece of glass was numbered, or something to that effect. Why?"

"That's a very interesting question and I'll go over that with you shortly," he replied, taking a sip of his cognac. "I also noticed that it's been wired up and from what I observed, very professionally."

"Again, that was my friend Al. He's a master electrician. He did all of the repairs, then wired and mounted it," I said. "It took him about a month."

"Given the complexities of the Cyclops, that's not a very long time," Harlan said surprised.

"Well, like you, he dropped everything," I said.

"And did he keep a repair log?"

"I honestly don't know, but I can find out," I replied.

"I can attest to his professionalism," David said. "I was very impressed with all the precautions he took when he fired it up."

"You turned it on?" Harlan asked, suddenly looking a little concerned. "What happened?"

David and I looked at each other. We were silent for a few seconds. David took a sip of his cognac and cleared his throat.

"It was the most astounding thing," David said, looking down into his snifter. "I've never experienced anything like it."

"He's right," I said. "When Al fired it up, it was—well, for lack of a better word—an experience. I mean, it's difficult to describe!"

"Please try," Harlan said, anxiously.

We both described at length what we had observed and experienced. David mentioned some things I hadn't noticed or just plain forgot, and when I spoke, David nodded his head in agreement and interjected every now and then. I agreed with his comments and was impressed with his total recall of that day—his powers of description were better than mine. Harlan listened, fascinated with our account of everything that had happened after Al flipped the switches on his panel.

"I'd love to see that for myself," he said. "My only concern obviously is that we could damage it. It sounds like it rotates at a very high velocity and balance is extremely important at high velocities."

"It's funny you say that because that was Al's number one concern," I said. "That's why he connected it to a control panel."

"He sounds like a very methodical professional," Harlan said. "You're lucky to have had such a conscientious friend do the work."

"He's definitely that," I replied. "His concern was that those two missing pieces were enough to throw it out of whack."

"It was okay for most of the test, but Al dialed it up to the point where we heard a loud crack. What happened was the support pole started to wobble and the plaster ceiling cracked. It wasn't the Cyclops itself that was damaged," David recalled.

"Well, you're very lucky. A few more seconds and it could have oscillated out of control and shattered into a thousand flying daggers."

David and I looked at each other like a couple of guilty school boys.

Harlan continued. "I strongly advise you to not turn it on again until those two replacement pieces are professionally installed and that the proper balance has been re-established. I'd be happy to provide you with some art glass from our archive, and we have a master craftsman on staff that I insist do the matching, fitting, and installation. It won't be the real McCoy but no one will be able to tell the difference."

"And what about those numbers?" David asked again.

"Right," Harlan said, opening the file he'd pulled out earlier. "I found some pretty fascinating information regarding the glass and, to my knowledge, this has never been done with a Tiffany object."

David and I leaned forward, very interested in Harlan's documents. "Every piece of glass was assigned a number that corresponds to this list I found," he explained as he riffled through the papers until he produced a list numbered from 1 to 1,026. "Each number corresponds to an individual piece of glass—the list details the colors, dimensions, and chemical make-up of each piece," Harlan said. "Two pieces," he continued, "numbers 217 and 449, are the ones that are missing. Now, take a look." He handed each of us a page from the list. "Scan down to those two numbers. What do you see?"

I scanned down to 217. Its chemical make-up had been redacted. David had the page listing 449. It too was redacted. We traded sheets and verified what we saw, then looked at Harlan, mystified.

"I know. It's strange isn't it? The only two pieces that have been redacted are the same ones missing from the Cyclops," Harlan said. "And gentlemen, it's my opinion that this is not a coincidence. During my inspection, I obviously noticed the two missing pieces and I wondered if those missing pieces were the ones that were redacted. I remembered the numbers, so when I stuck my head inside I wanted to see if that was the case—and it was."

"That's almost spooky," I said.

"Do you think it's possible the two missing pieces are locked up in some secret government repository?" David asked.

"Trust me, I looked," Harlan responded. "I didn't find

them. Remember, you had mentioned the two missing pieces in the packet you sent me."

"I remember," I replied, nodding.

"Honestly, they could be anywhere, or they could have been destroyed. We'll probably never know."

"Well, that sucks," I said.

"You obviously haven't found them here?" Harlan asked.

"Nope. But not for lack of trying."

"Daniel's allowed me to snoop around, too, and they haven't turned up under my watch either," David added.

"Well, if you don't mind, I'd like to have a go," Harlan said.

"Let me ask you this," David said. "Why do you think the information on those two pieces was redacted?"

"Take a look at some of the other pieces," Harlan said, sliding the list back to us. "Piece number 1, for example: It's composed of cobalt, copper, and iron-chromite, which tells me that it's primarily a cobalt piece with trace amounts of red and green. Look at all the other pieces and you see a few other chemicals and elements that give each piece its unique coloration. My guess is that pieces 217 and 449 might have been made with a radioactive element like uranium, for example, but I'm only speculating. Really, I have no idea, but, with your permission, I intend to find out!"

"So if the two pieces are made of uranium, does that mean if we find them and install them, the Cyclops will suddenly become radioactive?" I asked. "Will it make the Cyclops dangerous?"

"Generally no, but it depends. There's a ton of uranium glass out there and it's very collectable. The pre-war stuff has more uranium in it and it *will* register on a Geiger counter, but it's mostly harmless. Post-war uranium glass only has trace amounts. When you put it under an ultraviolet light source it glows green."

"So, the $100,000 question is: What's this Cyclops thing supposed to do and why was it made?" asked David.

"And that's the most fascinating thing of all," Harlan replied. "It was designed to render everything within its range invisible."

David and I looked at each other. I let out a startled chuckle.

"Seriously?" I said.

"Unbelievable!" David said, almost shouting.

He slapped his hands down onto the table then pushed himself away and stood up. I looked up at him and saw instantly that his lawyer wheels were turning. He paced a little then stopped and assumed the classic pose of someone deep in thought.

"To be honest, I wondered if that was the case," I said. "I mean, when I looked at my hands, I saw through my skin. When I looked over at David, I saw his spine and his turnippy little lawyer heart beating in his chest!"

"Very funny," David said, smiling.

"Hey, I'm a lawyer too!" said Harlan, also smiling. "And I resemble that remark!"

"Sorry! *Mea culpa!*" I pleaded, mockingly.

They laughed. Harlan started playing with his now empty snifter.

"So, it almost worked." Harlan said. "You could see through yourselves or, rather, into yourselves, but you weren't quite invisible."

"Yes," I said.

"So, based on your experience, it *almost* works."

"Yes, almost," David said. "Do any of those documents you found say anything about it working back when the original tests took place?"

"Yes. It looks like they achieved invisibility but, hold on a second," Harlan said, as he riffled through some other papers. "Here it is. It says, 'When code name Cyclops' ultraviolet filaments are activated, a phenomenon quickly manifests...' then two lines of redaction, then the text continues after the redaction, '...and the unanticipated phenomenon has thus far proven to be insurmountable, negative, and wholly unacceptable, which completely negates the otherwise completely successful...' then the rest is redacted."

"You surmise that 'completely successful' means invisibility?" David asked.

"There are other documents that, when you piece the information together, you come to the conclusion that they were successful in achieving their goals. I have a copy for you to read, but I think it would be wise not to share this information with anyone."

"You have nothing to worry about on that count," David said. "And If I were you, Daniel, I wouldn't share this with Paige—not just yet anyway."

I thought about this for a second and nodded as a disturbing image suddenly flashed into my consciousness: Charlie and a small coterie of Indian Village eccentrics enjoying themselves in the ballroom, bathed in the glow of the Cyclops' eerie chaos, amazed at their temporary transparency. I shuddered. Not that Paige would ever tell Charlie—or anyone for that matter—but it was perhaps a good idea to err on the side of secrecy for now.

"Do the documents give any detail on what those negative things might have been?" I asked.

"No," replied Harlan. "There's nothing on what the author meant about negative and unanticipated phenomena."

David reached for the packet and Harlan handed it to him. David scanned the documents and stopped at a blurry photograph that looked as though the camera had been jostled while the shutter was open. It was a photograph of what looked like three dark figures standing in chaos.

"This looks familiar, doesn't it?" David asked me, handing me the photograph.

"Yes, it does! Here, check this out," I said to Harlan, handing him the photograph. "This is actually what the room looked like while the Cyclops was going full bore."

He took the photograph from me and looked at it.

"Now imagine all that chaos in just about every color you can think of, and then some, and you get a pretty good idea of what the ballroom looked like when we turned the Cyclops on," I continued, as Harlan studied the photograph.

"These dark figures are certainly not invisible," Harlan said.

"Maybe that's what they meant by the negative phenomenon," David said.

"I'll do my best to find out. That is if you'd like me to," Harlan said.

"I would like that and, if it helps, I'll give you complete access to every file and crate on the other side of that door," I said, pointing toward the archive.

"Is that okay with you, Mr. Lawyer?" Harlan asked, offering his hand to David.

David accepted it and they shook. "That's fine, but the confidentiality agreement applies toward whatever you find down here as well. And please bear in mind that David, myself, Paige, and now you, are the only ones that know the archive even exists. We'd like to keep it that way."

"Of course."

"And it goes without saying that you'll share everything you find with Daniel and myself."

"Of course."

"And that you'll wear archival gloves…"

"David!" I interrupted.

"Yes, yes, David! I promise to wear archival gloves!" Harlan replied, laughing. "Anything else?"

"Yes," I said. "Paige and I would like you to be our guest for the evening. We have plenty of room here and it'll give you more time to peruse the archive—that is if you're still feeling up to it. We'll have dinner, then you can explore until your heart's content."

"That sounds like a wonderfully tempting offer, but only if it's no trouble."

"No trouble at all," I replied.

"And Mrs. Lintz? She's okay with this?"

"Paige is the one who suggested it. We've got too many empty bedrooms that need breaking in and we'd be delighted to have you as our guest."

"Then I gladly accept your hospitality," Harlan replied, a warm smile lighting up his face.

⛨   ⛨   ⛨

That first evening Harlan spent in our home was very enjoyable and we quickly became friends. Paige fell under the spell of his erudite personality and Elliot thought he was excellent, too. Harlan taught him some very cool but simple sleight-of-hand tricks that would surely dazzle Elliot's classmates during show and tell. We enjoyed Harlan so much that we decided to add him and his wife to the guest list for our much-anticipated open house.

After a fabulous meal prepared by Paige, Harlan and I retired to the archive to do some more searching. Although Harlan found some other, rather inconsequential documentation relating to the Cyclops, we didn't find the two missing crystals.

Based on what he was able to piece together, Harlan ascertained that the Cyclops was in no way dangerous with crystals 217 and 449 missing. We did learn, however, that the missing crystals were absolutely instrumental in the successful attainment of invisibility and without them it was basically rendered useless. We never found any additional information regarding their chemical make-up, only that without them all we really had was a very fancy optical instrument that, when activated, provided an incredible but harmless light show.

When I called David and told him that Harlan would be giving a demonstration during the party, I thought he was going to have an embolism. I was able to calm him down a bit when I told him that we now had documentation verifying the Cyclops' safety. We had also taken other precautions; on David's advice we insured the Cyclops, and installed an elaborate, museum quality security system in the ballroom that required us to punch in an access code and slide a magnetic card through a slot before the pocket doors would slide open. In spite of these elaborate and expensive precautions, David's attitude went only from panic to guarded optimism.

⇧　　⇧　　⇧

True to his word, Harlan flew the museum's master craftsman in from Cornell to install two color-appropriate replacement crystals. These new crystals would not enable invisibility—they were strictly aesthetic but, more importantly, they provided perfect balance. We also hired a team of engineers and brought Al back with his panel to assist in fine-tuning the balance of the Cyclops.

Al agreed to help out with the demonstration that we planned on having during the party, as he had become something of an expert on the intricacies of powering it up and down.

We had learned a few things about the Cyclops since our first test. One of the three filaments on each of the bulbs was composed of an alloy other than tungsten that would give off ultraviolet light when powered up. Al made a few more connections to his panel to ensure that the ultraviolet filaments would activate.

I thought about having the crack in the plaster ceiling medallion repaired but decided to wait until after the tests. I wasn't ruling out leaving the crack intact, as a battle wound of sorts; it did resemble a lightning bolt, which I found symbolic of my great-grandfather's genius.

In addition to achieving perfect balance, the Cornell engineers made some improvements to the complicated universal-joint pole from which the Cyclops hung.

⇑ ⇑ ⇑

Al, confident in all the upgrades, slowly turned his knobs and we watched as the Cyclops' upper and lower halves began to spin faster and faster in opposite directions. It slowly tilted upward then orbited around the pole. Its newfound balance made it perfectly silent in spite of the unimaginable rotational velocity, and the effects emanating from the Cyclops were even more spectacular. When Al switched on the ultraviolet filaments, they caused a fiery, iridescent aura to emanate off every surface.

Each of us was surrounded by our own aura that flickered, undulated, and changed color as we moved about and raised our arms. Al stepped away from the panel and spun in a circle causing his aura to quickly form into a whirl that spun above, then it whipped upward, melding into the atomic and molecular chaos that filled the ballroom. I drew pictures in the air with my fingertips and the fiery iridescence trailed my patterns. The pictures lingered for a few seconds before lashing upward into chaos.

Slowly, the unmistakable scent of ozone began to fill our nostrils, and I told Al to bring it down. He turned the knobs on his panel back toward zero slowly, and the chaos dialed down, transforming toward a uniform, spectral color as the Cyclops slowed its orbit around the pole and gently tilted back downward, both upper and lower halves slowly coming to a stop. The room darkened to black and soon, only the work lamp's glow aimed down on Al's panel lit our small corner of the room.

The Cyclops and its power was something I would never grow weary of, but I still wondered what invisibility would have been like and regretted that we never found crystals 217 and 449. The replacements, though, provided perfect balance and it was more than incredible how they enhanced the depth of all the effects—the chaotic dervishes, the whirls of light, and the fantastic and iridescent auroras that danced, hovered, and followed our every move. I wondered what other effects we would discover with further experimentation, and I was only mildly alarmed by the fine, white powder that covered my skin after this second, more intense session under the Cyclops.

Harlan could not be there for the test so I made a short movie on my smartphone that I narrated as we took the Cyclops through its motions. I sent it attached to a text telling him that naturally the video didn't do the spectacle justice compared to actually being present.

He called me immediately and instead of thanking me, he told me that under no circumstances was I to activate it again until he was present. I was a little surprised at his ire, but I understood his concern.

⇑   ⇑   ⇑

I'm usually not good in large groups, and I've never liked big parties with people who seemed like they were born to attend such events, but our open house was different. I wasn't completely at ease, but I wasn't in a paralyzed state of self-conscious paranoia either. I was actually having a pretty good time, and there were about 20 people who were being paid somewhere just north of minimum wage to take a lot of the worry off our shoulders. In spite of the fact that I felt completely out of my league, I was more than holding my own.

Two photographers walked around snapping pictures of people. I followed them with my eyes until they aimed their cameras at Charlie and some very chic woman. Who was she with the slicked back blonde hair wearing the tiny, black cocktail dress talking to Charlie? I had no idea. She looked so stylish snatching martinis off a passing tray for her and Charlie; and Charlie—absolutely in his element, as he took on the role of co-host of our party.

A few weeks prior to the party, Charlie was given a key to the house, a magnetic card, and the security code to the ballroom. He was very involved in the planning of the open house and worked closely with Paige. He had recommended Helen, the caterer, and at some point it just became easier to give Charlie complete access. In the days prior to the open house, he practically lived in the ballroom and we had trusted him to come and go as he pleased. Paige also came to learn that Charlie could be a little possessive and would sometimes get just a little miffed when she didn't give him the requisite time and attention he required.

Whenever he called it was expected that she drop everything. He was a jester in need of a queen, and Paige had been coronated into this role. Watching Charlie and the chic woman enjoying themselves, I was relieved for Paige that he had found someone else to dote on.

A skinny 20-something-year-old kid in a white ruffled shirt, bowtie and black pants walked up offering a silver tray filled with sizzling hot scallops wrapped in prosciutto, and their aroma was intoxicating. I took two of the toothpick-stabbed *hors d'oeuvres* and popped one into my mouth.

There must be an unwritten rule that says only one person is allowed to wear an ascot at any given party and Charlie won the honor. Very few people can wear an ascot and not look ridiculous; Charlie however, looked great wearing his. The woman in the little black dress whispered something into his ear after someone named Bobby Grossmeijer walked by them. Apparently Bobby Grossmeijer was an actor of some repute a thousand years ago who crashes events like these, and when he shows up, the party is deemed a success. I couldn't help but roll my eyes and smile. The woman in the black dress snorted and Charlie brayed as they downed their martinis. I watched and marveled at their effortless and unselfconscious party skills. I hoped Charlie wouldn't get too drunk too early, but as it turned out, I had nothing to worry about: People in ascots know how to hold their liquor.

Other people were standing by a round reproduction Louis XV table adorned with a giant flower arrangement; they stopped mid-conversation, posing for one of the roving photographers. A lot of new furniture arrived a few days before the party and our home, impressive as it already was, was transformed into a museum under the artful eyes of Charlie, Paige, and Helen, who, in addition to her skills with *hors d'oeuvres*, was a much sought after interior decorator.

Elliot and three other children ran into the foyer from the crowded library and bolted up the stairs. Elliot looked like a kid on a short visit home from prep school. His crisp white shirt had come untucked and his belt barely held up his rumpled blue pants.

"WALK!" I shouted in their direction but they ignored me as they turned left at the top of the stairs and disappeared down the hall, parting sophisticates in their wake.

Couples walked into the grand foyer, looked around and nodded their approval. I wasn't sure if it was the usual suspects they were scrutinizing or the house, or perhaps a combination of both. A cute female college student with a tiny nose piercing, dressed identically to the boy passing out the *hors d'oeuvres*, handed our guests coat tickets in exchange for their overcoats with Burberry scarves stuffed into the sleeves, hats, gloves, and fur wraps both real and faux, then added the stylish gear to the closets on either side of the entryway, which were already bulging with expensive outerwear.

Charlie broke off from the woman in the black cocktail dress and interrupted the chatter of the fabulous assembled in the library, the foyer, and the dining room. Slowly he urged the groupings of three, four, and six to trek upstairs.

Paige sidled up next to me and put her arm around my waist. She looked up at me and gave me a "Can you believe this?" look.

"Who *are* these people?" I asked in my best Thurston Howell III voice.

She smiled and pushed me in the direction of the stairs. Paige, too, was wearing a little black dress, rating very high on the chic list herself; I made a mental note to keep an eye out for cads and philanderers.

"The band's been playing in the ballroom for an hour," Paige said, "And the last time I checked there were only a few people up there listening. I almost feel like it was a waste to hire them."

"Ask Helen. Aren't bands obligatory at events like these?"

"I guess," she replied.

"I bet there aren't too many people used to trudging up two flights of stairs to an attic ballroom these days."

"With this crowd you never know."

"Now I get why the attic ballroom thing fizzled in the last century," I said. "It's a pain in the ass herding people upstairs."

"It's not like we're going to host parties every weekend," Paige said, wincing at the idea.

"Whatever do you mean, Lovey?" I replied aghast, swirling my martini.

She laughed as we walked by Elliot's open bedroom door. The woman in the little black dress was in his room, holding the children in rapt attention with what looked like a story.

"Who is that woman?" I asked, and Paige quickly glanced in.

"That's Charlie's niece. Her name is Polly. She's in from L.A. for a few days."

A traffic jam formed at the entry to the double-winder stairway and I heard the clickety-clack of high heels stamping up the wood stairs. Up ahead, some obnoxious swell let out a "Moo" and laughter followed. I felt a large hand fall onto my shoulder and looked up to see that it belonged to Judge Evans, our neighbor.

"You did a fine job on the restoration, you two," he said. "Your home is one of the crown jewels of the neighborhood!"

"Thank you, Judge!" I said.

"That's very kind of you, Judge Evans," Paige added. He handed her a gift. "Go on, open it!" he said to her.

It was a framed, colorized photograph of our house taken when it was just a few years old. Paige looked at the photograph and, when she looked up at the judge, tears welled in her eyes. She stood on her tiptoes and gave him a peck on the cheek that clearly made his night. He looked like he could die a happy man.

The three of us were among the last to make our way up. It was hot in the stairwell and I worried that the ballroom would be stifling, but when we walked in, it was, much to my relief, comfortable. Someone, probably Helen, had the forethought to crack open the dormer windows and the curtains billowed slightly.

Helen had completely transformed the ballroom. Giant red velvet curtains, drawn back and secured with gold ropes and tassels, hung in royal fashion in front of the massive octagon window revealing the view of Seminole Street with its tall and stately elms, their branches backlit by the sodium vapor streetlights and, below the branches, a hundred or more of our guests' cars parked up and down its length.

The ballroom was splendidly decked out with small groupings of both modern and reproduction antique furniture that ringed a large empty space for dancing under the Cyclops, and decorative chrome globes of varying sizes hung from other parts of the ceiling.

Al was way off on the left side of the stage behind his control panel pretending to fiddle with his dials. In the center of the stage was the band—a jazz quintet called The Bradleys—skillfully covering a Coltrane song. A crowd stood just in front of the stage, entranced by, and swaying to the saxophone player's solo. Al could have been mistaken as the band's sound man standing behind his panel.

Paige took Judge Evans by the arm and introduced him to Harlan's wife Virginia, or Ginny as she preferred. She actually knew quite a few of our guests—I guessed it wasn't unusual for people like Ginny to know people like our guests from other cities. Maybe there was some social register where they all kept track of each other.

I looked around for Charlie as I was relying on him to keep things going, but I had nothing to worry about. It looked like the party was successfully running on autopilot. Helen had arranged a long buffet table that lined the north wall, and two bars were set up, one on either side of the stage. People lined up at the bars, the liquor flowed, and that made things go swimmingly. Al came up to me a little annoyed.

"Man, what a bunch of assholes!"

"Whatever are you going on about, young man?" I replied, channeling Thurston.

"Don't turn into these people on me now," he said.

"Or I'll have to kick your ass!"

"I hope you're not getting cold feet," I said.

"No way! Me and the boys are ready to go whenever."

I looked around and noticed three other guys with big handlebar mustaches similar to Al's gorging themselves at the long buffet table. I was relieved that they weren't dressed in straw hats and striped jackets.

"I'll let you make that call," I said to him. "And trust me, I'm not turning into *these people*." I looked around the packed ballroom. "I don't even know who half of them are, but I'm seriously glad you're here. I know you're gonna knock it out of the park."

My mind, however, was not on the positive reception of Al's quartet. I looked up at the Cyclops. It hung from the complicated pole—the giant globe and its thousands of individual pieces of glass melding into one unidentifiable dark shade, sucking in any light and energy that strayed too close. And it seemed like our guests were avoiding it. No one danced under it. Those dancing chose a spot closer to the stage instead. I noticed a couple of women looking up at it. One pointed and the other bristled and drew her cashmere sweater over her shoulders. They looked uneasy while they talked about it, like it was giving them the creeps. I was more than a little nervous about turning it on.

"Has Harlan gone over things with you yet?" I asked.

"Dude, you're so behind the curve! Of course! We rehearsed and everything. We're going to rock that light. Wait till you hear the script he wrote."

"I don't know. I'm starting to have second thoughts. Some of these people are gonna freak when you start turning your dials. Seriously, what do you think's going to happen? You've seen what that thing does," I said, looking up at it.

"Don't worry, it'll be cool. Harlan's going to make an announcement and warn people before we fire it up."

David's talk about lawsuits a few weeks prior had been reverberating around in my head all day and now I was the one with a serious case of cold feet. I excused myself and looked around for David and Harlan but couldn't find them. I made my way toward Paige and Ginny through the crowd and asked if they had seen them.

"David took Harlan away from us a few minutes ago," Paige said. "I think they headed toward the stage."

I looked and still couldn't find them. The Bradleys were now covering "Take Five," and the weird syncopation was serving as an appropriate soundtrack to my mounting anxiety. I hopped onto the stage and finally found David and Harlan off in the left wing, talking by the circuit breakers where the thick black cables were plugged in and ready to go. They personified comedy and tragedy when they looked at me as I walked toward them: Harlan was all smiles and David was the epitome of grave. They both offered their hands and I grabbed at them.

"Where the hell have you been?" David asked.

"I was about to ask you the same thing," I replied.

I turned my attention toward Harlan and noticed the drink in his hand. He set it on top of one of the old bar tables that obviously didn't fit in with Helen's vision of the ballroom. A bunch of unacceptable ballroom flotsam had been crammed back here and it was crowded. There was a folder on the table, too.

"Harlan, I've got to be honest with you," I said. "I'm getting a serious case of cold feet. I don't know about this anymore."

"I've been telling him the same thing for the last five minutes," said David, a little panicky. "This party's a who's-who of Detroit, and if one of these people gets hurt..."

We both looked at Harlan.

"Daniel, just say the word and we'll call the whole thing off right now. But before you do, at least read through this," Harlan said, handing me the folder that contained the script he'd written.

First, I scanned his masterfully written and very strongly worded warning: "No children... persons who suffer from vertigo, heart disease... by remaining in this room you're agreeing to..." and, "What you are about to witness has been thoroughly tested and is in no way dangerous." Then I came to the body of the script, which was a lovingly written homage—a testament—to the genius of my great-grandfather. It brought to life the work that had for too long been boxed up and forgotten down in the archive.

David looked over my shoulder and read along with me; this tribute was reminiscent of David's own words to me five years earlier in the private library. "Tonight we're introducing to you the accomplishments of a towering, 20th century genius whose work had been lost until this very evening, forgotten in exile, and stowed away in a dusty old archive." He went on and compared my great-grandfather to the other immortals of 20th century science and industry: Fermi, Tesla, Ford, Edison, and yes, Einstein! My heart swelled with pride. I looked back at David and he, too, seemed fairly intoxicated by the words on Harlan's script. But I could sense something else beginning to churn around in that lawyer mind: the highly litigious assembly of patricians here in the ballroom suddenly transformed into potential investors.

We looked at each other and, motivated by our own very distinct reasons, agreed to go ahead with the demonstration. I'd known David long enough to know when he was stressed-out, but to the uninitiated Harlan, it would have been difficult to detect. For me, though, it was obvious: He always tried to take control whenever he allowed stress to get the best of him. His expensive briefcase was on the floor under the breaker box and I wondered why he'd brought it to the party. He had something up his sleeve and there was no telling what he'd do. I made a mental note to keep an eye on him.

The Bradleys wrapped up their second set to hollers for encores and a few minutes later Al and his barbershop quartet mounted the stage. They were dressed in identical black pants and turtlenecks, all with their own, distinctly elaborate waxed mustaches and old-timey facial hair. It was a little outlandish and I had to stifle a laugh.

The din in the room quieted to a murmur and I was suddenly worried for my friend. The guys in Al's quartet did not walk around unnoticed and the jaded revelers were curious as to what was about to transpire. Al blew into a pitch pipe and his quartet suddenly busted out the craziest rendition of the Sex Pistols' "Anarchy in the U.K." that I've ever heard. Then came the Ramones' "I Wanna be

Sedated," and a little Motown for good measure with Marvin Gaye's "I Heard it Through the Grapevine."

Listening to Jonny Rotten's vile sentiments sung in four-part harmony was too much, and the crowd of 30, 40, and 50-somethings went absolutely wild. Most everyone got the irony of a barbershop quartet singing punk rock, but I noticed also that a few of the more hip among us thought it was just a little too precious.

Al passed out a lot of cards that evening, and he and his quartet became something of a minor overnight sensation.

Charlie mounted the stage after Al's group took their final bow and it was obvious that a lot of people knew him when the applause redoubled and a few people shouted his name. He gave a thumbs-up and said something I didn't quite catch and everyone roared with laughter. He looked like a politician standing there basking in the adoration as he waved and pointed at various people. He raised his hands and when the applause died down, he began his off-the-cuff speech.

"Ladies and gentlemen, welcome to Daniel and Paige Lintz's open house. I've been asked to help out as co-host, and, well where are they now? Paige? Daniel? Come on up here."

I walked out from the wing and Charlie offered Paige his hand and helped her onto the stage. Everyone began to applaud and the three of us stood there with our arms around each other. The applause died down and Paige and I looked at each other and, with quick gestures, worked out that she would speak first. Paige pulled a petit notebook from a small hidden pocket in her little black dress and read from it.

"Thank you all so much for coming to our open house. From the moment we moved in and began the difficult task of putting this house in some semblance of order, the many wonderful people who've lived here in Indian Village for years slowly and unobtrusively began to introduce themselves and welcome us to the neighborhood. They offered their warmth and friendship, and many came bearing gifts. Over time, we came to know the definition of neighborly through their bountiful acts of kindness, support, and love; and without them it's doubtful that we would have been able to endure the many frustrations, setbacks, and unanticipated expenses it took to turn this house into our home."

A sigh rose up from the crowd as her voice began to crack. She took a moment to compose herself then continued off script, swallowing back her emotions.

"And this wonderful man here!" she said, as she put her arm around Charlie, "This guy here! What can I say except, Charlie Hintermann!"

She gave Charlie a big hug and peck on the cheek and I looked out at the room and watched as our guests broke into another warm and spontaneous round of applause. I put my arms out for Paige and she walked into my embrace.

Now it was my turn. I thanked everyone for coming, acknowledged the hard work of all those who helped in the renovation, a few of whom were assembled in the ballroom, and gave a shout-out to Helen and her staff for their efforts in ways both seen and unseen. Helen, a very heavy woman, was taking a break on one of the overstuffed chairs around the dance floor; when I mentioned her there were a few whoops and hollers. She smiled and waved up at me from her chair. I thanked Al for his expertise both as an electrician and musician, but mostly as an electrician, and the Bradleys for providing a musical backdrop for an evening that, second only to our wedding, was the most enjoyable I've ever had. Then I turned it back over to Charlie and he proposed a toast to home, hearth, love, and friendship.

Then it was Harlan's turn.

"We have a treat for you this evening," Charlie said. "Dr. Harlan Lappe, the curator of the Tiffany Glassworks Museum in Cornell, New York, is here and has graciously offered to give us a demonstration of this magnificent and strange chandelier hanging in this gorgeous ballroom. Now from what I understand, this isn't your everyday, run-of-the-mill chandelier. It's something special and perhaps we'll all understand just a little more about it after he speaks, so without further ado, I present to you, Dr. Harlan Lappe."

Both Harlan and Al walked out from the wing. Al took up his position at the control panel and Harlan took center stage.

"Ladies and gentlemen, I don't enjoy starting off demonstrations by sounding alarmist, but before we begin I'm going to ask that you all take a very honest self-assessment by asking a few questions: Have you ever suffered from vertigo or do you have a history of heart disease? Now this next one is important: Are you epileptic? If you can answer 'yes' to any of these questions, I'm going to ask that you, for your own safety, excuse yourself from the ballroom at this time. Daniel and Paige have a bar and some other treats set up in the first floor library for those of you who would prefer not to stay during the demonstration."

After Harlan said this, two people headed toward the pocket doors. One of Helen's staff met them by the doors and offered to escort them down to the library.

"Thank you for being honest, folks, we'd rather err on the side of caution." Harlan continued, lightening it up a little by asking who in the room avoided roller-coasters. He paused and a general murmur arose in the room, and a few people laughed and looked at each other nervously.

"What you are about to witness is something that has only been seen by a very small group of scientists and engineers almost a hundred years ago, and again, as recently as today. I assure you, there is absolutely nothing in any way whatsoever that will pose a risk to your health when this instrument is turned on."

Harlan had everyone in rapt attention and, other than the random creak in the floor and clearing of a throat, the room was silent.

"Yes, you may find the spinning lights to be slightly disorienting and it might be a good idea to either sit down, lean against a wall, or hold on to someone, but, again, I assure you that nothing this device does will pose a risk to your…"

Suddenly David walked out onto the stage with a stack of forms in his hand. Paige and I looked at each other.

"What's he doing?" she asked.

"I don't know," I shrugged.

David got the attention of a couple of Helen's staff members and instructed them to start passing out the forms. Harlan, surprised at the intrusion, picked up on David's actions, but it was too late to do anything about it so he reluctantly acquiesced. He took the microphone off its stand, snatched a form from David and read it. David whispered something into Harlan's ear. Harlan gave David a thinly disguised, "Really!? You're not actually doing this," look then glanced over at Paige and me. Paige was livid.

"This is it!" she said, elbowing me in the ribs. "He just broke the camel's back with this one!"

Harlan handed David the microphone then walked toward us.

"Did you know anything about this?" Harlan asked in a half whisper.

"Absolutely not!" I said.

We watched as David introduced himself and floundered on, briefly explaining that what was being passed around was a consent form. Evidently he had prepared for this moment.

"You'll find cups filled with pens on every table in this room. Please read over the form, sign it, and then pass it to a staff person," David explained to the captive audience.

As if on cue Helen's people began to mingle around and offer assistance.

I looked over at Judge Evans and Ginny as they carefully read their forms. The Judge's eyebrows arched. Ginny began to speak to him and he nodded, taking in what Ginny had to say. It was evident that Ginny knew quite a bit about the Cyclops, as she pointed up at it while talking.

I was a little surprised when the Judge took a pen out of a cup, signed it, and handed it to one of Helen's helpers. Ginny also signed.

I looked over at the two women who seemed afraid of it. They read their forms then put them down. They were animated as they spoke to each other and glanced uncomfortably up at the Cyclops. The ladies looked back down at their form and winced as if it had been smeared with something disgusting. They did not sign.

A lot of people knew Judge Evans, and a small group gathered around him and Ginny, perhaps to seek a little impromptu legal advice. Judge Evans and Ginny spoke to the assembly with reassurance, which prompted each person to sign. Within a few minutes, many of the forms were collected and brought to David. He held the stack above his head.

"By a show of hands who didn't sign? There's no shame if you didn't, but you may not remain in the ballroom for the demonstration if you chose not to."

A general din broke out when more than a few hands went up. David raised his voice trying to regain order.

"I'll have to insist you leave if you didn't sign."

An elderly couple was escorted a little too inelegantly from the room and someone blurted out that "this was some serious bullshit." David's surprise intrusion on the evening had completely changed the energy in the room, and to borrow Paige's observation from a few weeks ago, it was a total buzzkill. The two ladies who bristled when they looked at the Cyclops walked toward the doors.

No one expected to have to sign a consent form at an open house, and why should they? Bobby Grossmeijer was standing by the south bar. He smiled, cool and detached through his sunglasses.

"Fuck this," he said, loud enough for many to hear.

He set his drink down on a table and headed for the doors. A few other people followed him out in solidarity. Harlan grabbed the microphone from David and attempted to salvage the evening.

"Ladies and gentlemen, I apologize for the clumsy way we handled the intro to this demonstration, but I can assure you it's only because, above all else, we don't want anyone to get hurt."

"You mean you don't want anyone to get sued!" shouted someone in the crowd.

Charlie walked up to Harlan and put his hand out for the microphone.

"Allow me," he said, and Harlan gave it to him.

We stood there on the stage and watched the mayhem escalate.

"I don't understand what's happening," Paige said. "Why don't you do something?"

More people walked out. Charlie slowly walked toward the foot of the stage with the microphone in his hand. He began to tap on it and the amplified THUNK filled the room. Slowly the mayhem died down and everyone turned and looked up at Charlie. He stood there at the foot of the stage smiling then raised the microphone to his lips.

"Now then, where were we?" he said with a gentle mix of sarcasm, humor, and admonition, and we watched amazed as he saved the evening. His energy was the antithesis of the negativity that, until that moment, had permeated the room. "Oh, I remember! We were going to watch what will probably be for each and every one of you the most amazing thing you'll ever witness in your entire lives. And how does good ol' Charlie know this?" He quickly glanced at us and winked then proceeded with a giant fib. "Because earlier today I got to witness it for myself and look at me!" He twirled in a circle then posed for his audience. "Fabulous, huh? If anything, I feel ten years younger *and* I was told by many of you as I mingled around earlier how great I look tonight. Far be it for me to attribute it to the effects of this fancy chandelier but, you know, one never can tell!" He drew the microphone closer to his mouth and lowered his voice an octave. "Now why don't you all chill out, put your drinks down, find somebody to hold on to—that alone sounds like fun, doesn't it?—and enjoy what we've got in store for you!"

Charlie played on the vanity of our guests and quickly gained back their trust. Some people put their drinks down and headed toward the walls, others sat down, and within a minute all of the chairs, sofas, and settees were occupied. An excited optimism filled the room and leaked out into the stairwell. A few of the people who had left minutes earlier mingled back into the ballroom, including Bobby Grossmeijer who sauntered back in slowly and quietly. He took a place against a wall near the draped octagon window and took his sunglasses off. David walked up to Paige and me looking pretty satisfied with himself.

"I think there are still a few people here who didn't sign. I'll mingle around and see if I can get some more signatures," David said.

"Seriously David, don't bother," Paige said, not disguising her irritation. "I'm sure it'll be okay."

"Don't you remember what we discussed?" David asked. "You can't..."

"I remember, but I think we'll be fine," Paige interrupted.

David looked at me bewildered.

"David, in case you didn't notice, your little speech almost emptied this room," I said. "Paige is right, don't worry about it. We'll be fine, and we really don't want to hear another word about it!"

He wanted to say something but the words caught in his throat. Instead he put his hands on his hips and cocked his head, genuinely puzzled by our attitude. He turned on his heels and walked toward the wing where he had left his briefcase, muttering something about it being our asses and not his. He emerged with his briefcase, stepped off the stage, and walked toward the exit, and no one noticed as the thin, elderly gentleman with the slight limp, who had tried to make everyone sign some document, walked through the pocket doors and out of the ballroom; and no one gave him a second thought as he disappeared down the stairway.

Charlie handed the microphone back to Harlan. Upon Harlan's signal, the pocket doors and curtains were closed and the lights dimmed. Al was at his place behind the control panel stage left, while Paige, Charlie, and I stood stage right.

"I think we should hold hands," I said to them.

They looked at me wide-eyed with a hint of fear. I smiled back in reassurance and we clasped hands. They had no idea what to expect and, looking out from my vantage, I saw a similar look on the hundred or so faces in the ballroom. The lights went down a little further as Harlan walked over to Al and his control panel. All eyes were glued to the Cyclops. Harlan lifted his notes and began to read.

"In 1915, the United States Government commissioned a group of scientists and engineers, led by Alois Lintz, Daniel's great-grandfather, to invent an instrument that would render everything within its range invisible."

A gasp rose from the crowd and Paige looked at me concerned. I squeezed her hand and told her not to worry.

Harlan continued, "The government demanded two things: The result would have to prove to be 100 percent safe with no residual side-effects, *and* temporary, that is, the state of invisibility must terminate immediately upon deactivation of the instrument. Please bear in mind that in 1915, the harnessing of electricity and the invention of artificial lighting was still in a relative state of infancy, and it boggles the mind when one ponders what an accomplishment this instrument is in its precision. The many different disciplines that came together, and the synchronicity of application it took to create it, clearly represents an engineering feat that is, even by today's standards, virtually unprecedented. This instrument is, without a doubt, one of the greatest inventions of the 20th century!"

Charlie's interest was perked. He let go of Paige's hand and walked over to Al and Harlan. He stood behind them and watched fascinated as Al slowly turned his dials.

Charlie had more than just people skills; he was also a retired engineer so I could only assume that he was still very interested in technology. A 100-year-old instrument with more moving parts than a Swiss watch—one that required a great deal of engineering—would certainly enchant anyone with Charlie's professional background.

Harlan continued on about my great-grandfather, the many important positions he held in academia, science, and industry, and how in the years leading up to World War I and thereafter, his was a household name. But as his work, discoveries, and the contributions he made to science and technology diminished, his fame also diminished, to the point where no one remembered him at all. What Harlan didn't say was that my great-grandfather's passing into obscurity was not an accident.

As dedicated as my great-grandfather was to his life's work, he devoted an equal amount of energy into making sure that his memory and work would be forgotten—wiped clean from mankind's collective memory. The official story was that Alois Lintz suffered through many personal tragedies that eventually took their toll on him. A rare article about my great-grandfather in an old defunct magazine from the 1950s called *American Technician* read that, "Alois Lintz abruptly resigned from public life, became a recluse, and died years later a forgotten man." Nothing in the article mentioned that once he *resigned* he immediately got to work, meticulously archiving his life's work, boxing it, filing it, and locking it up, making damn sure that, like his name, his works, too, faded completely from memory. No one would devote more time and energy

toward engineering their own public demise than Alois
Lintz. But why?

Al turned the ballroom lights all the way off as he
adjusted the dials for Cyclops. He had improved his skills
with the panel and was able to coax even more spectacular
phenomena as the Cyclops suddenly pulsed to life from its
uniform black—the colors emanated from deep within,
surfaced quickly, then recessed back only to be replaced by
another unidentifiable color.

"As you're about to see," Harlan said, over the hum of
the panel, "invisibility will not be completely achieved.
There are a few key elements that have been removed from
the instrument, but what you'll witness will be no less
impressive."

Al continued to fiddle and the warm tones and hues
grew in magnitude. The Cyclops resembled a giant
cuttlefish as patterns formed and dissipated, undulating
iridescently, and the very surface seemed to transform in
texture and consistency. Pinpricks of light appeared on
every surface and every face in the ballroom, twinkling,
dancing, vibrating, and morphing in tone and hue. Al
turned another dial and the upper and lower hemispheres
slowly began to spin in opposite directions and the
pinpricks of light began their circular trek around the room.
The effect was immediately bewildering and many people
steadied themselves and held on just a little tighter, oohing
and ahhing. The globe spun faster and faster and the
thousands of pinpricks became razor sharp stripes of light.
Al turned another dial and the Fresnel lenses at the equator
of the globe lit up and started their spin. They accelerated
rapidly and slowly the Cyclops tilted upward on its axis

until it was parallel to the support pole. Then it began to orbit slowly around the pole.

Al hit the switch that activated the ultraviolet filaments and now the chaos. Shards of undulating plasma fingered their way toward the decorative metallic globes that Helen had hung from the ceiling, each globe unexpectedly amplifying the chaos and quadrupling Cyclops' effects. The plasma streams beamed off and careened, splitting into shards of multi-colored lightning that oscillated downward, seeking the higher surfaces, the centerpieces, and the heads of everyone in the ballroom. The beams struck everything and everyone, and I watched astounded as everyone became translucent.

I heard someone scream.

"There's nothing to fear," Harlan said, in reassuring tones. "The energy you're seeing cannot hurt you. That you can now see through yourselves is harmless. Enjoy it!"

I watched as a brave, skeletal couple walked hand-in-hand directly beneath the Cyclops and began to dance. A nimbus of gassy lightning whipped off their transparent bodies and joined the chaotic fray of electrons above them. Eddies and whirls of energy danced and whipped around the room. I looked at Paige and saw through her skin. She looked at me and let go of my hand. She held up her hand and looked at her bones and watched as blood pulsed through her veins and capillaries. She clenched and unclenched her fist, amazed at the delicate workings of the dozens of bones in her hand.

I looked back out at the assembly of people and a force had taken hold. It was almost spiritual. Some slowly spun around while inspecting their transparency. Others walked out onto the dance floor and swayed. It was impossible to recognize anyone as facial features and body fat seemed to melt away. We were an assembly of anonymous skeletons with our organs, circulatory, and nervous systems identically arranged in a temporary state of transparency. While the only thing that distinguished one person from another were variations in height, it was still easy to discern the men from the women.

I looked back at Paige and through her. I looked at her bones, her organs, and her uterus. I was shocked when I saw the embryo of our unborn second child floating safely in its amniotic sanctuary. I took her by her hands and drew her closer. I waited for her to turn her attention away from the dancers.

"You're pregnant!" I said.

She looked down, then back up at me. I watched as liquid filled her tear ducts then ran down the translucency of her skin.

"I love you," she said.

"I love you too."

I looked back down at our developing baby and noticed that its tiny eyes were flashing in a multitude of kaleidoscopic colors and patterns. I took Paige by the arm and led her to the stage right wing to get her and our baby out of the Cyclops' chaos.

PART III

Paige was determined that this pregnancy would be a healthier experience for her and the baby. She was very disciplined. She consulted with a nutritionist who specialized in working with pregnant women. She monitored her blood pressure and kept it normal with diet, exercise, and avoiding stressful situations as best as possible. She completely altered her (and our) diets, and everything brought into the kitchen was practically analyzed with a magnifying glass.

We bought only local, organically grown fruits and vegetables, and Saturday trips to Eastern Market were compulsory. She immersed herself in gardening, tearing out bulbs and various other plants that had long grown in the garden beds that circled an old backyard fountain, and replaced them with herbs and vegetables.

Charlie was mortified, telling her that herbs and vegetables had no place in a formal French garden. Paige, down on her knees, ignored his pleas and admonishments while yanking out fistfuls of the floral refuse. Charlie warned that this time around, he would think twice about our participation in the annual home and garden tour, even while taking the dirty, wilting clumps from her and tossing them into another biodegradable garden bag.

Elliot said that our food had to pass Mommy's yucky test, meaning if it was yucky, it was okay to eat.

Paige started working closely with her therapist and expressed her desire to draw closer as a family, ridding ourselves of unnecessary distractions and not allowing the small things to escalate. We ate healthier, talked more, and took walks. I lost weight. We talked about the soon-to-arrive baby and how different our lives were now compared to when she was pregnant with Elliot.

The inheritance had turned our world upside down, but we had accomplished so much since Elliot was born and had long settled into a normal life with stable, predictable patterns. We were happy and a lot more ready for a baby this time around, but, in spite of the precautions, our daughter Chelsea was born with an extremely rare birth defect.

It was explained to us that the malady was genetic, and that a regressive trait hidden in the coding of my DNA was the likely cause, although the doctors could not be absolutely certain. There was nothing that could have been done to prevent it, and the defect was impossible to detect. It did not show up on the ultrasounds during Chelsea's development because it was hidden within the orbs of her eyes. Chelsea was born without retinas, rendering her blind. Although I kept it to myself, I was fairly certain that Chelsea's in utero exposure to the Cyclops' bizarre lightshow was what actually caused the birth defect. Her condition, however, was curable and her prognosis for sight was good, but she would need retina transplants along with an experimental stem cell procedure. She would be the first person ever to go through this procedure and there were a lot of concerns. Timing was also critical. If we waited too long, the optic nerve and those parts of her occipital lobe involved in sight could atrophy. Her specialist told us that the ideal window would be when she was between 24 and 30 months old. A further complication was that a suitable donor would have to manifest in that optimal time period. We could only wait and hope for the best.

Other than her condition, Chelsea was a very happy baby. Since she was born this way, she had no idea that anything was wrong. Paige and I were devastated at first but we quickly came to terms with Chelsea's condition, and that was mostly because of Chelsea herself. She was an inspiration. She didn't have to see us to know when we walked into her nursery. She would be in her crib, cooing and reaching out for us to pick her up, smiling in anticipation. She loved being held in the rocking chair, especially when we sang softly to her, and she was crazy about Elliot. She loved touching his face and pulling his ears and she laughed when he feigned an "ouch" if she happened to pull too hard.

I was very concerned about Paige in light of what she went through after Elliot was born, but the precautions she took had a huge, positive impact on her mental and physical health. She was a rock—a champion for her daughter—and loved her with all her heart and soul from the very second she unexpectedly found out she was pregnant during the ballroom demonstration.

Elliot still suffered occasional seizures, but his doctors

were never able to figure out why. One strange harbinger of an impending seizure was that when one was about to happen, the monitors set up throughout the house would suddenly snow out, and in spite of all of the expensive security devices that prevented unauthorized access into the ballroom, I would always find him up there staring at the Cyclops, the pocket doors open just enough for him to slip through.

Elliot did not have the code, nor did he know where we kept the magnetic cards. I kept mine in my wallet, Paige had hers tucked safely away, and the card that we had given to Charlie—I was 95 percent certain that Paige had gotten it back from him, but I had to remind myself to ask her if indeed that was the case.

I assumed that whatever was causing the monitors to snow out was also causing the ballroom security system to fail. We experienced occasional brown outs and maybe there was a connection—some electrical short or other technical phenomena was causing the electronic devices in our home to malfunction. Al would know for sure and I would call him soon to come over and figure it out.

The last time I found Elliot in the ballroom he was talking to the Cyclops. I slipped through the doors quietly and watched, but he must have heard me coming up the stairs. The upper and lower hemispheres were slowly spinning in opposite directions. He stopped talking but continued staring up at the Cyclops. Finally he turned and looked at me blankly, completely devoid of emotion.

"They're not the right ones."

"Elliot, how'd you get in here?" I slowly walked toward him.

As I drew closer the Cyclops came to an abrupt stop. I looked over at Al's control panel on the stage. It was covered with a sheet.

"You have to put the right ones in," Elliot said, staring through me.

I got down on my knees and took his hands into mine, alarmed at how cold they were.

"Elliot, it's not okay that you're up here. You have to ask me or Mommy if you want to come up here to play, do you understand?"

He shifted his gaze up at the Cyclops.

"She can't see with the new ones."

"Who, Elliot? Who can't see? Who's telling you these things?"

"She's up there, Daddy!" he said, pointing. "In the light trying to look through the glass, but she says they're not the right ones."

"Elliot, did you turn the light on? Were you messing with the dials on the panel over there?"

"No."

"Then can you tell me why it was spinning when I first walked in?"

"Yes," he said, averting my eyes.

"Well, I'm waiting."

"She likes when it spins. When it spins the others come to visit."

Elliot was getting a little too big to carry, so I took him by the hand. We walked out of the ballroom. I slid the doors closed then pushed a sequence of numbers on the number pad and the bolts slid into their locked position. I slid my magnetic card through the slot and another set of bolts loudly slammed into their chambers. Elliot was standing in the dim at the top of the stairs a few steps behind me. I turned to him.

"Elliot, I'm going to ask you again," I said, more firmly than I meant to.

He started crying. I got down on my knees and took him by the shoulders.

"Listen, you're not in trouble. I'm not going to punish you, but I have to know. Who let you into the ballroom?"

He looked at me with tears streaming down his cheeks.

"I don't know. I don't remember!"

I drew him to me tightly. His small body shuddered while he sobbed. We walked down the stairs, down the hall, and into the bathroom. I sat him on the toilet and took his shoe and sock off. During our walk toward the pocket doors, I had noticed the familiar limp in his stride. We sat in silence as I cleaned and dressed his big toe.

🏛   🏛   🏛

It was well into November when we received a letter from the Michigan Department of Transportation. The letter described in detail a plan for a massive expansion of the Coleman Young International Airport. The airport's primary runway would be improved and lengthened due to an increase in air traffic and also to accommodate larger cargo and commuter jets. But, for this, the state needed land. Since this was the oldest of the major airports that serviced Metro Detroit, it was completely surrounded by an old, well-established eastside neighborhood; the State determined that the only land available for expansion was the beloved, very large, and well-tended Mt. Olivet Cemetery. It would be necessary to raze a significant part of the cemetery to make way for the runway expansion.

My great-aunt Nora was interred in the part of the cemetery that had been procured for the planned expansion. The letter stated that the Department of Transportation understood the extreme sensitivity of this controversial project and promised that the reinterment would be taken care of with the utmost sensitivity and professionalism. The letter included an approval form for us to sign, have notarized, and return to the State. After this, within a couple of weeks, we would receive a voucher that could be used to defray all of the expenses involved in Nora's reinterment.

Paige and I thought it would be best to have Nora reinterred next to my grandmother at Mt. Elliot Cemetery, which was not very far from Seminole Street. On the appointed day I went to Mt. Olivet to accompany Nora's remains to their new resting place.

I drove slowly down the winding narrow lanes of the cemetery. A lot of caskets had already been disinterred and piles of dirt stood sentry next to rectangular holes. I turned a corner and up ahead the cemetery workers had finished their work and were moving on to another grave.

I parked behind a county truck and got out of my car. Nora's coffin was out of the ground and temporarily resting on two saw horses. It was a cloudy, late November day, and large old oaks towered over the graves and swayed in the wind, their brown, mottled leaves curled tightly into rusty sleigh bells that jingled dryly as they shook high in the branches. The guy from the county introduced himself.

He had me sign a document on a clipboard and tore a copy off along its perforated line and handed it over, instructing me to show it to the administrator at Mt. Elliot. Before he left me alone with Nora's coffin he told me that he had just spoken to the driver of the hearse and that it would be arriving shortly. I thanked him. He climbed into his truck and drove off to another gravesite.

I walked up to Nora's coffin. It was small, about five feet long, lacquered white, and decorated in gold filigree with matching handles. Because it had been contained in an underground concrete vault, it was in excellent condition and very clean.

I walked around it. The wind blustered and I worried for a second that the precarious assembly would be knocked over and, as I stood in front of it, a chill went through my body as another gust suddenly blew up and rocked the coffin slightly. Then I heard a whisper:

"My eyes, Papa!"

I whipped around and peered at a tall, granite, obelisk capped with a roman helmet. My hair stood on end. *I heard it! I know I heard it!* My mind screamed. It came from behind that obelisk that had "GAVISTON" chiseled into its polished surface. I shifted my gaze to Nora's small, white marble gravestone propped against the pile of dirt that had filled her grave. The stone's surface, carved with a sleeping lamb in relief, was dirty with grime and the cursive letters had eroded to the point of being blurry and difficult to read. It, too, would be relocated to Mt. Elliot Cemetery. It read:

NORA LINTZ
Daughter & Sister
1903 – 1919

"Find them!"

I heard it again! This time it came from the jingle in the tree above… or was it whispered from behind another nearby gravestone… or carried in on a gust that whipped the branches? It was faint, almost imperceptible, more like a memory, and it came from everywhere and nowhere.

The sky darkened. Off to the west sunlight broke through the clouds painting them in a shock of red-orange. The gravestones glowed, reflecting the dim fire of the setting sun.

"My eyes, Papa! They're in the box."

I looked down at the small coffin glowing in the late afternoon light. I bent down and put my ear on the lid. Further off in the dim I saw the workers; a small backhoe, the county guy, and his truck were all backlit in silhouettes, their voices and laughter faint and far off, each occupied in the task of exhuming another mortal coil.

I peered down into the grave and after my eyes adjusted I saw a dried bouquet tied with a small ribbon. I was seized with the need to retrieve it. It should go with Nora, but it was too deep and I wouldn't be able to climb back out of the grave without help.

A puff and chill entwined through my fingers and I felt its cold envelop, like an icy, blue, hand latching onto mine. It pulled me toward the coffin.

"They're in the box, Papa!"

I grabbed the edge of the coffin lid and lifted upward

but there was something resisting my pull. The lid was thin and the weight of the thing was unexpected. I pulled with more force and the lid angled upward, opening on its hinges. Nora's spindly hands and arms rose upward with the lid, and all at once her fingers released their brittle hold, coming untangled from the torn and ripped satin that covered the underside. Her arms fell down on to her chest in a cloud of dust.

I covered my mouth, horror-stricken.

She'd been buried alive! Good God, she'd been buried alive!

I pulled the lid all the way open and stayed it. The creamy white satin underside of the lid reflected the remaining red daylight down into the coffin. It had been ripped to shreds and streaked with blood where her fingers had desperately clawed at it above her face. A small fingernail was imbedded in the coffin lid's wooden underside, glinting in the dim light. She was dressed in a maroon velvet, knee-length dress with a lacy collar and matching lacy sleeves. Her hair was black and bunches of it had fallen out and covered the small satin pillow in tufts, her mouth was wide open, frozen in a silent scream, and her gaping eye holes stared upward at the infinity of her predicament. One of her thin legs was bent at the knee and crooked outward, and her silk stockings bunched down at her ankles. Her shiny, black, brass-buckled shoes were scuffed at the toes where she had kicked at the lid.

"I'm sorry. How in God's name… I'm sorry, Nora. I'm so, so sorry," I said, looking down at the horror in the box.

I noticed something next to her right hip. It was dark

and small and oddly shaped. Was it a cameo that had come unpinned during her struggle? No, it didn't look like jewelry. It's common for objects to be buried with people. Is it a rosary? No. But wait, there's another one, differently shaped, but similar in size. I looked closer and my heart started slamming in my chest. I reached in and snatched them out of the coffin. I looked closely and turned them around in my hands. I looked at their smooth sides. One was numbered 217, the other 449. I was holding the two missing crystals.

Bright white light suddenly interrupted our brief meeting, illuminating the terrible and hidden calamity that had been buried, boxed and forgotten for over 90 years. It was the hearse, its headlights bobbing their way down the winding path through the black headstones and trees. I carefully wrapped the pieces with a Kleenex and stuck them in my jacket pocket before closing the lid.

After seeing Nora off to her new resting place, I drove home. It was a short drive—almost walking distance from Seminole. We buried her next to Grandma Beatrice, Nora's older sister.

Poor Nora. How terrible and horrifying. Buried alive. I had to put it out of my mind. She died in 1919 during a later wave of the influenza pandemic that had swept across the globe. But was that how she really died—influenza? Obviously not! She died of asphyxiation trying to claw her way out of her grave! How could she have been buried alive? And why? I thought that by 1919 medicine had advanced enough for accidental burials to have become a thing of the past, especially for someone of Nora's status. She came from money. Was there so much carnage that hospital wards were jam-packed with the dead and dying, and could it be that her death was mispronounced by an overworked and exhausted doctor?

I couldn't help but wonder. Did you play, Nora? Did you enjoy parades? Would the Sears Roebuck dream book arrive in the mail, and did you wish that one day you would fill your own home with the dreams you saw on its pages? Did you cut paper dolls? Did you and Beatrice chase fairies and sprites through the backyard garden? Did you and your friends wear white gloves during tea parties? Did you study reading, writing, and arithmetic, and did you bring home good grades and show them to your Papa, and were you rewarded for your efforts with a trip to Hudson's, dressed in your Sunday best?

And the crystals... were those the eyes you've been searching for these 90 years? You had them this whole time! But why?

She wasn't at rest, and I had to finally admit it. I didn't believe in ghosts in spite of everything I had witnessed over the last few years, but if there was ever an excuse for a haunting, Nora certainly had a good one. Buried alive! I'd heard her song in a dream—but was it a dream? And Elliot. He'd heard it, too, and knew the song by heart. Those disturbing lyrics:

I had a little birdy
His name was Enza
I opened up the winda
In-flu-enza

I assumed that Nora's life had been a happy one until

she'd gotten sick. That she played, that she went to the movie houses and laughed at Charlie Chaplin, and got caught up in *The Perils of Pauline*. That she had her dreams, loved, and was loved in return.

I would come to learn that when it came to Nora, nothing could be further from the truth.

⇧   ⇧   ⇧

Against all the odds I finally had the two missing crystals in my possession, and what an extraordinary fluke of dumb luck it was. I brought them into the library where I sat at my desk and studied them to see if I could figure out why their chemical make-up had been redacted from Harlan's documents. They were irregular in shape and no different from the other thousand or so pieces, except for what they did when I held them, and turned them, and looked at them from different angles. I'd never seen anything like it.

When I held them straight on, they glowed in a dark, jade-green color, so Harlan was probably correct when he assumed that uranium was a part of their chemical make-up. But they had an iridescent quality too and, when turned slightly and looked at from a different angle, they became crystal clear and as flawless as a diamond. Turning them again, they completely disappeared in my hand—but placing them directly in front of my eyes, they exploded in a kaleidoscope of multiple colors. From another angle they became pitch black. It was as though an alchemist had distilled, mixed, then poured an impossible molten tincture, composed of every element on the periodic table, into two, small, irregular, molds and these two crystals were the result.

I wanted to know so badly what the Cyclops would do now that I had them. What would happen? I couldn't wait to find out. I went up to the ballroom and pulled out the scaffolding. It was very late, past midnight.

Paige, Elliot, and Chelsea were with Marian at her cottage up north on Houghton Lake for the weekend. Marian knew a world renowned eye specialist who practiced in both Chicago and Traverse City, and they had made a Monday appointment for him to see Chelsea at his Traverse City office. I could work uninterrupted and not be bothered. I couldn't help but wonder, though, if I should tell Paige about Nora being buried alive. I debated back and forth, but settled on it staying a secret. Should I tell her that I'd found the missing pieces in Nora's coffin? I debated on that one, too, but decided that I'd just tell her that I found them in the archive—a stroke of dumb luck— that they had been down there this whole time, tucked away behind a crate wrapped in a cloth, just waiting to be discovered. The truth was that she wouldn't like that I'd taken them out of Nora's coffin, and she'd rationalize that there was probably a good reason that the two crystals had been buried with her.

I climbed the scaffolding and opened the panel on the lower part of the globe. I had to locate Harlan's two new pieces hidden amongst the thousands of originals. It took over an hour, but I finally removed and replaced them with the originals from Nora's coffin.

Al's control panel was still on the stage and shrouded with a sheet, the thick black cables still connected, snaking into the stage left wing. Should I? I had fired it up a couple of times for Charlie, and watched Al fiddle with the dials a dozen times and knew the procedure fairly well; it would have been foolproof with his handwritten, step-by-step instructions still taped to the panel.

I was conflicted. I knew it wouldn't be a good idea to fire up the Cyclops with no one else here. What if something happened? Then the old photograph that Harlan had shown David and me in the secret library suddenly flashed into my consciousness—the three strange figures standing in chaos. What was that all about? They had an unfocused and otherworldly quality, like hazy thermographs: Figures out of time. And I remembered the tall, thin figure coming at me in the bathroom through the shower curtain and its resemblance to the figures in the photograph.

I was starting to creep myself out, and realized just how long the day had been, how tired I was, and that I should just go to bed. Too many things could go wrong. I would wait and turn it on later with Al. I also worried that I had thrown the Cyclops out of balance by messing with it, and I should have the engineering firm back over to run their tests with Al.

I started thinking that I should call David and invite him over for the inaugural firing up of the now 100-percent completely restored—what did Harlan's documents say the Cyclops was—an invisibility generator? Paige and I hadn't seen him since he walked out on us during the party in a huff. I missed him and hoped he was still okay. I had thought about him a lot over the two years since the party. Much had transpired, the most important being the birth of Chelsea. I really missed David, and he was the only living connection I had to my past. I had so many questions for him, questions I had never asked, and looking back I realized that I could have been a better friend.

I climbed off the scaffolding and took one last look at the Cyclops before closing the doors. The original crystals from Nora's grave winked and flickered in the dim of the ballroom. I trudged downstairs and collapsed on to the bed. I closed my eyes but all I saw was Nora, her body frozen in an eternal thrash against death and her sockets staring up at me—angry, accusatory.

The next day I called Harlan.

"You're not going to believe this," I said to him.

"What happened? You didn't break the Cyclops did you?"

"No, just the opposite."

"What?"

"I found them! I found the missing crystals!"

There was a long silence.

"You're kidding! Where were they?"

I knew he would ask me this, but I hadn't really decided how I'd respond, so I didn't answer his question.

"Are you there?" he asked.

"Yes, I'm here. I just found them. Let's leave it at that, okay?"

"How do you know that what you found is real?"

"I know they're the genuine article because they're numbered, 217 and 449, and I've never seen anything like them. They're incredible. I can't wait to show you."

"I can't wait to see them! Where are they?"

"They're here, safe and sound," I said, leaving out the part about installing them.

"It's serendipitous that you called," Harlan said, "because a couple days ago I received some more documents about the Cyclops, but I haven't looked through them yet. It's been on my to-do list, but I've been putting it off. We've got a major exhibit opening next week and I'm days behind, but I'll see if I can sneak in some time."

"No worries. Just get to it when you can," I replied.

"You're sure that what you found is real?"

"Yes. And I'll be honest with you," I hesitated. "I actually installed them last night. They fit perfectly—like missing pieces of a puzzle."

There was another long silence.

"Not one of your better moves, Daniel," he said. "I mean, you don't really know what you're doing and you could have inadvertently damaged it."

"I know it was stupid, but…"

"You didn't turn it on, did you?"

"No, not yet."

"Daniel, don't get any ideas about turning the Cyclops on with those pieces installed,"

His tone made me feel like a teenager getting lectured and I didn't reply.

"I'm serious, Daniel. We've had our fun with the replacement pieces and all the fabulous light shows, but this is different. Do you understand?"

"Yes, I understand," I replied a little petulant.

"Just hold off until we know more. We don't know what happened a hundred years ago back when the Cyclops was last tested intact. It might be dangerous. We have to err on the side of caution and assume that it *is* dangerous. Do you understand?"

"I got it, Harlan! I won't turn it on."

"Promise me."

"Jesus, Harlan! Give me a break!"

"Promise me!" he yelled.

"Okay! I promise!" I shouted back.

"I don't mean to sound paranoid, but I'm telling you that you have something completely different now. That thing is dangerous with those two pieces intact, and we don't know enough about it."

"I understand," I replied, but as difficult as it was to admit, Harlan was right.

I would have to wait at least until he finished reading the documentation he had received. He reiterated how interested he was in seeing the crystals and told me that he would fly out as soon as he could.

"You know, it's crazy, absolutely crazy that one of the most important scientific instruments ever invented is hanging from the ceiling in your ballroom. Please take every precaution you can in making sure it's safe, okay?"

"I will."

"And Daniel, please, don't get any ideas."

"Don't worry, Harlan. You've succeeded in scaring the hell out of me and I won't touch the Cyclops—at least not until you fly out."

♙   ♙   ♙

A few hours after the phone call with Harlan I went out for a while to run some errands and arrived back home just after sundown.

I came home to chaos.

At first I thought someone had broken in. The front door was wide open, the clocks were blinking the wrong time, and a low, electric hum pervaded throughout the house. The alarm had not tripped. If this had been a break-in, the alarm would have been blaring and the police would have been here already. I looked at the key pad in the foyer and saw that someone had deactivated it. It wasn't Paige. I had just gotten off the phone with her minutes prior to pulling into the driveway. They were driving through Kalkaska, a half hour from Traverse City.

Charlie! He was the only other person who knew the code. But why did he leave the front door wide open? Security in Indian Village had improved immensely over the last couple of years, but it was still insane to leave a door wide open with the house unattended.

The lights were off, but a glowing spectral phenomenon lit the spaces throughout the first floor in a strange twilight incandescence. It pulsed through the ceiling, emanating from an orb-like disc, roughly the size of a child's kickball, throbbing in bright yellows, blues, and shifting to oranges and reds then back to purples. It didn't make any sense, and it was very alarming that the orb followed me from room to room, the way the moon seems to follow on a night-time stroll.

I went outside and searched the grounds, the front yard, and the back yard, and trekked the paths through the garden beds, calling out for Charlie. I went back into the house and looked everywhere, yelling "Charlie!" as the weird disc of light followed above me. It got brighter when I walked up the stairs, and suddenly I realized what was happening. I looked down the hall, through the arch of the double-winder stairway and noticed a familiar molecular chaos showering down from above. Charlie was in the ballroom! He'd turned on the Cyclops! I bolted up the stairs, two treads per stride.

The pocket doors were wide open, but I walked in to find nothing. I literally saw nothing except for the Cyclops orbiting around the pole. With the two crystals from Nora's grave in place, it had transformed into something resembling a celestial body—a neutron star orbiting a black hole, while jets of bright blue plasma whirled behind like the tail of a comet. I walked out onto a floor that didn't exist and bumped into tables that were not there. I peered down through the floor and saw the second floor below cast in the colors of a photograph's negative, and through that, the first floor cast in similar colors but darker and fainter; every room below was dollhouse-like, small and strange from my vantage.

I felt my way through the room, my invisible arms out ahead, probing, like the antennae of an insect. I was blind to everything except for the Cyclops and its plasma orbit; everything else in the room was invisible. I looked up through the ceiling, the attic, the trusses, and saw the sky above with its few brighter stars twinkling through the pollution of city light.

"Charlie!" I yelled out over the pulsing chaos.

He did not reply. I felt around the ballroom but kept bumping into things I could only recognize by touch: furniture, a treadmill, a rack of weights, and an elliptical machine. I got down on all fours and crawled toward the stage. I knew every square inch of this space, but the invisibility and occasional wisps of chaos were completely disorienting.

Then I began to hear whispers, voices I'd never heard before, behind me, far off, and near, and another voice, this one familiar and calling out. It was a voice I hadn't heard since I was a boy, and I denied it. I winced and covered my ears to shut it out. I would not listen because it was not possible. But it called out to me, shouting:

"Daniel!"

I finally bumped into the stage. I stood and mounted it, very slowly walking in the direction of the control panel, my arms out like feelers, while the voice called out, pleading for me to reply.

"Daniel, I see you, why don't you answer me?"

I baby-stepped my way and suddenly felt the edge of the panel; I grabbed it as though my life depended on it. Even though I knew exactly where I was, it was no less disorienting. Perhaps it would have been easier for me to just close my eyes and walk toward where I knew the panel to be, but the phenomenon was mesmerizing. I steadied myself by holding the edges of the control panel. As I looked around, I seemed to be floating above and through the house.

I turned and looked through the upstage wall and into Judge Evans' house, next door. Through a geometry of squares and rectangles, I spied him, transparent, sitting in his television room, the glow of the big screen lighting his surroundings. He lived alone, a widower, but a tall, thin woman stood next to the chair he was sitting on. She stared up at me through the translucency of plaster, brick, and mortar that separated us, the look on her face, shocked and bewildered.

"Daniel!" Behind me, the voice of my mother. Persistent. It would not be ignored.

"Daniel!" Her voice was tinged with a quality that had grown accustomed to pain.

I reluctantly turned around to look, and under the Cyclops stood my mother. She was charred and smoke rose from her body. Her arms were out, waiting for my embrace. I fell to my knees and wrapped my arms around my head, my torso rocking involuntarily forward and backward.

"Mother, go away! Please! You need to leave! You're dead!" I whispered too afraid to speak.

"Daniel! Come to me!"

I heard shuffling and sensed that she was walking toward me.

"I called to you, Daniel! I called, but you wouldn't come! Where were you?"

"You left me, mother!" I yelled back, cradling my head in my arms. I could not look at her. "You went to that party, and you got burned, and you died!"

"Daniel!" she screamed.

I opened my eyes. She was standing at the foot of the stage, three feet in front of me. Half of her face was burned beyond anything resembling flesh, and her scalp was red, cracked, and blistered. Her clothing had been burned off and she stood there charred and naked.

"Oh my God! Mother! Mother!" I crouched, horror-stricken, and buried my head back into my arms and rocked.

A panic suffused the room and other voices whispered, angry and accusatory. I couldn't understand, but their tones were malicious and hate spitting.

Something was knocked over. I looked up and my mother was flailing around the room, engulfed in flames. She tripped over invisible obstacles, then got up and ran, trying to extinguish herself, arms thrashing. She fell and rolled.

"Daniel! Help me!"

I couldn't watch, and the only thing I could think of was turning off the Cyclops. I felt around for the correct knobs to power it down, but I couldn't concentrate. I groped around the panel but couldn't make sense of it. I remembered that Al had reached around the back and simply turned off the main power switch. I reached for the back of the panel and felt around, but something grabbed my hand.

"I knew you would find them, Papa! I can see you now. Do you want to hear my song?" Nora pulled me away.

She was in her maroon dress and black buckle shoes. The tips of her fingers were dripping blood and the lace around her wrists was soaked in crimson. She took me by both hands and yanked me away, spinning me in circles. Her head twitched and her mouth opened wide, frozen in a macabre joy.

"Come, Papa! Let's play ring-around-the-rosy while I sing to you."

I tried to push her away but her hands would not let go. She held tight and spun faster. I was completely disoriented, but knew I was still on the stage. I managed to release my hands from her grip, but she grabbed onto my sleeves and tangled her fingers into my shirt.

"Where are you going, Papa? Don't you want to dance with me?"

I remembered again what grandmother wrote in the letter: "The best way to deal with them is to ignore them." I closed my eyes and stood stock still. I focused on the panel, trying to regain my senses.

Then I thought about Charlie.

What happened to Charlie!? He must have seen something terrible. He fired up the Cyclops not knowing that I had installed the lost crystals. Charlie must have come up here and turned it on, unsupervised and without permission. He had asked me on numerous occasions if he could see the Cyclops activated, and I indulged him on two occasions. We'd stood there, bathed in the maelstrom, marveling at the unbelievable phenomena. He became fascinated with it and truly believed that while immersed in its chaos, it was having a positive effect on his health, coming to believe in the malarkey he had made up that it was making him look younger. I just didn't know for sure, until now, that he still had the key to our house, as well as the access codes and magnetic card. Paige had obviously never gotten it back from him, and why should she have? I was the one who gave him access. I started to wonder how often he had come up here by himself. Would he just watch and wait for us to leave, then simply let himself in? Apparently so.

I opened my eyes. No one and nothing. I knew I was still on the stage. If I could face Judge Evans' house, I'd have my bearings and the panel would be off to my left. I slowly turned in a circle and finally came to face the judge's house, the translucent construction of brick, mortar, plaster, and lath. The woman who before was standing next to the judge's far off chair now stood staring across the chasm between our houses. She was tall and thin with dark circles under her eyes. She was wearing a blue dress, but no shoes and her fingers compulsively kneaded the beads of a rosary. Was she attracted to the Cyclops?

I closed my eyes, turned left, and walked slowly, but even with my eyes closed I still saw flashing images and molecular chaos: Faces jumping into view then disappearing into the fray of electrons. I put my arms out, probing. Unspeakable horrors scratched, poked, and tried pulling me off course, but I made it to the panel. I groped around and found the master switch. I opened my eyes. Nora and my mother stood at the base of the stage, staring at me. I flipped the switch and the room became pitch black and suffocating, silent as the grave.

⛓   ⛓   ⛓

I woke up on the floor, looked around and waited for my eyes to adjust. Eventually streetlight and moonlight leaking in through the slits between the curtains revealed a room where nothing was amiss, and the geometry of the large octagon window glowed through the giant, red velvet curtain.

I stood and turned on the panel's work lamp. My sleeves were ripped to shreds and streaked with blood. I was bruised. Scratches and welts ran down the length of my arms. Something glinted on the floor not far from the panel, but I didn't bother taking a closer look—I already knew it was one of Nora's fingernails. I walked into the wing and snapped a bunch of breakers on and the recessed ceiling lights flickered to life. I yanked the panel's cord out of its socket, unthreaded the thick, black cables from their plugs, and dropped them to the floor. I disassembled Al's panel, and stowed it back in its case, then coiled the cables and stashed them in the case too.

I walked around the ballroom and found everything was in its place. Only the strong scent of ozone lingered. I let myself fall into a bright red chair and buried my face in my hands and wept.

What was that horrible thing hanging from the ceiling? It hung there on the pole, waiting, its thousand pieces of glass melding in a shiny, uniform perfectly black sphere. God, it was beautiful, but the things it brought to life… how?

And my mother. Was it a shadow of her last moments playing out that I saw, or was she locked in this perpetual inferno? I sat there for an hour and waited for something to happen, but nothing did. No sounds or bumps. No shadows or vaporous fogs. Just the silence after the storm.

I thought about my mother, the way she looked the last time I saw her, getting ready for that party long ago. I had sat there sullenly on her bed, watching her. She had made a big bowl of popcorn for me and told me that I could camp out in her room and watch *The Ghoul* on her small black-and-white TV. She said I was big enough and didn't need a babysitter anymore. I remember how beautiful she was, her long brown hair, and the dress she wore. She had bought these shoes with straps that crisscrossed all the way up her calves. I thought she looked like a model. She sat at her makeup table looking in the mirror, putting her earrings on. She saw my reflection and smiled at me. I buried my face in a pillow.

"C'mon, honey. It'll be fun. You'll have a good time."

This image I had of her was now replaced forever by the specter of her last moments alive, lost and burning in an inferno, calling out to me.

Charlie suddenly popped into mind, defending himself from whatever horror may have terrorized him. In the time we knew him, he had never given us any reason to be concerned regarding our property. He was a man of impeccable character, but this accidental slip-up, the inadvertent revelation of his surreptitious visit, put a wrinkle on things; it changed my opinion of him ever so slightly, but still, I panicked, terrified at what may have happened to him. Paige loved him. I loved him too, in spite of this. He had become such a good friend—our best friend. He was eccentric, and a decidedly possessive and demanding friend, but very giving in return. He may have been a diva at times, but he was so much fun. He introduced Paige to all of the right people, and it was largely because of him that she was able to successfully form a small start-up as a buyer and stylist—her clients, most of them wealthy friends of Charlie.

I got up, ran down the two flights of stairs, bolted out of the house, and headed toward Charlie's. I crossed the street and stared up at his house—it was one of the smaller homes on Seminole street, a dignified arts and crafts bungalow.

It was early, maybe an hour from sunrise. His lights were off, but it didn't matter. I had to know if he was okay.

I ran up to his front door and pounded, but there was no answer. I peered in through the leaded panes of the front room window. I saw only a small, overly decorated room, brimming over with a mish-mash of thrift shop treasures and Gustav Stickley pieces, but no Charlie. I walked around the property and peeked into the windows that were low enough to look through. I stepped back onto the porch, pulled out my phone, and dialed his number. His cell phone, which I saw laying at the foot of the stairs, lit up and its ring tolled faintly through the window. I waited nervously, but Charlie didn't walk downstairs to answer. I hung up when I got his voicemail. He still had a landline and I called it, hoping he would answer the phone I pictured on his nightstand. Again I heard ringing through the window and, again, he didn't answer, but this time I left a message.

"Charlie, it's Daniel. Please call me. I want you to know I'm not angry. I just want to make sure you're okay. Please call me back when you get this message. It's very important!"

I walked back home. I changed the security codes to both the house and ballroom. I reset the clocks then went to bed.

🏛   🏛   🏛

My ringing phone woke me up. The curtains were shut and it was dark, but the numbers on the alarm clock glowed 11:02 a.m. I couldn't believe I had slept that late. I fumbled for the phone on the nightstand and answered. It was Harlan, though I had hoped it would be Charlie.

"Hey Harlan, what's going on?"

"Whatever you've got planned today, drop it. My plane touches down at 2:40 p.m. We've got to talk."

"What the hell are you going on about? I thought you had an exhibit, or something," I replied, shaking off the sleep.

I staggered to the curtains and snapped them open. It was the first bright, sunny day in a long time and I winced, shielding my eyes.

"This is way more important. That's why I'm flying in. I've got to show you what's in that new batch of documents I told you about. Your call the other day piqued my curiosity, so I brought them home last night and read them. I couldn't believe what I was reading. I'm warning you right now, it's very disturbing, and I'm going to make some recommendations you're not going to like. You still haven't turned it on, have you?"

"No. *I* didn't turn it on."

"What's that supposed to mean?"

"I left yesterday to run some errands and when I got back home it was going full bore."

"Oh my God! What happened? Are you okay? How...who got in? Who turned it on?"

"I'm 99.9 percent certain it was Charlie. He has a key to our house and he's the only other person with access to the ballroom."

"Jesus Christ, Daniel! I thought I told you to make sure that room was secure!"

"I forgot that Charlie had the fucking key, all right? Jesus, get off my back! I'm stressed enough as it is!"

"Sorry!"

"I went to his house last night to check on him, but he didn't come to the door, and I've been calling him non-stop ever since, but he won't pick up."

"You've got to get over there! You've got to make sure he's safe. Do it now!" Harlan ordered. "I'm on my way. I'll be there in a few hours."

"All right. Call me when you land," I replied. "Hopefully I'll have some good news."

I got dressed and walked back over to Charlie's. I pounded on his door. I called his cell phone, then his landline. Again, no answer. I tried the doorknob. It was inexplicably unlocked so I walked in. The room was cluttered but orderly and the faint ammonia tang of a cat litter box pervaded throughout.

Charlie loved cats. He had a soft spot for animals and had raised a lot of money over the years for various pet charities; I remembered that he had been talking to Paige about hosting a fund raiser in our garden come spring for the Michigan Humane Society. He had adopted three strays and one of them, a giant Russian Blue, was a real lover, so I was a little surprised when he didn't meet me at the door like he usually did.

I picked Charlie's cell phone up off the floor. The glass was cracked. I pushed a button and all the calls he had received in the last few hours lit the screen. There were two from me, one from Paige, and six from his niece, Polly.

I put his phone on the coffee table and continued looking, calling his name. I went upstairs and peeked into the bedrooms and bathroom. He wasn't up there and the bed in the master suite was still made. Maybe he hadn't come home after he left my house. I went back downstairs and looked again, calling his name.

Through the dining room window I saw that his Fleetwood was still parked in front of the garage. I started getting really worried. I walked into the kitchen and, through the basement doorway, heard a moaning whine that stood my hair on end. It was the cats. They were in the basement sounding very agitated, and I thought for a second that maybe they had accidently shut themselves into a confined space, or trapped some vermin they couldn't get at. As I descended the steps they heard me and stopped their commotion.

The Russian Blue appeared at the foot of the stairs, saw me and crouched, hissing, his ears pasted flat. I walked past him and he bolted ahead of me around a corner. I followed him into Charlie's media room and the blood drained from my face. One of the cats hopped onto a big recliner and let out a low, otherworldly moan. Another one saw me and bolted out of the room.

This space had not been used in ages. There was a giant old Sony TV set on a stand against the back wall, an impressive stack of stereo equipment from the 70s, and loud speaker towers that sat at the four corners of the room. Everything was coated with dust and a few cobwebs spanned diagonally from this object to that.

The Russian Blue changed his tack and traipsed a figure-eight between my legs. He looked up at me, still very agitated, then looked over at Charlie, who was hanging from a rope in the middle of the room.

⇧　　⇧　　⇧

Some detective asked me a thousand questions and I answered them to the best of my ability. I didn't think I was in any trouble; at least that's what he said when I flat out asked him. He wasn't accusing me of anything; he was just methodical in his work and said that in his business it was always best to dot the i's and cross the t's. Still, I thought it would be a good idea to contact David just in case. I needed him to know everything that had happened in the past 12 hours or so. I rehearsed it: Charlie had apparently come into my home, went up to the ballroom, got spooked by something, and left abruptly, leaving both the ballroom and house unlocked. I came home shortly afterwards to an unsecure home. I then went to Charlie's to make sure he was okay, but he didn't answer his phone or his door. The next morning I went back to his home, found that his door was unlocked, went in, and discovered his body hanging in the basement.

A small crowd of neighbors had gathered around Charlie's house, and many were crying as his bagged body was wheeled out through the front door on a gurney and deposited into the coroner's van. Judge Evans was there, too, and wanted to know everything. He stood by a squad car talking to a couple of police officers. When I made eye contact with him, he abruptly turned away. There were two news vans parked along the curb as well—Charlie's suicide would be reported widely in the local media.

I looked down the street and noticed a car pulling into my drive. It was Harlan. I walked up to the Judge.

"This is a terrible thing," I said looking up at his ashen

face. "I don't think I'll ever understand."

"It is indeed a terrible thing and a great loss to the neighborhood," he replied looking away, his breath steaming in the crisp, cold air. That I'd just been questioned by a detective did not escape his scrutiny.

"Why don't you drop by later," he said. "I think we need to talk."

"I'll do that, Judge," I lied, having no intention of suffering through another interrogation.

I met Harlan next to his rental car.

"Don't tell me!" he said, with a look of shock on his face as I walked up to him. I put my arms out and we embraced and I started weeping.

"Charlie's dead! He hung himself!"

"Oh, God! Oh, God, that's terrible! I'm so very sorry, Daniel. I know you were close."

"I've got to call Paige and tell her," I said, getting some of my composure back. "She doesn't know."

"Can I make a suggestion? Maybe you should wait until she gets back home."

"I thought about that, but I'd rather she hear it from me than the news, or from someone else. I've got to tell her. And another thing: One of Detroit's finest just finished asking me a million questions. I called David because I think I'm going to need a lawyer."

"Well, don't worry about it. I've got your back and that's a promise." Harlan gestured toward the house and we walked to the front door. His satchel was bulging more than usual.

As soon as we walked into the house Harlan requested what he'd been waiting to do for hours.

"I'd like to see the Cyclops if you don't mind."

"I'm not turning that goddamn thing back on if that's what you're asking me!" I replied, still haunted by my earlier experience with it.

"Hell no! I never want to see that thing turned on! Not with the original crystals intact, and not after what I've read!"

We walked up the two flights of stairs and stopped at the pocket doors. I punched in the code and slid the magnetic card through the slot. The bolts unlocked and we walked in. The room was just as I had left it, but it was unnaturally cold. I shivered and looked at Harlan for any indication that he too felt the chill, but he just took his jacket off and draped it over the back of a stool.

We set the scaffolding up together and Harlan climbed up with his satchel hooked over his shoulder and got to work. He located the hidden panel, opened it, and within minutes found and removed pieces 217 and 449. He climbed back down. The closed stage curtains billowed from right to left as though someone had just walked along behind them.

Harlan held the pieces in his hand and gazed down at them reverently, like a priest holding a holy relic. He turned them and brought them up to the light. He took a jeweler's loop out of his satchel and studied them for a long time.

"You were right. These are incredible. I've studied crystals and glasses of every kind. I know everything there is to know about lenses, prisms, mirrors, you name it, I've seen it all, but I've never seen anything like these! Unbelievable!"

"It's what those things do that's unbelievable," I replied.

He very carefully handed me the crystals, then opened his satchel and took out a small, shock-proof box. He put on a pair of cotton archival gloves and took the crystals from me. He took out a kit filled with vials of solutions, spray bottles, and swabs, and began to carefully and meticulously clean each crystal. When he was finished, he wrapped each piece individually, and placed them into the shock-proof box.

"C'mon Daniel, fess up. Where'd you find these? You and I both know they weren't in the archive."

"Follow me," I replied.

He stood behind me and watched as I locked the pocket doors, then I took him down to the library where we went to my desk.

"I'll take the crystals," I said, holding my hand out.

"Where are you going to keep them?" he asked, handing me the shock-proof box.

I stuck it into a drawer and locked it.

"Daniel, that's not a very secure place. Don't you have a safe? Better yet, why don't you let me take them? I'll put them in the museum's safe. I'm the only one with the combination."

"Don't worry about it," I said.

"What's going to stop you from reinstalling them?"

Something about the way I looked at him made him back away from me.

"I will *not* reinstall them," I said.

"Daniel, do you really want to take that…"

"Harlan! Just stop, okay? Seriously! Stop!"

I opened another drawer and handed him the letter we had received from the State concerning the re-interment of Nora. He read it.

"I don't understand," he said, looking at the document.

I looked at him cockeyed. He blinked.

"You've got to be kidding!" he said, putting two and two together.

"No, I'm not kidding. They were buried with her."

Harlan was silent, his eyes fixed on whatever it was he was thinking about.

"Does this make any sense to you?" he asked. "Where you found them, I mean?"

"Nothing makes sense," I replied, thinking about Charlie.

He put his hand on my shoulder.

"Why don't we go down to your great-grandfather's library? We need to talk."

⇑　　⇑　　⇑

We sat at the big table with the accountant's lamp. It was a little early but, in light of everything that had transpired, I opened the bar and got a couple of snifters down and poured us each a dram of great-grandfather's cognac. I wished at that moment that David was with us. It wasn't the same without him sharing in this ritual. I still had not heard back from him and worried that he had decided to just write us off and, looking back, who could blame him?

Harlan pulled some papers out of his satchel. He separated them into individual sheaves and handed me one.

"What am I looking at?" I asked.

"This is a report on what transpired during and after the first and only test of the Cyclops," he replied. "There were seven people present. Within one week, four had committed suicide, two were admitted to sanitariums, and the other, your great-grandfather, resigned from all his corporate boards, left the university, and, well, you know the rest."

I looked through the papers.

"What you have is an account of a Captain James Arthur Mueller, Jr. Captain Mueller was an officer in the U.S. Army and had served in France during the First World War. When he was a lieutenant, his company commander ordered him to lead a charge out of the trenches into no man's land, where they ran into a small detail of Germans who were repairing a section of barbed wire. A nasty little engagement of hand-to-hand combat ensued. The Germans were killed, and two of Lieutenant Mueller's men were grievously wounded. Although the objective was not achieved, the charge was deemed a success. The lieutenant was promoted to captain. He was awarded the Distinguished Service Cross for valor and his men were awarded the Purple Heart.

A couple of months later, Captain Mueller, because he was a college-educated engineer, was rotated back to the States and assigned to the research facility where your great-grandfather was hard at work developing code name Cyclops—the instrument that now hangs in your ballroom. From all accounts, his was a sterling career and he was on a fast track for a promotion to major. Then everything changed for the captain."

"I don't like where this is going," I said.

Harlan paused and looked at me.

"You saw something terrible last night, didn't you?"

I cupped my head in my hands. "Yes."

"Are you okay? Do you want me to stop?"

"No, keep going. I need to hear this."

"He was one of the two who was committed to the sanitarium. Nasty places back in the day. Everyone present at the test experienced something different. We'll never know what happened to the four who committed suicide—their stories obviously went to the grave with them—but within a few weeks, the captain was ready for a debriefing. What you have is a transcript of the interview."

I read while Harlan spoke.

"He claimed that within seconds of the Cyclops' activation two very gruesome, bloody, and hacked-up beings suddenly manifested from out of the invisibility. At first they appeared to be in a state of shock. They looked bewildered and lost, but as soon as they saw Captain Mueller, they reacted immediately and violently. He was convinced that these entities were the two German soldiers he killed during the hand-to-hand combat in no man's land. They pushed, pulled, and shoved him. They were enraged, completely mad. They shouted and wailed, and Captain Mueller never forgot the things they said during the incident. Look on page three, there's a quote."

Ich habe einen Sohn! I have a son! *"Können Sie mir helfen, meinen Sohn zu finden?* Can you help me find my son?

The other soldier was more confrontational, angry. *Sie haben mich verletzt! Ich bin verloren! Wo sind die anderen? Bringen Sie mich zu Ihnen!* You hurt me, and I'm *lost. Where are the others? Take me to them!*

I looked through the papers. Captain Mueller was released from the sanitarium after the war, but never really regained his footing. My great-grandfather was a compassionate man and kept tabs on him over the years. I guessed that he felt responsible for what had happened. Captain Mueller became a horror-stricken man and died before his 40th birthday.

"Last night I read some of the medical reports that were made on Captain Mueller over the years," Harlan said. "He had developed a strange wasting disease and became weak and emaciated; he later admitted to one of his doctors that he was often accosted by German soldiers, but these were dismissed as paranoid delusions attributable to having been shell-shocked during combat."

I went back to the papers. They recounted that the places where Mueller lived would suddenly get cold and dank, and a stench would rise up for no reason. Shadows would form and darken the rooms. A chill ran down my spine as I read. Sometimes he was awakened by the hissing of guttural German—angry whispers and heated, angry conversations that emanated from darkened hallways or different parts of the house. Harlan handed me another folder.

Jonathan Wingate was an optics specialist and the other survivor committed to the sanitarium.

When he was a boy, he and two of his friends had developed a fascination with trains, which led to a foolish game of dare, where they would dash across the tracks just in front of speeding trains. One day his playmates decided it would be fun to up the ante by tying their shoelaces together before attempting the dangerous crossing. It was on that day that Jonathan watched his playmates die.

During the test, he claimed that his mangled and bloody friends came to him. One boy's head was bashed-in and his right eye dangled by its optic nerve. The other boy's spine was snapped in two and he hobbled toward Jonathan in a freakishly unnatural gait. When they saw him they taunted and teased him for being a coward, for chickening out at the last minute. Jonathan, too, was eventually released from the sanitarium and went on with his life as best he could.

He claimed that he was often awakened by the specter of the two boys jumping up and down on his bed, laughing and teasing him, and his rooms were also infected with an icy chill and rotting stench. I looked up at Harlan.

"Some of the things about these stories are familiar."

"What things, specifically?" he asked, taking a small sip from his snifter.

"You're the first person I'm telling, okay? I thought I was crazy, you know? When the shadows would close in. One time I heard someone taking a bath, but when I snapped the lights on, the tub was empty."

Harlan looked fascinated by what I was telling him.

"Did these things happen before you installed the two pieces?" he asked.

"Oh, yes. Long before. But they didn't happen very often. Sometimes I thought it was nothing. What did Scrooge say in *A Christmas Carol*? 'just a piece of humbug'?"

"Something like that," Harlan replied.

"I thought the same thing and I kept dismissing it. But

sometimes what happened would be so over the top."

"Like what?" Harlan asked.

I thought about his question for a minute. I trusted Harlan. He had become a good friend by now.

"I feel like I was manipulated."

"Manipulated?" he asked, puzzled. "How?"

"I never would have found the Cyclops if it weren't for Nora."

"Who is Nora, exactly? What is she to you?"

"She was my grandmother's younger sister."

"Your great-aunt."

"Yes."

"The one who was disinterred?"

"Yes. I wasn't going to tell you this... I wasn't going to tell anyone, but when I opened the lid of her coffin, I discovered that she'd been buried alive."

"That's horrible!"

"I didn't know who she was, for sure—this ghostly girl in the maroon velvet dress that I had been seeing—until I opened her coffin."

"Did you see her last night?"

"Yes."

"Daniel, what else did you see?"

"It's too hard. I can't talk about it."

"I'm worried about you," Harlan said. "I don't think you've seen the last of these phenomena. I'm going to stay with you until Paige gets back."

"If you think that I'm going to do myself in..."

"I don't know that you won't! Look what happened to Charlie! The four scientists all those years ago! Within a week they were dead! All of them! By their own hands."

"I don't understand any of this! Why is this happening?"

Harlan took another sip of his cognac then exhaled. He then gathered up the folders that by now littered the top of the table.

"I have a theory, but it's only that—a theory," he said placing a few of the folders back into his satchel.

"What's your theory?" I asked.

"That instrument upstairs was designed to make everything within its range invisible, but there's a problem—a very serious flaw—a dangerous and unintended anomaly: It draws open the curtain between the living and the dead—the dead who have attached themselves to the people who were present at the moment of death."

"Are you crazy? I wasn't present during Nora's death. Hell, I wasn't even born!"

Harlan grabbed another folder and riffled through it.

"Here, look at this," he said, upon finding a photograph. He showed it to me. "This is a photograph of your great-grandfather, taken, I'm assuming, when he was about the age you are now. Look at it. The resemblance is uncanny."

I looked and I had to admit that he was right. It was me wearing an old-fashioned suit with shiny hair parted down the middle and a waxed mustache.

"Perhaps Nora attached herself to this house, or the Cyclops, at the moment of her death. I don't know. But when you moved in, and because you're so closely related, *and* because you resemble your great-grandfather…"

I interrupted. "That makes sense because she always

calls me Papa."

Harlan leaned in and his eyes widened.

"I have to ask you Daniel, and I know you're not comfortable telling me, but I think it's important. Who else did you see last night?"

I bit my lip and looked away.

He persisted. "Who else did you see?"

"I can't tell you."

"Was it your grandmother?"

"No."

"Your great-grandfather?"

"Goddammit, Harlan!"

"Who was it? Tell me!"

"I can't!"

"Did you witness someone die?"

"No!"

"Was it Charlie? Oh my God! Did Charlie come to you last night?"

"No!"

"Who came to you, Daniel?"

"Goddammit, Harlan!"

"Who came to you?" he asked pounding his fist on the table.

"My mother! My mother came to me last night, and that means your theory is fucked and doesn't hold water!" I shouted back. "I wasn't there when she died! She died in a fire at her fucking boyfriend's house in 1977! She left me alone and went to that fucker's party! She died and he escaped and left her in that house to burn, and that motherfucker is still alive! She came to me last night, Harlan! She came to me and she was burning, and smoldering, and flailing around, and calling out to me!"

Harlan went pale. I thought for sure he'd drop it. But he continued.

"You see? She was calling out to you!"

I looked at him incredulous.

"I can't bear to know that she's stuck in that state! So your theory sucks Harlan, don't you see? I wasn't there! She left me for that motherfucker!"

"But she was calling out for you!" he persisted.

"So!"

"You were the last thing on her mind! She *did* attach herself to you, Daniel! She loved you! She called out for you!"

"But I wasn't there!"

"In her dying moments, she called out for you!"

I got up and kicked my chair over. I covered my ears and for the second time within an hour I started crying in front of Harlan, but these were tears of rage. I pointed at him daring him to challenge me.

"But I wasn't there, Harlan! I wasn't there for her!"

"Jesus Christ, Daniel! How old were you? Ten? Eleven years old?"

"I wasn't there for her!"

"It's *she* who wasn't there for *you*!"

☖ ☖ ☖

Polly flew in to take care of the funeral arrangements and to settle Charlie's estate, and from the moment she arrived Paige was by her side.

She told Polly stories about Charlie, how quickly they

had connected, and how their relationship blossomed into the most natural friendship she'd ever had, and that she felt privileged to have gotten to know such a wonderful man—that she missed him terribly.

"He was really the only friend I had here and I don't know what I'm going to do without him," Paige said.

They sat in the sunroom in their yoga pants and turtlenecks, their legs covered with an afghan. Chelsea played with large colorful plastic blocks at the foot of the sofa on a blanket on the floor.

Through the leaded window panes the fallow garden slept. Only the holly bushes and clusters of rosemary stubbornly held onto their green in a setting of washed-out yellows, tarnished stalks of silver and tawny golds. The fountain was wrapped in waterproof canvas and the surrounding beds were covered over with hay.

They held hands and cried, but it was a comfort to watch Chelsea play.

Paige told Polly about Chelsea's retinas and the hope we held for her impending surgery. They shared a pot of tea and a box of Kleenex.

Polly had stories to share, too. She told Paige how dysfunctional her childhood was, that her mother was an alcoholic, that her father abandoned them when she was four years old. Charlie was the one, solitary stable influence in her life.

"He was a lot older than my mother and sometimes she resented him, thinking that he meddled too much, but she loved him in her own way. He looked in on us often. He was very generous. He was always just a phone call away, but mostly I didn't even have to call because he had a sixth sense of when to swoop in and take me away from all the craziness. I was relieved when I'd see him pull into the driveway. He worked for GM and always arrived in a different car. He had a whole fleet to choose from and on the days he came to get me, he always picked an extra fancy car, usually a Cadillac, and he would make a big production in the driveway by opening the door for me like he was my personal chauffeur, but I especially loved it when he pulled up in a Corvette. Sometimes the outing lasted only a few hours—dinner at a nice restaurant, a movie, or a walk in a park. Other times it was the whole weekend and I'd have to pack an overnight bag. He was always so funny and talkative. And he was interesting, you know? He brought sophistication into my drab world. He made me feel special. He'd tell me about his theatre group and what plays they were working on. Sometimes he would take me to the theatre and I'd look at the sets they were building, and they were giant and magical, and the people at the theatre were so friendly. I remember this one set that sparkled when the lights hit it, but when Charlie took me backstage I realized the magic was just an illusion, that the set was really just an assembly of carelessly cut pieces of plywood taped together and propped up from behind by slats of wood, and if you weren't careful, you could trip. I learned that everything facing outward was beautiful and magical, but the stuff on the inside barely held it together. After he dropped me off I would find a small envelope that he had stuck into my jacket pocket or my purse when I wasn't looking, with a card inside thanking me for a most enchanted evening—that's how he talked. He used words like 'enchanted.' And there was always a $20 bill folded neatly inside, 'your allowance,' he wrote. It was exorbitant, but that was Charlie. I still have every one of those cards."

We loved her stories about Charlie and wanted to hear more.

We learned that he was a junker through and through. He loved flea markets and garage sales and so many of his possessions had memories attached to them. Polly often went junking with him and he taught her what to be on the lookout for and to always feign indifference whenever you happened upon a treasure you knew you had to have, and to never, ever let the dealer have their asking price. You had to bargain with these people. It was expected. It was part of the game.

Polly told us that years ago, when she was in college, Charlie was in the midst of a Roseville Pottery bender. Charlie told everyone he knew, including Polly, that he was crazy about Roseville and to be on the lookout for it. By this time, Polly was also an avid junker, thanks to her uncle, and one weekend while out junking, she found a piece of Roseville: A vase with a water lily motif glazed in garish turquoise and corals. It was small and rather squat, and the handle seemed too big—aesthetically awkward—but she knew Charlie had to have it. She coughed up money she didn't have and bought it. She packaged and mailed it to him. A few days later she got a phone call from him. The vase had arrived and he was crying because it was the most beautiful thing he'd ever seen in his life and it was going in a place of honor. What he didn't tell her was that when he opened the package the vase was broken. Polly found it centered on the fireplace mantel on a little platform in front of more elegant, valuable, and stately pieces. It had been glued back together.

She told us that there was a framed black-and-white photograph of her beaming in a cap and gown with Charlie giving her a giant kiss on the cheek. He saw to it that she went to school, stuck to her studies, and rose above her dismal upbringing and strengthened those slats that propped it all up. He taught her to see the beauty, the sparkle, and the shine in life.

Polly explained that it was largely because of her Uncle Charlie that she was the owner of a prestigious art gallery in Los Angeles. Her opinions and appraisals on fine art and antiques were the gold standard and the walls of her gallery were primo real estate for any artist, but, in spite of her expertise, she could not objectively appraise Charlie's collection.

She saw his pottery, the milk glass, the atomic age ash trays, bowls, and lamps. The folk art on the walls, the porcelain coated tin signs, and the Indian baskets propped up and displayed on the shelves and curio cabinets in Charlie's living room. His Stickley furniture. Virtually all of it, mass market antique goods that had peaked in value years ago; and other than maybe three or four outstanding pieces, there was nothing remarkable about Charlie's collection. That was the reality. But when it came to Charlie, there was no reality.

To Polly, Charlie's small arts and crafts bungalow was a palace, and the knick-knacks amassed inside were priceless artifacts that would make Aladdin swoon. She couldn't bear to part with any of it.

Paige talked Polly into staying with us for as long as

she needed. Polly agreed that it would make things a lot easier. We put her in grandmother's old bedroom suite.

🛡   🛡   🛡

The thought of Charlie breaking into our house kept me awake all night. I felt violated. As soon as I closed my eyes, the image of my mother burning, flailing, and falling over unseen objects popped into view. It wouldn't be this way if Charlie had been capable of putting a leash on his vanity. I loved the guy, but he was the cause of all of this chaos.

I wanted to find out why Polly had called Charlie so many times on the night of his suicide, but I had to figure out a way to delicately ask her. On one hand, it wasn't any of my business, but on the other, it sort of was because whatever pushed him was brought on by what happened after he let himself into our home.

He obviously called her before he killed himself and whatever he said must have scared her; clearly that's why she tried calling him back all night. What did he say to her? I wondered if he had told her anything about sneaking into our house and turning on the Cyclops. And what had he seen? What horror drove Charlie to suicide? Nothing about Polly's demeanor indicated that she was blaming us or suspected that his suicide had anything to do with his surreptitious visit. But I had to know for sure. I'd rest easier knowing.

🛡   🛡   🛡

Paige and Polly's deep affection for Charlie was a commonality I did not share, so I mostly stayed out of the way. I did, however, do what I could to be a good host. I made sure they were comfortable. I brought them tea and made it a point to always be nearby in case they needed anything. Not to mention it made it easier to listen in on what they talked about.

Polly worried about Charlie's cats—that they would have to be separated—but Paige let her know that that was out of the question and insisted we adopt them ourselves. The second we let them out of their crates they dashed into the library toward my desk and circled it, zeroing in on the drawer where I had temporarily stowed the crystals. They crouched and hissed, their ears pasted back, their fur standing on end. Paige, Polly, and I watched the strange incident.

"What do you have you hiding in that desk?" Polly asked.

"I have no idea what's happening here! Lingering scents that we can't smell? Maybe there's a dead mouse in one of the drawers," I replied.

"Okay, that's gross!" Paige said, her nose wrinkled in disgust. "I'm officially adding, 'clean out desk' to your honey-do list."

"Yes, dear," I replied, slumping over, my posture betraying the resignation of a thousand endured years of marital tyranny.

Polly laughed, and then as if hearing some piercing, ultrasonic whistle, the three feline heads snapped in unison in the direction of the grand foyer. The cats fled out of the library, dashed upstairs, and disappeared into the labyrinth of the upper stories of the house. We didn't see them again for a few days.

I put food and water in their dishes; they would have to eat eventually.

I had to tell Elliot to leave them alone because they had to get used to their new surroundings. They had been through a lot over the last week and needed time to get acclimated. He called out for them, going from room to room, occasionally spying one down the hall. It would invariably see him, hiss, and vanish into the darkness. I explained to him that they were not used to being around children and his exuberance was scaring them.

The Russian Blue (Tsar was his name) did warm up to Chelsea. One day he suddenly appeared out of nowhere and sidled up to her on her blanket in the sunroom. She dropped what she was doing and froze, stock-still, astonished at the feeling of this lithe, living, soft, and purring thing. She tentatively held out her arms and Tsar nuzzled her hands with his warm, moist nose, then sauntered in and rubbed against her. He then turned in a couple circles and sat just out of reach and purred, his tail slowly flicking this way and that. This was Chelsea's first encounter with a cat and it was fascinating to watch her reaction. Tsar stared at her and she stared back at the sound of his undulating purr, as though some great secret were being imparted.

⛪   ⛪   ⛪

I woke up to the acrid stench of burning flesh.

"Daniel!" My mother's scream came from somewhere

in the house, her voice far off and pleading.

I jumped out of bed just as I heard a crash and pandemonium above in the attic, like someone falling, flailing, and rolling, followed by a low groan that pulsated throughout the house. *Is it the attic trusses burning and collapsing?* I couldn't help but think. The sounds were loud enough to vibrate pictures on the wall, but in spite of the rumbles and noises, Paige didn't stir. She lay on her side, sound asleep.

A layer of hazy smoke cut through the dark, floating shoulder level, and when my head ascended into it, my eyes immediately burned and watered. I stumbled, coughing and gasping toward the wall switch and snapped it on. The smoke and stench instantly disappeared, but I didn't notice in time to stop what I had set into motion. I rushed over to Paige and shook her awake.

"What? What's going on?" she rolled over halfway, lifting her head, slightly pissed-off and very groggy.

"I think the house is on fire!"

No other statement is capable of stimulating a more visceral reaction: It cuts to the core, and Paige was out of bed, in her robe, out of our room, and on her way to Chelsea, all in the span of seconds.

"I'll get Chelsea! You get Elliot!" she yelled to me from down the hall. "Oh my god, Polly!" she added, half panicked. "Tell Polly! We've got to get her, too! Help her, Daniel!"

I stood there in a daze and listened to the commotion of Paige rousting Chelsea out of her crib. It felt like my head would split open at any second, but at least I was cognizant, belatedly so, that the house was, in fact, not on fire. Paige came back to the doorway carrying a very confused, scared, and crying Chelsea.

"Are you sure the house is on fire?" Paige asked. I stood there stupidly in my pajama shorts not knowing what to say.

"Daniel?"

"I… I don't know anymore. I thought I smelled smoke. What are the smoke detectors doing?" I asked, wondering about the ringing reverberating around in my head.

She looked down the hall at the evenly spaced smoke detectors, their green LEDs indicating desirable battery levels.

"Nothing, Daniel. The smoke detectors aren't doing anything. I think everything's okay."

Chelsea sensed Paige's worry and continued crying. I heard grandmother's door open down the hall and Polly suddenly appeared in sweats and a t-shirt.

"Is everything okay?" she asked. "I heard a ruckus."

"Daniel thought he smelled smoke."

They looked at me, waiting for me to say something. Tsar padded up and swiped his cheek against Paige's ankle then looked up at Chelsea. He began to purr and she stopped crying.

"I'm really sorry we woke you," I said. "It's obviously a false alarm, but I'm going to take a look around anyway."

"Well, I'm going to wake up Elliot," said Paige. "I want us together just in case."

"That's fine," I replied, trying to disguise the fact that I felt like a complete idiot. "Why don't you guys wait in the foyer till I give the all clear?"

They looked at each other and nodded.

I headed toward the double-winder stairway, quickly looking back to see Paige hand Chelsea off to Polly. She said something to her in front of Elliot's bedroom door. I snapped on the stairwell light and, treading up, I felt an icy current flowing down the stairs.

The pocket doors were wide open but no stairwell light penetrated into the vast space. It was as if a black screen had been placed in front of the doorway. Inside, the air was icy, dank, and corrupted with a stifling, earthy rot. I stepped into the billowing darkness and suddenly the smallest of Charlie's cats, the calico, jumped out from the inky black of the ballroom, latched onto my leg, and sank its razor teeth into my calf, injecting a searing pain that shot up my leg. I lost my balance and fell into the dark, crying out. The cat detached itself then shot off. I reached down and felt blood running down my calf, a whoosh of nausea rolling over me, and a searing, high pressure steam in my head wouldn't stop whistling as I looked through the opaque fog toward the stairwell entry. It was as if a black, lacy bunting was cloaking the door. It rippled and diminished growing dimmer and smaller, a cover descending, lidding out the fog, now a sliver, then pure, stifling, suffocating blackness.

There was a dull thud; something hard and hollow landed on the parquet floor. I stood still, trying to determine where I was in the deafening silence that followed the thud. Then there was knocking and scratching. Something struggled. Kicking and scratching, gurgling and desperate short breaths. More knocking and scratching, and ripping, struggling, kicking and the scuffing of buckle shoes. The cold, dank morphed into something warm and sickly sweet. I inhaled hard, gasping, but the air was running out. I spun and put my arms out trying to feel for something to grab on to. I took small, tentative steps and swept my arms from right to left, feeling and reaching. My foot suddenly struck something hollow and wooden, and I lost my balance and fell forward.

I heard Paige's footsteps running up the stairs.

"Daniel, Elliot's not in his room! Daniel?"

She stopped at the entry and would not go further. The billowing black that covered the entryway dissipated enough for me to see her shadow swirling in the opaque fog. She stood ten feet from me and stared into the black, but, in spite our close proximity, she couldn't see through the swirling veil that shrouded the room. She hugged herself and shivered.

"Daniel? Are you in there? What's happening, this doesn't make sense!"

I would not be able to explain this away because it defied the laws of motion and light. I stepped back into the stairwell, materializing before her as though a magician had just performed some trick. She looked at the blood running down my calf and into my slipper.

"Jesus, what happened to you?"

"It's nothing. Just one of the cats. I didn't see it and stepped on its tail," I lied.

"Elliot's not in his room! He's not up here?" she asked, worry lines etched into her forehead.

She was panicking and I had to bring her down, but something was gnawing at me, wanting me back in the ballroom—calling me. I felt cold wisps from behind, wrapping around my arms, torso, and legs, pulling me in.

"You know he sleepwalks sometimes," I said. "He's probably curled up on one of the sofas in the library. I've found him there before. I'm looking around up here, but it's a big room."

"Why don't you turn the lights on?" she asked, puzzled.

"I have to go backstage and turn the breakers on. Why don't you and Polly check the library and the other parts of the house?"

I didn't want her up here. I didn't know if it was safe, and I didn't want her seeing anything in the ballroom that might freak her out. I had no idea what was happening and I wasn't sure if the darkness had anything to do with the Cyclops' new capability. Even though the pieces had been removed and safely tucked into a desk drawer, I wasn't sure if it was still capable of stirring up other horrors. I gave her more impetus to vacate the ballroom.

"And make sure he didn't walk out of the house," I said. "I found him in the backyard once."

She stood there assessing me. I had gone too far. She turned and trotted halfway down to the landing. She looked back up at me with anger, then shouted down.

"Hey, Polly?"

"Is everything okay up there?" Polly replied.

"You must think we're crazy, but would you do us a favor?"

"Anything. What do you need?" Polly asked from the foot of the stairs.

"Elliot sleepwalks sometimes. Could you check the library and see if he's there?"

"Um, okay. What should I do if I find him?"

"Nothing. Just let him be. We're going to have a look up here, but I'll be right back down, I promise," Paige said reassuringly.

I wouldn't have blamed Polly if she would have marched up the stairs, handed Chelsea to Paige, then packed her bags and high-tailed it out of here, but she didn't. Paige walked back up to me and grabbed my hand.

"Let's go," she said.

We plunged into the darkness, but as we crossed the threshold, I could make out shapes and outlines of objects. Light now leaked into the room from the dormers and I saw the octagon window through its curtain. The room was no longer cold and dank. We slowly made our way to the edge of the stage.

"I'll wait here," she said. "Go turn the breakers on."

I climbed the stage and through the dim I made my way to the breakers. I opened the box and snapped them on. The lights flickered to life.

"Elliot!" Paige shouted, terrified.

I walked back out and Paige was on her knees before Elliot who was lying on the floor directly beneath the Cyclops. I hopped off the stage and ran to them. I got down on my hands and knees next to Paige. Elliot was unconscious and foaming at the mouth. His skin was pasty and moist, and his extremities trembled. Placed over each of his eyes were the crystals from Nora's grave.

⚜ ⚜ ⚜

Paige sat next to me in the hospital waiting room as I ranted on with my bizarre story. She may have been listening but her eyes were staring at something a hundred miles away. I told her I didn't understand that, in the pitch black of the ballroom, I was hearing Elliot in the throes of a seizure and not Nora's last moments in the grave. I finished my account of what happened after I fell into the darkness, and I realized I wasn't making any sense. She didn't have any context. I had left out everything that had happened prior. She looked at me like I was some disturbed cretin that had just propositioned her at a bus stop. She got up from her seat next to mine and moved down to a seat further away. I looked at her but said nothing.

Marian had already come to pick up Chelsea from the hospital and take her back to our house. We had left in such a rush that we didn't have time to organize. Paige rode in the ambulance with Elliot and I followed behind with Chelsea strapped into her seat. I had forgotten to bring Chelsea's diaper bag, and when Paige realized that I had forgotten it, she told me she was nominating me for idiot father of the year. She made me go to the nurses' station and ask where I might find a diaper. It was embarrassing, but their reply was rote; it wasn't the first time the night nurses heard someone ask for a diaper.

Elliot's doctor had just finished telling us that his seizure was brought about as a result of a fall. He had a closed-head injury and was in a coma. Paige began weeping and asked the doctor about his prognosis. I just sat there feeling stupid and responsible. He said that children bounce back from incidences like these better than adults do, but he was careful to let us know that his condition was gravely serious. It was life-threatening.

Elliot could emerge from the coma in days or years from now, or not at all. There was a lot of swelling and they had to relieve the pressure by opening his skull. He was in a very vulnerable place and the risk of infection was high—too high for us to see him. The doctor could not tell us if Elliot would survive once he was off life support, it was too early to know; we just had to take it one day at a time. He asked us if we had any other questions. We were too numb to respond. He took a couple steps backward, looked at Paige in her seat, then me in mine, then turned and awkwardly walked out of the room.

We stared out of the fifth-story window at a vast parking lot where icy sunlight glinted off the chrome of a thousand cars.

Then I started talking.

I told her about the house. I told her about the incidences I'd had in the house: the bathroom, the archive, the ballroom, the wheelchair, and how Nora had come to me and thought I was her papa, and for me to help her find her eyes. I told her about the connection between Nora and Elliot's big toe. I told her about the Cyclops and what it was originally designed to do, but that there were unanticipated anomalies. I told her about the crystals and where I had found them. That Nora had been buried alive. I told her that I had installed the crystals and that afterwards, while out running errands, Charlie had snuck into the house and turned on the Cyclops. I told her about Harlan's visit, why he had flown out, and everything I had found out about Captain Mueller and Jonathon Wingate. I told her about the four scientists who committed suicide.

Then I told her about Charlie; that he had probably

experienced something that was so terrible that he fled from our home and promptly hung himself in his basement. I told her about my experience with the Cyclops—about my mother and Nora, and how I woke up to the smell of smoke, crashing noises, and my mother calling out to me.

"All while you slept," I said.

I told her everything until I didn't have anything left to say.

"Please talk to me," I pleaded.

She wouldn't even look at me. Instead, she grabbed her purse and fished around for her cell phone. She stood up and bolted out of the room, fresh tears running down her cheeks. I sat there for a minute before I got up and looked out of the window. I walked over to the vending machines and absently noted the horizontal rows of junk behind the glass. I walked to the door and watched Paige through the narrow window. She spoke intensely into her phone while her free hand punctuated the air, her eyes red and tired from crying so much. My belated revelation was nothing short of an outrage. I knew that we were finished. She had every right to hate me. I knew it was all my fault.

She glanced over and saw me looking at her and, without missing a beat, she walked up to the door and slammed the window with her fist. I flinched and backed away, and when I looked again, I saw her disappear around the corner. I sat back down and cupped my head in my hands. A few minutes later Paige stormed back into the waiting room.

"You allowed my mother to take my daughter back into that house. They're alone in that house right now because you didn't say anything," Paige seethed.

"You're right," I replied, weakly.

I wanted to crawl into a shell and escape. I wanted to go back home.

"My son is in a coma, and I'm not taking that chance with my daughter. I told my mother to pack mine and Chelsea's things and get the hell out of there." She walked to the door and turned to face me. "We're moving out, Daniel. My children and I are never stepping foot back into that hellhole, do you understand? If you love that place so much you can stay there all by yourself, but I will not allow you to put my children in jeopardy! How could you? What the hell is wrong with you, Daniel?"

⇧   ⇧   ⇧

Elliot emerged from his coma six days after arriving in intensive care. I knew how lucky he was; and how lucky we were.

I walked to Charlie's house to tell Polly that Elliot was doing much better; that he had taken his first steps in physical therapy today.

"Thank god," she said. "I was so worried, but somehow I knew he'd pull through. He's a scrapper, isn't he?"

"He's a lot tougher than his dad," I replied.

Polly had moved into Charlie's after the accident. She figured she only had a couple more days' work before she would ship everything to L.A.

I told Polly that Paige was at the hospital helping him write a thank you card to his classmates. They had sent him a giant "Get well" poster and starting Monday he would be able to attend his elementary classes online via a link set up between the school and hospital.

Paige had calmed down to the point where we could occupy the same room now. She was friendly to me around Elliot, but when we were alone she still would not say much, and when we consulted together with his neurologist, or the physical therapist, she spoke to them without acknowledging that I was in the room, blocking me out. It was subtle, but I think the staff could tell what was going on. They probably witnessed similar dynamics with other patients' families: Parents who blamed each other for accidents their children suffered.

I didn't want to burden Polly with our troubles. She certainly had enough of her own but it was a comfort confiding in her about Elliot. I also found myself confiding in her about Paige and felt guilty when I shared too much.

"You know, I care about my son, too," I had said to Paige earlier, catching up to her in the hallway.

"I'll believe it when you torch that hellhole," she replied, zooming ahead into Elliot's hospital room, leaving me in her dust.

"She couldn't have meant that," said Polly. "I understand why you love that house so much. You two really put your heart and soul into that place."

We sat in Charlie's living room amidst the boxes destined for L.A. She had made a pot of coffee and brought it to the living room on a tray with two mugs, cream and sugar, and some shortbread.

"Polly, there's something I have to tell you about Charlie," I said, changing the subject. "It's about what I believe may have happened to him." I took a deep breath and proceeded. "Charlie let himself into our house before he committed suicide."

Her brow furrowed at this revelation. She looked at me.

"What do you mean?" she asked, genuinely puzzled.

"I mean, he had a key to our house and let himself in while I was out running errands."

"Why would he do that? What do you think he wanted?" she asked.

I told her about coming home to chaos and that Charlie was the only other person with access to the house.

"He was obsessed with that instrument in our ballroom," I added.

This was all new to Polly so I had to be careful to not cast Charlie in a bad light. She was perplexed and the despair she had hidden away began to crack through and surface.

"You mean that whacky light you have up there? What about it? Why was he so obsessed with it?"

"Did he call you on the night of his suicide?" I asked.

"Yes."

"What did he say?"

"Daniel, I'm not very comfortable talking about this, it's too personal. Honestly I'd rather not share," she replied shifting uncomfortably in her chair.

I took a softer tone.

"Well, can you tell me if he seemed upset?"

"He was absolutely upset! He was hysterical; panicky. And I heard something. It sounded like choking noises, like someone was with him."

"What do you mean?" I asked.

She looked out of the window as tears welled in her eyes. The memory was painful and I was dredging it up with my persistence. She turned to me on the verge of anger.

"I mean I thought I heard someone choking. It was horrible."

I leaned in toward her. This was a huge revelation on what Charlie had gone through that night.

"What you just told me is key to figuring out what may have driven him to take his own life," I replied.

"This is crazy! What could that thing have to do with his suicide?"

"I don't know," I replied.

She threw her hands in the air, getting more and more agitated with the conversation.

"Then what are we talking about?" she asked.

"I know it's strange, but it's like a giant puzzle," I replied evenly. Right now you have some pieces and I have some pieces, but you'll need to give me your pieces before it starts making sense."

"Daniel, I'll be honest with you, this conversation's a little weird. We're talking about my uncle who killed himself. I'm a little raw, do you understand?"

"Do you want to know what happened to him?"

"Yes!" she said now crying openly.

"So do I!"

"How is that possible? It's not like he left a note! He was here one minute and gone the next," she said through tears.

I told her everything about the Cyclops, its history, the code name, the crystals—everything. I told her about the chaos I came home to and how I found Charlie the next day.

"Charlie had no idea that anything was different about the Cyclops. He simply turned it on and waited for the effects, but this time something different happened. Something terrible. Can you tell me anything about your last conversation with him?"

Polly took a deep breath.

"Charlie confessed something to me on the phone."

Between what Polly told me about her last conversation with Charlie, and reviewing the digital footage from the cameras that Paige and I had set up throughout the house years earlier, I was finally able to piece together an accurate picture of what had happened to him during his clandestine visit. Much of what I gathered was based on the footage, but some is pure speculation.

The grainy images of Charlie flailing down the hallway, practically falling down the stairs, then stumbling through the front door were difficult to watch, but there was something strange and unexplainable in those grainy images: A shadowy, child-sized figure clutched onto his back; clawing and jabbing at him violently. It seemed to be causing him a great deal of distress.

ON THE FINAL HOURS OF
CHARLIE HINTERMANN

Charlie woke up that morning feeling a little low. The dizzy spells were happening more frequently and he couldn't put off making an appointment with his doctor any longer. He was hoping it was something as simple as all the prescriptions he was taking: six different pills, with two of them three times a day. Maybe their interactions were the cause.

He drew the bedroom curtains open and looked down the street to see if Paige's car was in her driveway. It wasn't and that was a drag. Daniel's pickup was in the driveway, which meant he was home, and, although he was nice, he was just a little too quiet for Charlie. Daniel was always so serious—a bit of a stick in the mud, and Charlie's lighthearted banter was always reciprocated with some monosyllabic grunt. It was exhausting. Paige, however, was a joy; she was so much fun and she fell right into things in Indian Village. She had a carefree way about her, very relaxed with an easy, unselfconscious elegance.

Some people just had it, and Paige had it in spades. Daniel, on the other hand, needed a little work. He was a great guy, but it was always a lot more fun with Daniel when Paige was present. He did have to admit, however, that Daniel had done an amazing job on the house. It was far and above the best looking property on Seminole and that was saying a lot. Their renovation also had the added bonus of motivating some of the other longtime residents to step it up.

Going upstairs to their ballroom had become something of an addiction. He was sneaking in whenever he got the chance. Daniel had classes that kept him on a schedule and Paige was probably off on an appointment with one of her clients, all of whom adored her as much as Charlie did.

"What a find!" Helen commented. "It's like she came out of nowhere!"

It was Sunday and Charlie wanted a "treatment" more than anything. That's what he called them: His "treatments." He would go up and turn the machine on, wait for the strange smell to permeate the room, then bask in the chaos for a few moments and wait for the magic to happen. He always felt refreshed afterwards. It put a spring in his step and he swore that when he looked in the mirror, the crow's feet were less prominent, the wattle under his chin seemed a little tighter, and the powder that formed on his face was just like having a chemical peel.

A real chemical peel cost a fortune and, although he was sitting pretty, he had grown up in a time when frugality was the norm. He remembered his mother and father always arguing about finances. Except for when it came to

Polly and his beloved antiques, frugality was something that became ingrained.

Bothering Daniel was out of the question. He had, on a couple of occasions, asked Daniel if it would be okay if he could see a demonstration of the light. The first time wasn't a problem, and he made sure to watch very carefully the sequence of buttons and knobs Daniel manipulated on the panel. The second time Daniel seemed really put out. He remembered it was a Sunday, just like today, and maybe Daniel had things to do. He could have said no, but he didn't. He simply escorted Charlie up to the ballroom, turned the machine on for a few minutes, and then turned it back off. It was awkward, and besides, Daniel didn't leave the thing on long enough for it to work. Charlie knew that it only started working after the strange ozone scent permeated the room.

There was something else, too. There were things in the light that he couldn't exactly identify, but they seduced him somehow. It wasn't sexual. There were brief, flickering images of things within the chaos. The wisps of plasma would form shapes that seemed to harmonize with certain memories and gave him peace. There seemed to be a consciousness, or perhaps it was his own consciousness, that gave the shapes their meaning. The wisps of plasma would form these feelings, linger there for a few seconds, as if they were making an effort to make their presence known to him, then quickly morph into chaos and join the craziness above. He thought that the phenomenon of the plasma whipping off his body and forming these peaceful feelings was the most important aspect of the treatments. Not only was it an invigorating fountain of youth, but it was also spiritual. If only Daniel could manufacture more of these machines and set up shop. He would make a fortune!

Daniel didn't have classes on Sunday, so Charlie would have to be on the lookout. Sneaking in on a Sunday was taking a chance, but if he heard Daniel trudging up during the treatment he would just power down the instrument and pretend that he was up there working out on the exercise equipment.

Paige had been on Charlie to start getting into better shape and she did give him permission to use the equipment. They worked out together, but mostly it was Paige who actually exercised. Charlie would hop onto the treadmill and set it to what Paige jokingly referred to as mosey, then proceed to mosey for, say, five minutes tops, before he would hop off with great fanfare and announce that he had broken his previous day's record by about a mile and a half. He would proceed to plop down onto the bench press or some other piece of equipment, dabbing at imaginary beads of sweat, and start a discussion, usually on where they should lunch. Plus, he was always leaving a trail of things behind wherever he went, and he was pretty sure that he had left his warm-up jacket up there. If Daniel was put off by finding Charlie in the ballroom, the warm-up jacket would lend some credibility to his excuse.

"I'm sorry Daniel, but I've been looking all over for this, and Paige said it would be okay."

It would be fairly easy to wriggle out of any trouble.

A few hours later, Charlie watched Daniel's pickup pull out of the driveway and head south toward Jefferson. Daniel taking the pickup was a good sign and meant that he was probably going to be gone for a while.

He let himself into Daniel and Paige's house then quietly walked up the two flights of stairs to the ballroom's pocket doors. He punched in the code, slid the card through the slot and listened as the locks unbolted from their chambers. He walked into the ballroom and looked up at the Cyclops. Did something seem different about it? He walked over to his jacket that was draped over a bench press.

He looked back up at the Cyclops.

He whipped the sheet off the control panel and walked over to the breaker box to turn on the appropriate switches. He flipped the switch on the back of the panel and watched the needles light up and bounce. He twisted the two dials that activated the complicated bulbs and the uniform black of the globe pulsed to life. But something was different. He looked down at the panel to make sure he was manipulating the correct dials, and he was. But the light issuing forth was different somehow. There was a uniformity to it, an order that was new. The million pinpricks of light no longer danced but were as focused as laser beams, more powerful somehow, appearing capable of burning holes into the walls.

He turned the dials that set the two hemispheres spinning in opposite directions and now the pinpricks caused the room to glow in a uniform blue. This was strange, but when Charlie double-checked the directions on the sticky note that Daniel's electrician friend had scribbled, he noticed that he was following the correct steps. For a second he thought that maybe he should stop—just turn the thing off and forget about the treatment—but now he was curious about what would happen next. He turned the dials that set the Fresnel band at the equator into motion and watched the globe tilt upward on the pole and slowly orbit clockwise. He then turned the ultraviolet filaments on and something astounding happened. Everything completely faded to the point where it no longer existed. The walls disappeared first, then the ceiling and floor. They were simply no longer there and he was suddenly left floating in thin air. He clutched the panel, terrified.

"What is this? This isn't right!" he said out loud.

He looked down and could just make out the lower floors as though he were hovering above some living blueprint. Where was the chaos? The wisps of plasma? He tried to get his bearings by looking at the panel he held fast to, but it was no longer there. Neither were his hands, arms, nor his body. Everything was gone.

He brought his invisible hands to his face and clasped them together, and felt reassured when he felt the flesh of his fingers and the bones beneath entwined in a double fist. This phenomenon was new and completely unexpected. He panicked thinking that he had perhaps taken too many treatments and invisibility was the result. Either that or Daniel must have made some adjustments.

He stepped away from the panel and almost lost his footing because it was very disorienting being invisible. He looked up at the Cyclops and it was now an eerie blue orb that left a blue trail of plasma in its wake, like a gassy, blue planet quickly circling a black hole. He walked slowly and cautiously toward the light but forgot about the ledge and fell off the stage, collapsing onto a floor that could not be seen. He grimaced in pain but, after flexing his ankles, knees, hips, elbows, and shoulders, he was fairly certain that nothing was broken.

"You're lucky," he said aloud to himself. "That's all you need right now is a broken hip."

He lay there on the floor for a minute, getting his bearings. He shifted to all fours and readied himself to stand. His side was sore and he would be looking at some ugly bruises in the mirror tomorrow morning.

A cackle cut through the air. Someone laughed. It had an adolescent quality. Was it Paige? Elliot? He looked up and standing off in the nothingness was a girl he had never seen before. She looked like an antique porcelain doll and stared at him through black bangs. She wore a maroon velvet dress with a lacy collar and sleeves, white stockings, and black buckle shoes.

"Hello, Charlie," she said, her voice coming from everywhere and nowhere.

He got up, forgetting about the pain and backed away until his heels hit the stage. She drew closer; her lacy sleeves were soaked in blood. It ran down her hands and dripped off her fingertips.

"Michael needs you, Charlie. He cries out for you."

She parted her hair and her large, empty eye sockets flashed brightly in a kaleidoscope of multiple shapes and colors. He heard the pad of small feet, scampering just behind and off to his left. And then he heard horrible gagging. Something was gasping and struggling for breath. Its airway was obstructed and it struggled, gasping, utterly unable to draw air.

He looked in the direction of where the horrible

gasping came, but saw nothing, only the faint shadows of Seminole Street.

He looked back up at the girl but she was gone. Instead Michael, Charlie's little brother, who died just after his second birthday, stood there in his red footy pajamas. Every cell in Charlie's body screamed, "run," but he stood there incapable of movement. The baby's hair was wispy, fine, and blonde, and his face was blue with dark circles around his eyes. His arms lunged out toward Charlie as he slowly walked toward him, his blue fingers, black at the nails, reaching out and grasping. His little mouth opened, forming a small "o," and his black tongue lolled around as he gagged and choked, desperately trying to draw air. Michael was choking and needed Charlie to clear the obstruction.

Charlie stared at Michael, his long-dead baby brother, when something popped in his chest, snapped up his shoulder, down his left arm, and boomeranged painfully in his wrist. His legs buckled and he landed hard on the floor. He had forgotten to bring his heart pills. He had to get back home and take them. But he just sat there, frozen, clutching his arm, watching Michael draw closer.

"You poor boy! You poor, poor boy—Oh, Michael! What have I done to you?" Charlie said as he watched his long dead little brother stumble closer toward him.

The scent of ozone permeated the air and a wisp appeared, hovering there, just out of reach. Charlie willed himself toward the wisp and followed it through the murk. The wisp became a dizzying, undulating ribbon that was hard to follow, but it soon morphed into a hallway that turned and banked. Doors opened on past transgressions, but the baby's blue fingers pointed and pushed him along the way, keeping him on track. The hallway shifted and turned, and stairways appeared that led toward black voids. But the end was near, Charlie knew it, and he kept going until a door appeared that opened into... Michael's nursery.

Charlie walked in and a long-buried jealousy and hate rekindled and surfaced when he saw Michael lying in his crib. Michael was awake and looking up at a mobile of little fluffy sheep and fences that hovered above his head, just out of reach. When mama wound the key, "Hush, Little Baby" tinkled on tiny bells, and the sheep went 'round and 'round, jumping over the little fences.

Charlie got down on all fours and crept up to the side of the crib and listened to Michael lying awake. Michael, who ruined everything. Michael, who mama loved more than him. They had only paid attention to Michael, and all he had heard was "Not now, Charlie!" and "Leave Michael alone, Charlie!" and "If you go near him one more time!" and "What did you do to your brother's arm?"

Michael drew his eyes away from the mobile, suddenly aware that someone was there, but unable to see anything but the closed door. Charlie suddenly popped up like a jack-in-the-box and shouted "Boo!" It scared Michael and Charlie watched Michael's face turn red and contort. Charlie realized his mistake and knew that he had to head off the scream before it erupted.

"Shh. I'm sorry, Michael! Shh, don't cry, baby, don't cry! It's okay, shh..."

Michael had heard these soothing sounds come from Charlie before, but he didn't trust him. He shimmied backward until he bumped against the bars behind him.

Charlie climbed into the crib and sat down. Michael struggled to sit up but it was difficult with his arm wrapped so snuggly in the heavy cast. He had to get away from Charlie.

"It's okay, baby, let me help you up," Charlie said, reaching, but Michael flinched away and Charlie slapped his little brother's hand and pointed at him.

"Stop being such a baby! Don't cry! I mean it!"

Charlie saw the terror in Michael's eyes and it made him feel powerful. Michael looked up at Charlie in his crib then looked over at the closed door.

"Ha-ha! Mama's sleepin' and she can't hear you."

Michael wanted to scream but if he did the boy would slap him again, so he shut up. He just wanted the boy to leave.

"Now, hold still," Charlie said, grabbing the cast and yanking Michael into a sitting position.

They sat there on opposite sides of the crib looking at each other. Charlie kind of felt bad for what he had done to Michael a couple days ago. Maybe a game would make everything better.

"Hey, wanna play patty-cake? Oh, you can't with that cast. What good are you, then?"

Charlie looked around. He needed something to do. It was getting stupid just sitting in the crib with Michael.

"I got an idea! Wanna play hide-n-seek? Yeah, let's play hide-n-seek!"

Charlie grabbed the blanket and covered himself up to his neck.

"You count to ten and I'll hide, okay? Wait, you're just a baby, you can't count. Okay, I'll count for you then."

Charlie covered his head with the blanket and quickly counted to ten.

"Okay, come and find me!" He sat there under the blanket knowing full well that Michael knew exactly where he was and he felt stupid, but the baby was even more stupid for not trying to find him.

He whipped the blanket off his head and shouted, "Surprise!" In spite of what had happened earlier, Michael laughed.

"Oh, you like that game? All right, it's your turn. I'll count to ten and you hide, okay?" Charlie covered his eyes and counted, "One, two, three, four, five-six-seven-eight-nine-ten!"

He uncovered his eyes and saw Michael just sitting there with a stupid look on his face.

"You're 'sposed to hide, don't you know anything?"

Charlie looked for something that Michael could hide under.

He saw the pillow.

"You can hide under this, okay?" Charlie placed the pillow against Michael and it almost covered him completely. Michael caught on to the game and he thought that he could make Charlie laugh, so he kicked the pillow and it fell down.

"Bah!" Michael shouted, laughing.

"No! Don't kick it, you're supposed to hide!"

Michael was confused. He wondered why his brother didn't laugh. Charlie covered Michael again, and again Michael kicked the pillow, but this time he connected and the pillow flew at Charlie's face. This was just too funny, and Michael really laughed now. He was enjoying this game with the pillow, but Charlie grabbed the pillow and slammed it down onto his lap and Michael saw the rage on Charlie's face. He stopped laughing.

"You don't want to hide? Let's start over. You're just a stupid baby so I'll help you find a hiding spot."

Charlie got up on his knees and crawled toward Michael and grabbed him by his good arm and shoved him down onto his back, but Michael's cast ricocheted upward and struck Charlie in the face.

"Ouch! That hurt!"

Michael looked up at his big brother, terrified. Charlie watched Michael's face turn red and contort in a silent scream and he knew that it was too late to stop him from crying. He brought the pillow down onto the baby's face.

"You wanna play hide-n-seek? This is how you play! I'll count to ten while you hide!" Charlie felt Michael struggle under the pillow and it enraged him.

"Stop squirming or I'll find you!"

Michael's arms and legs really started thrashing now, so Charlie laid down on top of the pillow and began to count slowly,

"One, two, three, four…"

Michael's body humped and convulsed and Charlie was surprised at how strong the baby was, so he put his full weight down onto the pillow.

"You made me lose my count, so I have to start over again. One, two, three, four, five, six." Charlie noticed the struggles get weaker. "That's a good baby! Just hide and I won't find you—six, seven, eight, nine, aaaannd TEN! Ready or not here I come!"

Charlie lifted himself off the pillow and looked around

the room. Michael finally understood the game because he was staying perfectly still under the pillow.

"Hmm, where could that baby boy be? Is he in there?" Charlie asked, pointing at the closet door. "No. Is he behind that?" He pointed to the dresser. "Nope, not there, either! What about under this pillow?"

Charlie lifted the pillow and looked down at Michael. He didn't look right. His eyes and mouth were wide open and his tongue kind of stuck out of his mouth, and he was still—very still. Charlie tapped Michael on the shoulder.

"Tag! You're it!"

Nothing. Michael just lay there. Charlie tapped Michael on the shoulder again.

"I found you fair and square, now get up!" Michael just lay there, motionless, and Charlie watched his little brother turn blue.

"Hey, wake-up! Wake-up, baby! Heeeyyyyyy! Wake-up, Michael! Wake-up! Wake-up! Wake-up!"

Charlie looked down at his baby brother's lifeless little body. He poked his shoulder again, just a little harder.

"Ollie, Ollie, oxen free!"

He got down closer to the baby's face and looked into his eyes. Michael just stared back at him, or rather through him. It was like the eyes couldn't see anymore, like he had fallen asleep with his eyes open. He climbed out of the crib and looked and now the baby was even bluer than before. The game made the baby tired and he fell asleep. Charlie reached over the bars and covered Michael with the blanket, then he picked up the pillow and put it on top of Michael's head.

"There, baby. That will keep you nice and warm till

mommy comes and wakes you."

The door swung open. Charlie turned and saw the wisps curling and undulating into the room, reaching for him. They wrapped around his neck, arms, and legs, tightened their grip, and pulled him out. The nursery door slammed shut, and as he was pulled further and faster down the hallway, the door diminished, fading from view completely. Charlie streaked past the darkened stairwells, pulled along by the wisps, and the other doors whipped by. The hallway twisted, banked, and turned. It faded and became a ribbon, then a wisp, and he was suddenly back in the invisibility of the ballroom, but now something pinched and dug into his legs, causing excruciating pain.

Michael was at Charlie's feet and latched tightly to his leg. His face was bluish-black, contorted and twisted, desperately trying to draw a breath. He reached and pulled himself up toward Charlie's waist. He climbed higher until he was on Charlie's chest. Michael's small fingers latched onto Charlie's shoulders and he climbed higher yet, staring blankly into Charlie's eyes. Charlie screamed and tried to pull the dead thing off, but Michael's fingers dug into Charlie's shoulders; the stench of Michael's corpse mingled with the ozone and Charlie began to gag. Michael wrapped his tiny arms around Charlie's neck and squeezed. Charlie grabbed Michael under his armpits and with all of his might he managed to yank himself free of Michael's grip. Michael flailed and thrashed, suspended on Charlie's outstretched arms. Charlie swung and tossed Michael off into the void before he blindly ran, bumping into and tripping over unseen obstacles. He stumbled then fell down wincing in pain and utterly horrified by the unbelievable manifestation of his long-dead little brother.

He pulled himself up and, looking down through the floor, could just make out the second story of the house below, cast in negative tones. The layout of the faint images began to make sense—the load-bearing walls, the hallway, and stairs, and he was able to orient himself. He limped toward where he thought the pocket doors were, but he heard Michael's gagging close behind. Charlie tripped and flailed his way toward the pocket doors, but Michael was too quick and latched onto his leg again. Charlie's mind flashed to his house. If he could only get back to his house, he would be safe. Maybe Michael wouldn't be able to follow him.

Charlie limped along, his arms stretched outward, trying to feel his way. Finally he bashed into the wall and, skirting left, found the pocket doors, but Michael was climbing up his backside, his fingers digging into Charlie's skin with every upward pull.

Charlie stumbled out of the ballroom, lurched down the double-winder stairway, and limped down the hallway. He passed an antique mirror and stopped at the sight. He was no longer invisible, but a bizarre lighted disc followed above that flickered multiple colors, and it was in this light that he just barely discerned Michael's small spindly arms burrowing, now elbow-deep into his shoulders. Michael was sinking into him. Charlie was absorbing his dead sibling, and he felt the small fingers reaching in deep, probing, and grasping at his muscles and sinew. He burst out of the house, stumbling toward his home.

⇮   ⇮   ⇮

The doorbell rang one day a couple months after Charlie's suicide. It was Judge Evans. He had turned out to be a valuable ally throughout the lengthy investigation and it was in part, thanks to him, that I was cleared of any wrongdoing in Charlie's death.

Judge Evans still had a lot of connections in the city.

"Here are some documents that I thought you might find interesting," he said, handing me a folder that he had brought with him.

After Judge Evans left I beelined into the library and tore through the folder. One of the investigators found a cassette tape in an older model answering machine in Charlie's bedroom that had activated during a phone call between Charlie and Polly on the night he committed suicide. Apparently the answering machine was defective and would activate during both incoming and outgoing calls. I found a transcript of Charlie and Polly's last telephone conversation in the folder.

P. Ridge: Hello?

C. Hintermann: Polly?

P. Ridge: Hey Uncle Charlie, what a surprise! How are you? What's happening?

C. Hintermann: Oh, sweetie! How wonderful to hear your voice. I'm... I'm... um.
(unintelligible/garble/choking)

P. Ridge: Is everything okay? What's going on?

C. Hintermann: Oh Polly! I'm, I'm not good. Things are.

P. Ridge: Oh no, Uncle Charlie! What's wrong? Are you... do you need a doctor?

C. Hintermann: Polly... wait, no. I just... I just need to talk. Everything's fine.

P. Ridge: It doesn't sound like everything's fine. What's wrong? Talk to me.

C. Hintermann: I just... I don't know how to... oh, God! Help me!

(unintelligible/choking/garble)

P. Ridge: Are you crying? What's that noise? What's happening to you?

C. Hintermann: Oh, God! What-have-I-done-what-have-I-done-what-have-I-done!

P. Ridge: Uncle Charlie! You're scaring me! Calm down! Please, calm down and talk to me! You have to tell me what's happening!

C. Hintermann: I'm sorry. I'm so sorry for scaring you! I think, um... I think I'm having a panic attack and I need to hear your voice.

P. Ridge: Are you sure? Should I call an ambulance for you?

C. Hintermann: No! I don't need an ambulance. Just... just listen to me, please! I just need to talk. I need to tell you something. If I tell you, if I confess, maybe it'll go away.

P. Ridge: Okay... you're not making any sense! Calm down, please! I want you to sit down and take some deep breaths, okay?

C. Hintermann: Yes! That's good! Okay, I'm sitting

down.

    P. Ridge: Breathe! Are you breathing?

    C. Hintermann: Yes. I'm breathing. That helps.
Thank you. Thank you, Polly.

    P. Ridge: Are you sitting? Do you need water?

    C. Hintermann: No. I'm good. I drank some water
earlier.

    P. Ridge: Are you comfortable?

    C. Hintermann: Yes, it's better now. Oh God! I just
need to hear your voice.

    P. Ridge: Do you need me to fly out? Just say the
word and I'll drop everything and take the red eye.

    C. Hintermann: No sweetie, you're very sweet for
offering; I just... hearing your voice has helped
tremendously!

    (Intelligible/garble/choking)

    P. Ridge: Jesus, what's that noise, Charlie? Are you
choking? Are you having a heart attack?

    C. Hintermann: Honey! No! I'm, I'm fine! It's not
me, it's... it's the television."

    P. Ridge: The television?

    C. Hintermann: Hold on, I'll turn it down.

    P. Ridge: You don't watch TV. Are you telling me the
truth?

    C. Hintermann: If I was having a heart attack, do you
think I'd be able to talk to you? C'mon! You're the one
who needs to calm down now!

    P. Ridge: Okay, okay, I believe you. What's
happening, then?

C. Hintermann: Oh honey! I love you so much! I just want you to know that I love you. Don't cry, I'm sorry.

P. Ridge: I can't help it! You're freaking me out! What's wrong, Uncle Charlie? Tell me, what's going on? What's happening?

C. Hintermann: Sweetie! I have to confess something to you. I've never told anyone. I've never told a soul. Now listen to me, but first, tell me... do you love me, sweetie?

P. Ridge: Of course I love you!

C. Hintermann: Don't cry honey, please!

P. Ridge: I can't help it!

C. Hintermann: I have to tell you something. It happened a long time ago. So very long ago. Are you there?

P. Ridge: Yes!

C. Hintermann: Polly?

P. Ridge: I'm here! I'm listening!

C. Hintermann: Okay. Okay. I'm going to tell you now. You know that I had a little brother, right?

P. Ridge: Oh man! I think... uh... I think I recall seeing pictures at Grandma's house.

C. Hintermann: Michael. His name was Michael.

(-end of tape-)

PART IV

I put the Cyclops on permanent loan at the Tiffany Glassworks Museum. Harlan convinced me that it was the right thing to do; basically I'd be an idiot to keep it around any longer.

"You lost your marriage, you almost lost your son, and one of your neighbors is dead. What else does that thing have in store for you?" Harlan had said to me.

And he was right. I was never more relieved to have anything out of my life. I also gave him the crystals, which he locked in a safe located in the basement at the museum. Harlan and I are the only two people on Earth who know their whereabouts. One day he will conduct a study of the crystals, but now is not the time. There's just too much going on at the museum—and the fall-out from Charlie's suicide and its connection to the crystals is still too fresh.

Harlan was correct when he said that the Cyclops' reemergence would cause a sensation, but that turned out to be an understatement. The Tiffany Glassworks Museum is mobbed—one of the top five most attended museums in the country. It also made it onto the cover of *Time* magazine along with a photograph of my great-grandfather with a caption that read, "The Forgotten Genius." The Cyclops now hangs in its own specially constructed gallery designed to optimize its effects. Harlan reinstalled the two replacement crystals, effectively neutering it back to a light show novelty.

No one knows more about the Cyclops than Al, so Harlan hired him as the museum's chief electrician, and Harlan conducts sold out demonstrations once a week with Al at the controls. Spectators watch from behind the protection of special, floor-to-ceiling panes of glass, ensuring that the whirls, dervishes, and jets of plasma are kept at bay, their hypnotizing effects diminished.

Al has acclimated well at Cornell, but sadly his personal barbershop crusade was met with only mixed results.

I was glad when the experts from the museum showed up and carted the Cyclops off; still I find it difficult walking up into the ballroom and looking at the cracked medallion to see only those two wires poking through the ceiling. I miss looking at it and I miss firing it up and being immersed in its mesmerizing chaos.

And I hate myself for it.

One day, with Polly's help, I will find another chandelier, but for now the ugly wires are serving as a kind of penance.

Paige is great about my visitation rights. I get the kids every other weekend and can pick them up anytime I want; I just have to give her 24-hours' notice.

It took a year, but she finally agreed to allow the kids back into the mansion. She became more comfortable with things once the Cyclops was gone, but I lied to her again, assuring her that absolutely nothing has happened since I had gotten rid of it. I sincerely hoped that it had everything to do with, and was solely responsible for all the unexplainable activity, and even though it's gone, things still happen.

The house is in no way cleansed.

I walk the hallways and shadows lurk in the peripheries; they whisper and whistle. Objects often roll out into the hallways, and at night I hear my mother's body flailing and falling over unseen objects, and her voice often wakes me in the dead of night, screaming out for me. I bury my head in my pillow to drive out the sound and to block the acrid stench of burning flesh. Heeding grandmother's advice about "ignoring them" is next to impossible.

The archive feels like a crypt, and I now know that it's so much more than just an assembly of rooms filled with the flotsam and jetsam of a long-dead genius. The scent of ozone still lingers in the ballroom, the curtains billow, and an earthen dank permeates the atmosphere of this seldom used room.

Elliot has not had a seizure in over a year and, although I'll never be able to prove it, I believe the Cyclops was causing them. I asked him if he remembered anything about the night we found him in the ballroom with the two crystals over his eyes.

"I only remember waking up in the library and the girl was floating next to your desk pointing at a drawer," he'd said.

Chelsea's surgery provided her with only limited sight. She can make out shapes and colors, but she remains legally blind.

⚉   ⚉   ⚉

Marian described an incident after she spoke to Paige on the phone the day after Elliot got hurt: She was in our bedroom packing some of Paige's things when she happened to look over and saw that Chelsea had the two crystals and was holding them up to her eyes.

"I had no idea where she'd gotten them, but she was looking through them like she could see clear as a bell. She tottered around staring at different things, but when she looked at the big Russian Blue, it hissed and ran away. That's when I saw what she was up to. She looked up at me and there were all these strange—I don't know how to describe it—colors and lights flashing brightly in her eyes, and I thought, 'that can't be good,' so I took them away from her and put them on top of the dresser. My God, how she cried and carried on! Then a little while later I turned around and she was in the hallway with the crystals at her eyes again! Now that dresser's high and there's no way she could have climbed it—I was in that room the whole time! I would have seen her! And there she is in the hallway, looking up, like she's, I don't know, engaged with someone, and that Russian Blue is going insane, hissing and crouching at something *I* couldn't see! Well, I walked up and snatched them away from her again, put her in her crib, then went downstairs and stuck them in Daniel's desk. And you know what? She cried and fussed that whole day—and that's not Chelsea! She never has tantrums! She cried in the car the whole way back to my place, and all night, right up until you arrived! She was inconsolable. I could not get her to stop crying and fussing. She wanted those crystals back, but there was no way! I mean, who knows what kind of damage those things could've caused! I understand completely why you don't want those kids in that house anymore!"

I loathed acknowledging it, but Chelsea and Nora had something in common: They were both born blind. Nora's addiction to the crystals transcended the grave and I needed to know why Chelsea became attached to them so quickly as well.

Great-grandfather was meticulous with his archive and I wondered if his obsession carried over into the possible storage of any records that might exist relating to Nora, so I began a search through the hundreds of drawers and miles of shelves. I looked through the library, the office, the archive, and even the bedrooms, but it was in the secret library where I finally found a trove of papers and medical documents relating to her.

There was not a lot regarding her first few years other than school records (she was an "A" student) and steps the family had taken to make her life as a blind person as easy as possible. Then when she turned 13 everything changed. According to the family doctor, she began to suffer "bouts of extreme hysteria." At first she was treated at home, but nothing helped. Her problems seemed to start around the same time my great-grandfather began his work on the Cyclops, and she became obsessed with the instruments of his occupation.

It became impossible to contain her erratic behavior and concerns were raised over her ability to function in an otherwise happy household. She was put on a regimen of drugs that would have been sufficient to tranquilize a horse, and my great-grandfather hired a live-in nurse but that arrangement did not last. A bevy of nurses were subsequently hired but none stayed on very long.

The most disturbing documents linked Nora to the death of her mother. My great-grandmother had fallen down the stairs and survived, but for the remainder of her life she was confined to a wheelchair. She swore that she was pushed by Nora—something Nora vehemently denied. Regardless, after the incident, Nora was removed from home and committed to the Northern Michigan Asylum, known also by a gentler name as the 11th Street Academy in Traverse City, Michigan.

The asylum's approach to care was a gentle administration of encouragement and therapy designed to improve the patient's self-esteem. Patients were not permitted to idle away the hours in their rooms and common areas. They were given jobs and tasks according to their abilities and interests. There was a small farm with livestock to care for, greenhouses, a cannery, even a small furniture factory. Nora worked in the greenhouses and thrived in the compassionate environment.

After a few months, convinced that the cure had erased her hysteria, her doctors released her back into the care of her father and she was sent back home. However, very soon afterwards, her fits and spells redoubled in number, and it was during that short stay that Nora's mother was found dead at the foot of the stairs. Her neck had been broken. Nora was found spinning in circles around her mother's body in the wheelchair, singing hymns she had learned at the asylum.

Once again, Nora was committed, but she never recovered her sanity. She was often found lurking the halls late at night laughing and singing and, according to some eyewitnesses, her eyes flashed in spectacular bursts of colors. There were accounts from some of the patients in Nora's ward, and even the staff, that Nora had a special pair of glasses that allowed her to see into their souls. She would go around and accuse patients and staff, even the doctors, of horrible atrocities and sins, of things she couldn't have possibly known. The other patients began to fear her and rumors abounded that she practiced witchcraft and consorted with the devil. Patients avoided her and those directly responsible for her care gave excuses why they were no longer attending to her needs. Eventually she was segregated from the general population and confined to a building where the most extreme cases were housed.

There was an outbreak of influenza and Nora was found, *allegedly* dead, in her room. The two crystals were found lodged in her throat. I use the word *allegedly*, of course, because of the discovery I had made when she was disinterred. Presumably, to avoid any potential scandal, great-grandfather insisted that the official cause of death be recorded as influenza. He accompanied her corpse back to Detroit on the train, and I could not find any announcement of her death, nor was there anything regarding funeral arrangements. I could only assume that her burial was a private, family affair. This only increased my suspicions that he knew she was alive when she was buried.

EPILOGUE

I was giving Elliot a tour of the archive. I wanted him to know everything about his great-great-grandfather and great-grandmother. It was important that he know where he came from and the stock he was made of. He was now old enough to learn about his family's past. We came to the room where the Cyclops had been stored and he looked at me with trepidation.

"Should we hold off on this room?" I asked. "It's gone, you know. There's nothing in here that can hurt you, I promise."

"I'd rather hold off," he replied.

My cell phone rang; it was a nurse from a luxury senior's community in Grosse Pointe. She told me that she had been spending a great deal of time with David DuMichelle and that he often spoke fondly of myself and Paige. She suggested a meeting and that perhaps she could set something up.

"I normally don't do things like this, but he's such a flirt, and I've kind of fallen for the guy."

"I know what you mean," I replied. "He's very charming."

She went on to say that he really perked up at the idea. He had recently had a couple of small strokes that had left him immobile; he probably did not have much time left. I almost laughed because I had heard this story before and never met anyone more resilient than David.

"Don't tell him I told you," she said. "But he's really looking forward to this."

⇧   ⇧   ⇧

"I know a few things about that house you've been living in—things I know you're not aware of. I think you're ready to hear about them now," David said while an attendant helped him put his shoes on.

We were in his apartment getting ready for a stroll around the grounds.

"Well I appreciate that, David, but you don't owe me anything; and you know, I've been a real shitty friend and I apologize."

"Yeah, I agree," David replied. "You have been shitty, but I accept your apology—if only out of loyalty to your grandmother."

"Why do you suddenly feel so compelled to share?" I asked as I held the door open for the attendant who pushed David's wheelchair. David leaned a little to the right in his chair and his speech was slightly impaired, but he was still sharp and observant. We exited the building and followed a cobblestone path through a lush park with fountains, benches, a pond, flowerbeds, and manicured lawns, surrounded on all sides by the buildings and cottages where the tenants lived.

We came upon the tennis courts and David motioned for the attendant to stop next to a bench just off the path. The attendant swiveled the chair, affording David a view of the courts. He locked the brakes and asked David if he needed anything else. David waved him off. I took a seat on the bench next to him and we watched as two elderly gentlemen in tennis whites hacked their way through a set.

"Jesus Christ, get a load of these clowns!" David said, assessing the low level of play. "Quick, somebody get Mack Sennett on the phone!"

I looked at him and smiled sadly. He was wearing a warm-up suit and his white, Velcro strap tennis shoes gleamed brightly in the crisp midafternoon light. He was so tiny now, a shadow of the man I first met more than ten years before, and I no longer laughed about his resilience.

"Well David, I don't know if there's anything you can tell me I don't already know," I said, getting him back on track to what he had started saying in his apartment.

He stared ahead at the comedy unfolding on the court.

"You don't know shit!" he scoffed. "By the way, how's your lovely wife?"

"She's not my wife anymore."

"That's too bad. Divorced?"

"Yep."

"Well, you're in good company. No marriage has lasted more than a couple of years in that house."

"It's my fault," I said glancing downward, unable to hide the shame that washed over me when David asked about Paige.

"Probably not completely. That place does not abide happiness. I'm not surprised at the demise of your marriage."

We sat there for a little while and I got bored watching the tennis match. I closed my eyes and tilted my head upward. The sun felt good on my face.

"What else, David? What's this big secret you've been keeping all these years?"

He unlocked the left wheel with his good hand and swiveled his chair to face me. He paused wanting to be sure that I was listening.

"What I'm about to tell you is inexplicable," he said, finally. "It can't be explained."

"Um, okay. I guess I'm ready. What can't be explained?" I replied turning to him.

"One day your great-grandfather went down into his basement, his beloved archive, and disappeared. He was never seen again."

I blanched, and the look on my face compelled him to carry on.

"I know you've spent a lot of time down there, but you've never found the room, have you?"

"What room?" I asked as a chill crept down my spine.

"There's another hidden room down there. A big, converted wine cellar."

"Where? Why didn't you show it to me when we did the inventory?" I asked, a little louder than I meant to.

"I was instructed not to," David said while a trail of saliva pooled at the corner of his lip and ran down his chin.

"You were also instructed to tell me to leave the archive alone, remember?"

"No, I wasn't." His eyes brightened as he continued. "I was instructed to plant a seed. To pique your curiosity."

"I don't understand." I said.

"Your grandmother told you in that letter to leave the archive alone, didn't she? What happens when you order a little boy to not touch the stove?"

"He touches the stove," I said, incredulous at what I was hearing.

"And touch you did!" he said almost gleefully.

"But that stuff down there... that thing I found! My son was almost killed! My neighbor..."

"I remember reading about him. I wondered," David said, his eyes darting upward.

"That thing is fucking dangerous! What is this, some test I'm being put through?" I said, not hiding my anger. It didn't matter how weak and frail David was—I suddenly felt like hitting him so I got up and took a few steps away to prevent that from happening.

"You know how it works now. You've figured it out, but it's only one piece of the puzzle. Can you get it back from the museum?"

"How'd you know about that?" I asked, reeling around to face him.

"Jesus Christ, Daniel! I'm not a complete invalid. I read the papers. They've got televisions on every wall in this joint in case you haven't noticed!"

"What about this room? What's in it?"

"Your grandmother used to refer to it as 'the holy of holies.' It's where your great-grandfather's *pièce de résistance* is kept," he replied, very satisfied with himself.

I looked at him sitting in his wheelchair. "Where is this room?"

"I'm not going to tell you," he said, enjoying the show he was putting on for me but, for a split second, I detected a hint of reluctance in his demeanor. "You'll find it eventually," he continued, "and when you do I can only hope that you'll be more careful."

"I don't even know if I want to find this room! It just sounds like more…"

"Oh, it is! Be careful! Be very, very, careful!"

♙   ♙   ♙

I couldn't sleep. I lay awake thinking about David. That son-of-a-bitch! He dropped a giant bomb on me and then up and died two days later. I pictured him lying there, drawing his last breath with a crooked, half-smile frozen on his face. He knew I couldn't live in this house knowing there was a room I had yet to discover.

I had been through every nook and cranny of the archive. I searched every room. I tapped on all the walls with a hammer and listened for any telltale hollow sounds. I pushed the shelves away from the walls and pressed on the random exposed stones, and on the bumps and flaws in the concrete, half expecting some part of the wall to suddenly yaw and grind open to reveal a darkened passageway. I even inspected the walls under the stairway. Nothing. I tapped on every square inch of floor with the expectation of finding a trap door, but there was no trap door. I completely ransacked the archive and once again became a man obsessed.

I lay in bed, racking my brains, mentally assessing the house, floor by floor. I imagined myself an architect engaged in the act of reverse engineering the structure, turning it into a blueprint. In my mind, I snapped on the accountant's lamp and unrolled this imaginary blueprint out on the big table in the secret library. *Where is the logical placement for a wine cellar?* The question reverberated around in my head, over and over again. Then it dawned on me that David did not specifically say that it was in the archive; this whole time I had just assumed it was.

The bar! I never would have known about the bar if David hadn't shown it to me. It was hidden behind large mahogany panels that swung open when a section of trim was pulled downward.

I bolted out of bed and ran down to the library. I conducted a quick study of the hidden panel that opened on the passage leading to the spiral stairway. It was seamless, perfect, constructed with the highest level of craftsmanship. I had often played in this room when I was a boy and never once detected its existence. I pushed the cleverly hidden button and the panel opened. I descended the spiral stairway and flicked the light switches on and walked over to the wall that hid the bar. I ran my hands along the molding and found the cleverly disguised latch. I pulled downward on it and the panels slowly swung open and the bar rolled outward on its hidden track. The lights flickered on, brightly illuminating the bottles, decanters, and glassware.

"Dad?"

I turned around. It was Elliot standing at the foot of the spiral stairway in his pajamas.

"Elliot, go back to bed, please!"

"What are you doing down here so late?"

"Nothing! Please son, just go back to bed."

He buried his face in his hands and began to cry.

"Elliot! Seriously, what's wrong with you?"

"I heard your bedroom door open," he replied, sobbing. "So I followed you and now I know why you came down here."

"Why do you think I came down here?"

"You came down here to open the bar because you need a drink! You're an alcoholic!"

"Oh, Elliot! No! No! That's not at all why I'm down here!"

I walked over and held him. I led him to one of the big tufted-leather couches, covered him with a throw and sat next to him.

"I'm just looking for something, son. That's all. I promise."

"What're you looking for?"

"I don't know if I want to tell you."

"Is it something that could hurt us?"

"I think it could. That's why I'm looking. I don't want it to hurt us. I don't want anything in this house to ever hurt us again."

He laid his head on my shoulder and closed his eyes.

"It's way past your bedtime, Elliot. You should go back to bed."

He lifted his head and looked up at me.

"There's no school tomorrow! Can I help you find it?"

"Absolutely not."

We sat there on the couch. I was getting chilly so I grabbed the throw and half covered myself and checked to make sure Elliot was still covered completely. I listened as his breathing fell into a relaxed, rhythmic pace and it was calming. My eyelids got heavy and my head drooped.

"It's really pretty down here isn't it, Dad?"

"Yeah. I think it's a really nice room," I replied, a little surprised that he was still awake.

"It's almost perfect," he said. "Too bad about those scratches on that wall. Maybe one of the carpenters can come back and fix them."

My head snapped up.

"What scratches? Where do you see scratches?"

"Right there," he said, pointing at the opened panels on either side of the bar.

"Wow, you're right. I've never noticed those before."

There were two sets of horizontal scratches that radiated outward from either side of the bar. They were actually more like gouges. The lower gouges were roughly a foot off the floor and the higher ones, roughly five. I got up.

"Stay right there," I said to Elliot, pointing at him. "Don't move a muscle, and that's an order, do you understand?"

"Okay," he replied, a little alarmed by my vehemence.

"I mean it!"

"Okay, I won't move!"

I walked to the right side of the bar and inspected the upper gouge; I noticed that the brass trim on the middle shelf was causing the horizontal gouge in the wood. I got down on my knees and noticed that the bar rail's finial was the cause of the lower gouge. I grabbed onto the side of the bar and pulled, walking backward. Just like the pulley doors that opened on the attic ballroom, both sides of the bar slid open in opposite directions and I heard the trim and finial digging into the panels as I pulled.

"Oh my goodness!" Elliot said. "I can't believe it!"

"You just stay there!" I said, pointing at him. "Do not get off that couch!"

He just stared at the newly revealed opening. I walked around the front and the bar was split down the middle into two identical halves, revealing a brick archway. It was too dark to see into it. I took a few steps in.

"Dad! I'm scared! Don't go in there, please!"

I heard him, but ignored him. I walked another five feet and stopped at a short, brick stairway leading down. I turned around and looked back through the dark arch of the newly revealed hallway and saw Elliot still on the couch. He looked worried.

"Stay there!" I shouted at him. "Don't move!"

He heard and nodded. I descended the three steps and walked another ten feet and the arched hallway suddenly opened into a very large, barrel-vaulted room of exposed brick and mortar. The room was lit by a large cube that hovered about a foot off the floor. It rotated very slowly on one of its vertexes, and its highly polished surfaces reflected the room. As it turned, the surfaces changed iridescently from one primary color to another.

I stood in the entryway and looked for something that might explain its rotation. Except for the cube, the room appeared to be completely empty. I entered and slowly walked around the perimeter, hugging the walls, careful to not get too close. I turned and faced the wall, hoping to find a panel. Something must be controlling it, but there was nothing—only the cube.

"Wow!" Elliot said, standing in the entryway.

Its spinning decelerated slowly then it came to a stop. The cube's surfaces darkened to black and all at once stars and galaxies twinkled brightly from within.

"Elliot! Turn around and get out!" I shouted. "Now!"

But it was like he didn't hear me. He slowly walked toward the cube and its million constellations contained inside.

"Elliot! Stop!"

I ran toward him as his arm stretched outward, reaching for the cube. I dove, hoping beyond hope that I'd reach him before he got to the cube. But I was stopped in mid-air by something—a force I could not see or explain— and I watched helplessly as Elliot touched the surface of the cube with his finger. The image of his touch mirrored on every surface. The force that held me frozen in mid-air released its hold and I dropped, hitting the brick floor hard.

Elliot was no longer in the room. He was in the cube. His image was identical on every surface and he had an amazed look on his face. He looked at me through every surface.

He smiled and waved and said something, but his voice echoed oddly and I couldn't understand him. Then he started getting smaller, and smaller, and smaller, at the same time receding further, and further, and further inward, disappearing deep into the cube's singularity.

I pounded on the cube. I touched the surface with my finger, replaying Elliot's actions exactly. I touched every surface, but it would not let me in. I ran out of the room, up the steps and out into the secret library. I felt wet. I had completely pissed myself. My son was gone! He had disappeared into the cube—floating off into the universe contained within, like an untethered astronaut. I ran and flailed around the room, vainly looking for something that would bring him back, but what was I looking for? I screamed his name over and over.

Suddenly, a blinding, multicolored light flashed out from the arched hall and I blinked. *He's back!* I thought. *He figured out how to get out! He's very smart, my little helper. My curious guy!*

I ran back into the arch, hoping that he was back, that he had gotten out. He must have. What else could those lights have been? I stopped at the entryway. The cube had resumed its slow spin, its surfaces reflecting the brick walls of the barrel-vaulted room, changing iridescently from one primary color to the next.

A man stood in front of the cube, facing it. Nothing made sense.

"Who are you?" I asked.

He turned around. His grey suit was old-fashioned, from another time. He wore a mustache and his hair, parted down the middle, was slicked down with pomade; he was coated in a white, powdery, substance. He looked down at his arms and conducted a general inspection of his appearance. He looked back up at me.

"What year is it?" he asked looking a little bewildered.

I told him the year, trying to contain my panic.

His eyes darted as he considered the revelation.

"Please, tell me who you are," I asked with fear and concern.

"My name is Alois Lintz. And who, sir, are you?"

"My name is Daniel Lintz. I'm your great-grandson. Please. Help me!"

ACKNOWLEDGMENTS

The idea for this book started a long time ago when I was a college student and rented a room in a very large and creepy old house that was built in the 1870s. Every now and then, and for no reason that my fellow tenants and I could ever figure out, the chandelier that hung above the dining room table would start spontaneously swinging on its chain. To add to this mystery, we would sometimes find two crystals from the chandelier strewn on the floor in front of the linen closet door in the hallway upstairs.

Six, eight, and sometimes as many as ten people lived in the house at any given time. Some were students, others had jobs in factories, or worked in restaurants, and one, the most popular, was a masseuse. Now and then a transient would arrive mysteriously in the middle of the night, stay for a week or two, then, just as mysteriously, leave without a trace.

We core tenants had many theories on how the chandelier would start swinging on its own: perhaps it was the freight trains that sped along the tracks just behind the backyard fence (plausible). Or maybe it was the giant 18 wheeler trucks that rumbled by delivering gravel to the landscape company just down the street (also plausible). But the theory we all *chose* to believe was that the ghost of a little girl inhabited the house. We surmised that she was fascinated by the chandelier and loved the crystals because they reminded her of her mother's beautiful jewelry. I guess this is how urban legends start.

One tenant claimed that he saw her lurking in a darkened corner of the dining room angrily waiting for him to leave so she could play with her beloved crystals. Other tenants were too afraid to open the linen closet door when they'd happen to look down and see the crystals laying at their feet.

I personally never saw our little ghost and I always laughed off my roommates' terrifying stories of their encounters with her, but I admit to being genuinely creeped out on those rare nights when I'd find myself alone in the house. I'm beelining through the darkened dining room, the hairs on the back of my neck standing on end as I ponder one of my roommate's dumb stories that suddenly didn't seem so dumb here alone in the dark. I nervously try laughing it off as I approach the stairway, but just as I mount the steps I turn around and, through the murk, notice the chandelier swinging on its chain.

Better Boxed and Forgotten is vastly different from these long ago memories, but here it is, the end result, the book you're now holding in your hand—a chandelier and two of its crystals—time, memory, and imagination meet, mingle, and percolate.

There are many people I owe a great debt of gratitude to for helping me see this book through to its completion:

Nancy Arnfield whose eagle eye caught every spelling and grammar error that slipped by my careless scrutiny. Pal Molnar for his notes, many consultations, and help in designing the cover. Philipp Lukacs for his thoughtful help with German grammar. Jeff Stine for his much appreciated IT expertise and for saving my third draft from oblivion by extracting it from a laptop with a fried motherboard. (Phew!) Fellow author and playwright, Cara Trautman whose sage advice and encouragement helped guide me toward the light at the end of the tunnel. Pam Malane, Joe Plamebeck, Carol Sue Stewart, Sara Wolf-Molnar, Bradley Stern, Brian Conway, Patty Morris, Susan Muller, Lynn Muller, Jeff Lark, Roland Stottmeyer, Linus Wennerström, and Charlotte Rebelein for their thoughtful notes and encouragement. A particular thank you to Ginny Lark Moyer for her brilliant editing and consultation. This book benefitted greatly from her many hours of careful attention, dedicated scrutiny, and bounty of great ideas. Ginny, you rock! Thank you Kelsey Turek for your very professional and timely edit. Above all, a giant thank you to Karen Lark, my wife and best friend, who read my drafts and encouraged my musings, dreams, and eureka moments. Karen also helped me see the folly of my more outlandish ideas and put up with a lot of far-off thinking while I mentally drifted through the basement, hallways, and ballroom of the house on Seminole Street. Karen, you are my rock!

About the Author

Andrew Charles Lark is a graduate of Wayne State University where he received his Bachelor of Arts Degree in English. His play, *Stop Up Your Ears* is a farcical account of a month in the life of Florence Foster Jenkins. It won Wayne State University's Heck-Rabi award and was produced at the Hilberry Studio Theatre in Detroit, Michigan. His other plays include *The Embrace of Redemption,* which received several readings and workshops, and *Ask Me! Tell Me!* which was professionally produced at the Ringwald Theatre's Gay Play Series in Ferndale, Michigan and also the Hudson Theatre's Play by Play Festival in Hudson, New York. *Better Boxed and Forgotten* is his first novel. He is busy writing book two of the Archive Series. Andrew lives in St. Clair Shores, Michigan with his wife Karen and terrier mix, Georgie. Maybe someday they'll live in a house much like the one on Seminole Street. He'll keep you posted.

A Short Note from Andrew Charles Lark

Thank you very much! It means a great deal to me that you took time out of your busy life to read my book. I sincerely hope that you enjoyed it. I am busy working on the second book of The Archive Series. To check for updates, blog ruminations, other works, and my plays, please check out www.andrewlarkbooks.com

If you enjoyed *Better Boxed and Forgotten*, it would mean the world to me if you would consider writing a review. Thank you, and happy reading!